"I love the way this man writes! I adore his style. There is something about it that makes me feel as if I'm someplace I'm not supposed to be, seeing things I'm not supposed to see and that is so delicious."
REBECCA FORESTER, USA Today Bestselling Author

This book "is creative and captivating. It features bold characters, witty dialogue, exotic locations, and non-stop action. The pacing is spot-on, a solid combination of intrigue, suspense, and eroticism. A first-rate thriller, this book is damnably hard to put down. It's a tremendous read."
FOREWORD REVIEWS

"A terrifying, gripping cross between James Patterson and John Grisham. Jagger has created a truly killer thriller."
J.A. KONRATH, USA Today and Amazon Bestselling Author

"As engaging as the debut, this exciting blend of police procedural and legal thriller recalls the early works of Scott Turow and Lisa Scottoline."
LIBRARY JOURNAL

"The well-crafted storyline makes this a worthwhile read. Stuffed with gratuitous sex and over-the-top violence, this novel has a riveting plot."
KIRKUS REVIEWS

"Verdict: The pacing is relentless in this debut, a hard-boiled novel with a shocking ending. The supershort chapters will please those who enjoy a James Patterson–style page-turner"

NEVER
TO DIE

R.J. JAGGER

THRILLER PUBLISHING GROUP, INC.

NEVER TO DIE

Thriller Publishing Group, Inc.

ISBN 978-1-937888-90-9

For Eileen

ACKNOWLEDGEMENTS

Thanks to the many wonderful readers, booksellers, editors, publishers, agents, audio producers, book reviewers, authors, groups (including International Thriller Writers and Mystery Writers of America), proofreaders and other kind-hearted souls who amplified my efforts and who encouraged me with positive vibes over the years. Without you this book would have never happened.

Chapter One
Day One—April 12
Tuesday Night

———————————

Rave Lafelle shifted her 24-year-old body nervously in the dark interior of her rusty VW and tried to convince herself that the headlights in the rearview mirror weren't following her. But when she turned onto Sheridan, and the other vehicle did too, she swallowed and decided that she could no longer fool herself. The car had been there for too long and for too many twists.

Rain poured down out of a black night sky, one of those Denver springtime gushers.

She kept one eye in the rearview mirror and tried to see the driver whenever the streetlights gave her a chance, but the storm kept her from picking out anything except a black silhouette. Suddenly, in spite of her better judgment, she pulled over to the curb and stopped.

The mystery vehicle edged in behind her.

The driver immediately got out.

And walked through the weather towards her.

Rave's first instinct was to wait until the person was almost at her door and then take off as fast as her four cylinders would let her. But now the silhouette took on the outline of a woman and caused

Rave to pause.

She pushed the door lock down and then cranked the window handle until the glass came down a crack.

The person turned out to be a strikingly beautiful black woman in her mid-twenties with long, straight panther-black hair that was already flattening from the storm. "My name is London. Your life is in danger," the woman said. She spoke in an English accent with a French overlay. "I'm here to help."

"What do you mean?"

"Not here. It's too dangerous," the woman said. "Follow me. We'll find a place to talk." Rave must have had a look of doubt on her face because the woman added, "This isn't a joke."

They zigzagged through side streets for ten minutes and finally ended up in a tavern on Colfax called the Mesa View Bar. The woman bought two glasses of white wine, handed one to Rave, clinked glasses and said, "You're going to need this." She reminded Rave of one of those perfect-body, perfect-skin island girls that sailors killed for.

They took a booth near the back as rain beat on the windows.

"The storm's getting worse," London said.

True.

It was.

"Why are we here?" Rave asked.

The woman retreated in thought, as if not quite knowing where to begin. Then she said, "When I was fifteen, my mother got a job in Paris as a historian, and we moved to France from Jamaica. During my mother's research, she learned that she was a bloodline descendent of a man named John Haigh from Yorkshire, England. He, in turn, was reputed to be a vampire."

Vampire?

Rave laughed.

The word seemed so weird.

"A vampire?"

The woman cast a stern look, so severe that Rave realized what was mysterious about the her eyes. They were blue instead of brown.

"Yes, a vampire," London said. "As was the custom in those days, a wooden stake was hammered into his chest and his body was burned to consumption in a bonfire. His wife, who was impregnated at the time, fled and started a bloodline that continues to this day. My mother is part of that bloodline and so am I."

A sudden flash lit the world outside and a deafening clap of thunder immediately followed, so near that Rave twitched.

"So what are you saying? That you're a vampire?"

The woman cocked her head.

"Maybe, but only to a point. I'm mostly just a bloodline descendent. To the best of my knowledge, there are no full-blooded, immortal vampires left."

"Does that mean you believe there were real ones at some point?"

London took a sip of wine and got a strange expression on her face.

Then she looked Rave directly in the eyes.

"I'm sure you're going to find this very strange, but yes, I do," she said. "I have lots of reasons to support that conclusion which I'll be happy to share with you later if you want. Right now, however, the thing you need to concentrate on is staying alive."

"What is that supposed to mean?"

"It means that you're just like me. You're also a bloodline descendent of a vampire. That's why your life is in danger. And I'm talking about immediate danger, as in tonight or even the next ten minutes."

Rave studied the woman and looked for lies.

She found none.

Her pulse raced.

"Danger from who?"

"Slayers. They're here in Denver, as we speak. They're coming for you."

Chapter Two
Day One—April 12
Tuesday Night

———————————

Tuesday night after dark, Nick Teffinger—the 34-year-old head of Denver's homicide unit—drove into a ragged industrial area on the north edge of the city and killed the Tundra's engine in front of an abandoned warehouse. A storm beat down. His blood raced and for a moment he thought about heading home and cracking open a Bud Light. Instead, he grabbed the flashlight and stepped into the weather. By the time he got the door open and stepped inside the structure, he was drenched.

He stood there for a second in the dark.

Listening.

Not hearing anything except the hammering of the rain on the metal roof.

He pulled up an image from last night, when he first came here—an image of a woman killed with a wooden stake through her heart, as if she was a vampire. The end stuck out of her chest four inches. Teffinger wiggled it to get a feel for how deep it was.

"Deep," he said.

Detective Sydney Heatherwood—a 27-year-old African American woman—held the flashlight steady. She was the newest member of the homicide unit—personally stolen by Teffinger out of the vice unit a year ago—but had already cut her teeth on Denver's worst.

John Ganjon

Nathan Wickerfield.

Jack Draven.

Aaron Trance.

Dylan Jekker.

She studied the stake and said, "This is too freaky."

"I'm guessing it goes all the way to her spine," Teffinger added.

"This isn't Transylvania," Sydney said.

Teffinger grunted and said, "It is now."

They were a considerable distance inside a lightless gutted warehouse. Teffinger moved his flashlight down the dead woman's body. She was tied securely with rope on her wrists and ankles, stretched in a tight spread-eagle position on an old rickety workbench that hadn't been worth hauling away.

She was naked.

Her eyes were open.

Fear was still etched on her face; a face that otherwise would have been nice.

Her clothes and purse were piled on the floor.

Teffinger guessed that she was in her late teens or early twenties.

"I don't see any other injuries to the body except for the stake," he said, meaning it was pounded in while she was still alive.

Sydney nodded.

Teffinger raked his thick brown hair back with his fingers. It immediately flopped back down over his forehead. "What a way to go."

"It wouldn't be in my top twenty," Sydney said.

Thirty minutes later they brought the crime unit in, set up lights, and started the arduous task of processing the scene. According to the victim's driver's license, she was 20-year-old Cameron Leigh who lived in the 1300 block of Race Street.

In her purse they found a vial with a screw-on cap.

Holding four or five ounces of a red substance.

A substance that looked like blood.

"So what's this?" Teffinger asked as he slipped it into an evidence bag. "A little vampire snack? Something to get her through the day?"

Sydney grunted and said, "We all have to eat."

Teffinger looked around, spotted Paul Kwak, waved him over and handed him the vial. "Blood," he said. "Let me know if it's animal or human. If it's human, let me know if it's hers or someone else's. If it's animal, let me know what kind."

Kwak scratched his truck-driver's gut.

"Weird stuff just finds you, doesn't it?" he questioned.

"Apparently so," Teffinger said. "You work with me, after all."

"Not funny."

"Not meant to be," Teffinger said, turning to leave.

"Where you going?"

"Coffee," Teffinger said.

"Coffee?"

"Right, coffee."

Kwak chuckled and said, "Why don't you just drink the blood? Save me some work—"

"Blood has no caffeine."

"Yours does," Kwak said.

"I mean besides mine."

Outside, there were no streetlights in the area and an oppressive blackness floated overhead. A full moon with an eerie ochre tinge hung in the east, flickering in and out of drifting clouds. Teffinger looked at it and said, "If I hear a werewolf, just one single werewolf, I'm going to wake myself up, take a long piss and then go back to sleep."

Sydney chuckled and then grew serious.

"So what's your theory?"

"My theory is the same as always. We need to find someone with a motive," Teffinger said. "And then figure out if this whole scene got staged to throw us off track."

"So you don't think she's a real vampire?"

"She is in a sense," Teffinger said. "She's going to come back from the dead, through me, to get the guy who did this to her. I guarantee you that."

That was last night, after the property's security company conducted its periodic inspection and discovered the scene. Now, alone and drenched, Teffinger maneuvered his six-foot-two frame into the ominous structure as he flickered the flashlight from side to side.

He didn't believe in vampires.

Or ghosts.

Or anything occult.

He never had and never would.

Still, the place had a creepy feeling to it. He pushed it down and headed deeper inside.

Chapter Three
Day One—April 12
Tuesday Night

_____

Trent Tripp crept through the French nightscape twenty miles south of Paris under a chilly moon. He should have his full concentration on the target—French model Diamanda—but the Paris prostitutes wouldn't leave his thoughts. When this was over, later tonight, he'd take his pleasant face and his perfect six-foot-four body to them for servicing one more time before heading to the airport.

Diamanda was going to be tricky.

A spiked fence encircled her estate.

She had a fulltime bodyguard.

Plus she was a vampire descendent, meaning she could have strength. The yellow Lotus parked in the circular cobblestone driveway indicated she was home.

Tripp carried no wallet or identification.

He left that in the glove box of the rental, parked a half mile up the road.

He carried no gun.

What he did have was an 8-inch knife with a serrated blade, a wooden stake and a mallet.

From what he could tell, the woman was alone in the master bedroom walking on a treadmill and watching TV. She wore white panties and a short black tank that left a flat, tanned abdomen well exposed.

Her strawberry hair bounced.

Her mouth hung open, taking in air, so, so sexy.

At the fence, Tripp hugged the shadows and listened for dogs. When none came, he muscled his way over and landed on grass with cat feet. Then he put on a black ski mask, latex gloves and crept towards the structure.

The sliding glass door to the deck off the master bedroom was open far enough that he could hear the pounding of his target's feet on the treadmill.

He muscled his way up to the deck.

Quietly.

Invisible.

Then he stood in the dark, listening.

Suddenly the whining of the treadmill stopped.

The door slid open.

And the vampire stepped outside.

Tripp stood there, frozen, not knowing if the woman heard a noise and came out to investigate, or whether she ventured out for an innocent breath of fresh air. He held the blade in his right hand.

Then he pounced.

To get the knife to her throat.

And keep it there until she calmed down.

She turned just before he got to her.

He expected her to scream but instead she kicked his arm and the knife flew out of his grip. The woman got her hands on his neck and pressed her thumbs into his throat.

She was strong.

He couldn't get air.

She was suffocating him.

He punched her wildly in the back. Instead of twisting in pain, she pushed her thumbs even deeper into his throat. He hit her in the stomach. She groaned but didn't let go.

He struck her again.

Harder.

Still no air came.

Then he dropped to the ground, rolled, and broke her grip. It was at that moment that a second figure appeared and kicked him in the ribs.

Chapter Four
Day One—April 12
Tuesday Night

———————

Rave's universe suddenly seemed creepy and eerie. She parted company with London at the bar and drove home alone in the storm. Her modest two-bedroom Lakewood bungalow appeared to be as she had left it, with no visible evidence that anyone had entered.

She poured a glass of wine, put in a Billie Holiday CD, forwarded to Track 4 and sang along to a lamenting tale of love gone wrong.

Lady Day.

The greatest.

End of story.

She was one of the reasons, if not the reason, that Rave grabbed a microphone four years ago at age twenty and never looked back, dropping out of college and everything else to bare her soul on stage every chance she got.

Maybe a stupid move.

Maybe not.

Time would tell.

Most people described her style as "soul." She agreed to an extent, but didn't think that any one term could pigeonhole her. Her sets included Billie Holiday's "Autumn in New York," Roberta Flack's "Killing Me Softly," Fiona Apple's "Criminal," and several from Alicia Keys. But her trademark talent was taking an eclectic mix of rock songs, slowing them down and giving them a sexy, sultry edge.

Meat Loaf's "Two Out of Three Ain't Bad."

The Beatles' "Girl."

Elton John's "Sorry Seems To Be The Hardest Word."

Nirvana's "Come As You Are."

Barbara Streisand's "Evergreen."

Tim Pepper discovered her last year in a smoky New Orleans dive. He hooked her up with first class musicians, called the group Rave Lafelle, and booked tours across the United States. He was on the verge of penning a stint at Storm, the newest mega-casino on the Las Vegas strip. More importantly, he was securing material for Rave's debut CD, and passing judgment on her own compositions—three of which he had already approved.

She felt like a rocket.

Just leaving the launch pad.

Headed for the stratosphere.

At least, that's how she felt until London entered her life.

Now there was talk of vampires.

And slayers.

She didn't doubt that living people could be traced to persons who may have been considered vampires in their day. But even so, why would anyone today care? She walked over to the window, pulled the curtain back and looked into the black stormy night. She didn't expect to see anything, but did.

The Jamaican woman.

London.

Sitting in her car under a streetlight.

Three houses down.

Doing what?

Stalking?

Guarding?

Rave let the drapes swing back and drank another glass of wine.

Fifteen minutes later, when Ms. Jamaica still hadn't left, Rave walked out the front door without slowing down to grab an umbrella and headed straight for the dark silhouette of the vehicle. The woman had her window down when Rave got there.

"What are you doing?"

London pulled a 9mm SIG out of her purse and flashed it. "Like it or not, I'm your guardian angel tonight, sweetie," she said.

"This is too bizarre."

True.

But not relevant.

"We don't know what they look like," London said. "One of them may be a skinhead with lots of tattoos, but we're not positive about that one way or the other."

"You're really serious about all this, aren't you?"

London said, "I'm sorry this is happening."

Rave said, "If you're going to be here, you may as well come inside."

Chapter Five
Day One—April 12
Tuesday Night

———————

Teffinger sat down on the workbench where Cameron Leigh had been killed and turned off the flashlight. The inside of the warehouse immediately turned blacker than black. The absence of light made the pounding of the storm louder.

His presence here baffled him.

The scene had already been processed and wasn't about to cough up any more evidence, even if he was looking for it, which he wasn't.

Something had pulled him here.

What?

The day had been unproductive. Teffinger ended up in endless meetings and didn't even get a chance to search the victim's house.

The day had also been strange.

Paul Kwak called shortly before five and said, "It was blood all right—human blood, not hers. I repeat—not hers. It looks like we got an honest-to-God vampire on our hands."

"Not hers?"

"Nope."

"Are you sure?"

"I'd bet my split-window on it," Kwak said, referring to his '63 Corvette.

"Well that's interesting."

"Very."

"Human blood, huh?"

"Right," Kwak said. "As in a species other than yours."

Teffinger chuckled and said, "Do me a favor and call the coroner. Have him check the victim's stomach to see if she drank any of it. For all we know, someone just planted it in her purse. If that's the case, this same someone may have killed someone else too, besides Cameron Leigh."

"Well that's optimistic," Kwak said.

"What do you mean?"

"What I mean is, the first thought that enters my head is that she killed someone to get it," Kwak said. "For all we know, there's a body lying out there somewhere with bite marks in the neck. Maybe that's why she's dead—revenge."

That was earlier today. Now, thunder cracked overhead. Teffinger laid down on his back on the bench, in the same position that

Cameron Leigh had been found, and pictured the death process. The wooden stake would shatter her ribs and sternum, causing unimaginable pain. Then it would penetrate her heart and immediately stop the functioning of that organ.

Blood would stop flowing through her body.

The dying process would be slow.

Her brain wouldn't shut down right away.

Maybe the stake clipped a lung and filled it with blood.

And maybe it lodged against a nerve.

What was he—or they—doing the whole time?

Shinning a flashlight in her eyes?

Taunting her?

Now Teffinger knew why he had come here. He needed to go through the dying process with the victim. He needed a calm moment that wasn't jammed up with the hustle and bustle and the thousand little thoughts that came during a crime scene investigation. He needed an imprint in his mind—and more importantly in his heart—of what had actually happened here, and how horrible it had been.

Now he had it.

He sat up.

Then he said, "I promise."

And went home.

Chapter Six
Day One—April 12
Tuesday Night

_____

French women understood their sensuality. It was always there, in the way they walked and tossed their hair and parted their sexy little lips. They had an intuitive animalistic underpinning that didn't exist anywhere else.

They ran hot.

They understood lust.

They weren't afraid of it.

Or embarrassed by it.

Tripp cruised the edgier streets of Paris where the whores walked, pulled up to a petite blond in a short black skirt, and powered down the passenger side glass.

She leaned in.

"Do you speak English?" he asked.

She did.

Very well, in fact.

"How long have you been out tonight?"

"I just started, why?"

"Where were you beforehand?"

"Getting ready."

"I mean before that."

"Sleeping, why?"

"By yourself?"

"Yes."

"So I'm your first customer?"

She nodded.

"I'm squeaky clean, if that's what you're getting at."

"What's your name?"

"Rozeen."

Tripp smiled.

Rozeen.

He paid her up-front in cash for the whole night. She was hungry, so he took her to Le Tambour on rue Montmartre, a chatty place with a vintage transportation-chic style, slatted wooden banquettes and bus stop sign barstools. They ended up in a long room that had a retro city map on the wall.

"No one's ever taken me out to eat before," she said. "On the clock, I mean."

Tripp shrugged.

"Their loss. Tell me about Rozeen," he said. "Who is this beautiful woman I'm with?"

She turned out to be an art student, on her own since age seventeen, who lived alone on the west side.

Tripp liked her.

He liked her face.

The way she moved.

The way she talked.

"Do you feel like getting crazy?" she asked.

He did.

She took him to Rex, a high-energy nightclub on bd Poissonniere. They inhaled drinks and she teased him on the dance floor to pounding music until they were both covered in sweat. Then she took him back to her place—a small apartment without much.

No WC.

That was at the end of the hall.

She gave him the best blowjob of his life.

Then passed out.

At dawn, she woke up and crawled on top.

And stayed there until she came twice.

Before Tripp left he said, "What time did I pick you up last night?"

She shrugged.

"I don't know, 10:30, maybe."

He opened his wallet, pulled out a thousand dollars in American money and handed it to her.

"Actually, I think we were together since about 7:30, in case anyone ever asks. Wouldn't you agree?"

She took the money and smiled.

"Yes, it was 7:30. I remember clearly now."

Tripp took a picture of her with his cell phone, programmed her number into the phone's memory, and called to make sure her phone rang. It did. He promised he'd be back again someday and kissed her goodbye.

Then headed out the door.

Chapter Seven
Day One—April 12
Tuesday Night

———————

Rave lit a joint, took a deep drag and passed it to the Jamaican woman sitting next to her on the couch. "Columbian," she said.

Good stuff.

Grabbing Rave's brain almost immediately.

Highlighting the exotic edges of Billie Holiday's voice.

London took a hit and said, "I shouldn't be doing this. I need to stay sharp."

"Right, for the slayers," Rave said.

"Let me ask you something," London said. "Do you have any powers?"

Rave laughed.

"You mean vampire powers?"

London nodded, obviously serious. She wore jeans and an aqua T-shirt that played well against her light-brown skin. The gun sat in her lap. "Right, vampire powers," she said. "Lots of the descendents have them, watered down of course—way watered down, in fact."

"How so?"

"The most common is a dislike for the sun," she said. "Don't get me wrong. Everyone can tolerate the sun. We don't spontaneously burst into flames or anything like that. But some of us just don't like the sun."

Rave considered it.

"I like the night better than the day, but that's probably because I'm a singer and that's when all my fun happens," she said.

"But you don't mind the sun?"

"No, not at all."

"You don't need to wear sunglasses?"

Rave shook her head.

"Not really."

"Me either," London said. "Maybe 'powers' is the wrong word—'symptoms' might be a better one. How about strength? How would you classify your strength? Were you a track star or gymnast or anything like that?"

Rave chuckled.

"No, but ever since I was about three, I've been able to turn into a bat and fly. Did I mention that?"

London punched her in the arm and said, "Come on. I'm serious."

"I know," she said. "That's what scares me."

Lightning exploded outside.

Immediately followed by the slap of thunder.

Rave took a deep drag on the joint and said, "I'm not a vampire. I don't have any powers or symptoms or whatever you call them. I'm just a normal person."

London studied her and said, "I wouldn't say that. Look at you. You're stunning."

Rave chuckled, waved the fire tip and said, "No more of this for you."

She had never thought of herself in terms of stunning, but had to admit that she had a sexy, sultry face and a nice, solid body. Thick blond hair cascaded down her back—a pain to wash and keep untangled, but worth it. Her manager, Tim Pepper, called her a "man-melter."

London asked, "Have you ever come back from the dead?"

The words shocked Rave.

Not because of the question.

But because of the answer.

"That's a strange question because there actually was an incident when I was small," she said. "God, I haven't thought about it in years. When I was about eight, living in Florida, a hurricane blew in one night. Afterwards, in the morning, after everything calmed down and we were all outside checking out the damage, I waded into a ditch that was filled with water. It turned out that a high voltage line had come down into it. I immediately stiffened and fell. Everyone in my family said I died. They said I wasn't breathing and my pulse wasn't beating and that they had actually gotten to the point where they had given up trying to save me. Then all of a sudden I opened my eyes and stood up."

The joint was short and about to burn her fingertips.

She mashed the tip in an ashtray.

"Freaky," London said.

"Like I said, I don't remember it," Rave said. "It could be that I just got knocked out for a while and everyone overreacted." She chuckled. "It was just one of those things. Trust me, it's not because I have any latent vampire powers."

London retreated in thought.

Then she put the gun in Rave's hands.

"Have you ever fired one of these before?" she asked.

"No, are you crazy?"

"This is the safety, right here," London said. "You got to flick it like this to get it off."

They listened to music and chatted for a long time.

Then the buzz of the wine and pot wore off and their eyelids got heavy. Rave left London to sleep on the couch. Then she staggered into the bedroom, closed the door and flopped onto the mattress without even taking her clothes off.

The world went away.

At some point later—it could have been ten minutes or three hours—something pulled her out of a deep sleep.

A noise.

The storm?

She let herself wake up just enough to study it.

Yes—the storm.

Beating on the roof and windows.

She rolled to her other side and was almost out when a crash came from the living room, something like a lamp falling. She opened her eyes and held her breath.

There!

Again!

Something was happening in the other room.

She ran to the door and opened it. Two black shapes were in a desperate struggle on the floor. She flipped the wall switch. The room burst into light. London's face was wild and covered in blood. The other person was a white man with a shaved head and lots of tattoos. Blood poured from his nose.

Rave stood there.

Frozen.

Then the man sprang up and charged her.

She knew she should move.

Run.

Do something.

But she didn't.

The man's fist swung and caught her on the side of the face. Her left eye exploded in pain and closed shut. Then more hurt came, from her abdomen—so severe that vomit shot into her mouth. She doubled up and dropped to the ground.

London hit the man in the back and he swung around.

He punched her in the face.

And she fell to the ground.

It was then that Rave spotted the gun on the floor not more than two feet away. She suddenly had it in her hand, a cold steel object. She wrapped her fingers around the grip and got her index finger on the trigger.

Then she stood up and pointed it at the man.

He didn't notice.

And when he finally did, he froze. Then he got up slowly and said, "Give that to me."

Rave suddenly remembered the safety.

And flicked it off.

"Stay back!"

Then something caught her eye—a wooden stake and a wooden mallet, lying on the floor near the edge of the couch. When she focused back on the skinhead, he was a step closer.

"Stay back I said!"

Suddenly the man lunged.

And Rave pulled the trigger.

Chapter Eight
Day Two—April 13
Wednesday Morning

Wednesday morning, Teffinger pulled himself out of bed before dawn, popped in his contacts, and jogged three miles up and down the Green Mountain streets through a black chilly rain. The storm fingered its way into his clothes and into his eyes. As soon as he got home it stopped, naturally, because that's the way his life worked. He showered, dressed, and ate a bowl of cereal in the Tundra as he cruised east on the 6th Avenue freeway to headquarters.

The sun broke over the horizon and hung there as Teffinger came up on Wadsworth, blinding him as best it could.

He didn't care.

The Denver motor-heads were already making their maniac moves.

He didn't care.

He punched the radio buttons and couldn't get a song to save his life.

He didn't care.

This morning he would search Cameron Leigh's house.

And get some answers.

Being the first one to work, as usual, he kick-started the coffee machine and then called Dr. Leigh Sandt, the FBI profiler from Quantico, Virginia, while the pot gurgled. She answered on the second ring. He pulled up an image of a classy woman, about fifty, with the best legs on the planet.

"Hey, it's me," he said. "I got something bizarre. Someone pounded a wooden stake into a young woman's heart, as if she was a vampire. Have you heard of anything like that happening anywhere else?"

A pause.

"Who is this?"

He grunted.

"Not funny," he said.

"What is it about that Rocky Mountain air? You get the most bizarre stuff out there, I swear."

"No disagreement," he said. "So do vampires ring any bells or what?"

No.

Not even close.

But she'd check around and get back to him.

"How are the women treating you?" she asked.

He grunted.

"They aren't."

"Really?"

"I'm in a dry spell like you can't believe."

"You?"

"Think Sahara," he said. "Even the dogs in my neighborhood are scared to walk the streets alone." He paused and when she didn't say anything he added, "You're actually pulling up a visual."

"Yes I am and it isn't pretty."

Sydney walked into the room at 7:00, nicely dressed in a white pantsuit, wearing a sleepy, pre-caffeine face. She saw one cup of coffee left in the pot and headed straight for it, as if Teffinger would grab it if she let him get half a step.

Teffinger stayed in his chair and said, "I saved that for you."

She rolled her eyes.

Then sprinkled creamer into a disposable cup, drained what was left in the pot on top and took a long noisy slurp.

Ah.

Good stuff.

"So what's the plan?" she asked.

"I'm heading over to Cameron Leigh's house," he said. "You want to come?"

She chuckled.

"Let me put it this way," she said. "Anyone who carries human blood around in their purse has my attention."

"So you heard?"

"Everyone heard."

"That reminds me," he said. "Sometime today, I need you to get in touch with the hospitals and see if any of their red stuff has turned up missing."

They made a fresh pot of coffee.

Filled a thermos.

And headed out.

Ten minutes later, they arrived at the victim's house, which turned out to be a 50-year-old brick box on Race Street, with no driveway or garage. Teffinger circled the area for five minutes before finally finding a street slot big enough for the Tundra, two blocks over.

He felt good.

The coffee had entered his bloodstream.

The few clouds remaining from this morning's rain were already burning off.

They entered the house using a copy of the key obtained from Cameron Leigh's purse. When they opened the front door, a solid-white cat trotted over and rubbed against Teffinger's leg.

He picked it up.

And couldn't believe what he saw.

The animal had one blue eye and one green one.

Just like him.

Sydney noticed it and said, "This is too freaky. It's like a little, furry you."

Teffinger put the animal in her hands.

Not amused.

And headed for the refrigerator.

"No blood in here," he said.

"Check the freezer."

He did.

None there either.

Nor were there any plastic bags in the kitchen trash. "There's no evidence that our mystery blood came from a hospital," he said.

"You still want me to call around?"

He nodded.

"Yeah, it's too important not to."

Ten seconds later she said, "Hey, over here."

She was standing at the living room wall to the right of the fireplace, a wall crammed with books, hundreds of them, on sagging wooden shelves dubiously stretched between cinder blocks.

"The mother lode," Sydney said.

Teffinger scanned the spines.

"Vampire books," he said.

"That's an understatement," she said. "I mean, look at all these things. I had no idea they even had books about vampires, much less billions of them."

"Interesting."

"This is way beyond an obsession," Sydney said.

True.

Teffinger leafed through a few of them and then headed back to the refrigerator and poured a bowl of milk for the cat, which immediately attacked it with a fast pink tongue.

"You own him now," Sydney said.

"Oh no."

"What are you going to do? Just leave him here?"

"This is animal protection's problem, not mine."

"Animal protection? He'll spend two weeks in a cage and then be put down," Sydney said. "Is that what you want?"

He grunted.

"He wouldn't do that to you, if you were the cat," she added.

"How do you know?"

"Because even I wouldn't do that to you, Teffinger."

He raked his hair back with his fingers.

"So you say."

Nothing of relevance turned up for some time. Then they found something interesting in a desk drawer—a handwritten family tree. At the bottom was the name "Rave Lafelle."

At the top was "Evan Radcliffe."

"1837-1871."

"Stake/Burned."

"So what is this supposed to mean?" Teffinger asked, pointing. "That this guy was a vampire? And she was related to him?"

Sydney cocked her head.

"Looks that way."

Teffinger shifted feet.

"I wonder if this thing is legit," he said.

"As obsessed as she was, she checked it twenty times," Sydney said. "You can bet your cat on it."

They tried to boot up the victim's laptop but it had a security password that didn't respond to Cameron or Vampire.

So Sydney tucked it under her arm.

And Teffinger tucked the cat under his.

And they headed outside.

"Wait a minute," Teffinger said.

"What?"

"Wait right here."

He ducked back inside the house and returned two minutes later.

"Alley," he said.

"Huh?"

"That's the cat's name—Alley."

"How'd you find out?"

"The grocery list on the counter says, Food for Alley."

"You're such a freaking detective sometimes," Sydney said. "It's downright scary."

He chuckled and said, "Yeah, once I even found my own nose. And get this part—in the dark."

Chapter Nine
Day Two—April 13
Wednesday Afternoon

———————

When Tripp landed at LaGuardia International Airport on Wednesday afternoon, he could still smell Rozeen in his clothes and taste her on his tongue.

He could go for a fulltime diet of a woman like that, no doubt about it. He didn't know how much he spent on her, but it had been worth every penny.

The U.S. soil felt good.

No, not good.

GOOD.

No doubt the French vampire's estate was swarming with police and Paparazzi right now—poor Diamanda, not just killed, but brutally beaten to death, and stabbed through the heart with a wooden stake.

Such a tragedy.

Such a waste.

Whoever did it ransacked the house, looking for something.

Tripp's cell phone rang as soon as he stepped out of the terminal and the voice of Jake VanDeventer came through. Tripp pulled up the image of a rough, tanned face and piercing blue eyes, something in the nature of a bad guy from an old black-and-white spaghetti western.

"We have a problem," VanDeventer said.

The man sounded stressed.

"How so?" Tripp asked.

"Abbot didn't call last night or today," VanDeventer said.

Tripp understood the implications.

Abbott had gone to Denver.

He was supposed to check in every night.

The same way that Tripp did.

Not doing so either meant that Abbott had been killed.

Or was in custody.

"What do you propose?" Tripp questioned.

"I'm catching the next plane to Denver," VanDeventer said. "I want you to meet me there."

Tripp turned around.

"I'm on my way," he said.

Chapter Ten
Day Two—April 13
Wednesday Morning

───────────

The shot to the skinhead's face last night blew away most of his nose and killed him on impact. Rave dropped the gun, sank to the floor, leaned against the wall and stared at the body. She didn't feel sorry. It was self-defense, pure and simple. But she did know that her life had just changed.

How big and how far, she couldn't tell.

But a change had come.

London turned off the lights, pulled the window curtain to the side and looked out. The surrounding houses remained dark, showing no evidence that anyone had heard the shot.

"Thank God for the storm," she said.

"I suppose we should call the police," Rave said.

"No."

The word surprised Rave.

"Why not?"

The Jamaican woman sat on the floor next to Rave, put her arm around her shoulders and said, "Lots of reasons. For starters, that gun is illegal as hell. It isn't registered and the numbers have been ground off. That's a felony offense, in case you're not aware."

Rave swallowed.

"Why?" she asked.

"You mean, why is it an illegal gun?"

"Right."

"In case I ever had to use it," London said. "I can't afford to get connected to a homicide."

"Why not?"

"Because I already got connected to one once before," she said.

"You did?"

"I'll tell you about it later. The important thing now is to figure out what to do with that," London said, referring to the body.

"I shot him, it's my problem," Rave said. "Just take your gun and leave."

"And then what? What do you tell the police when they ask where the gun is?"

"I don't know—"

"And what do you think they're going to say to that? Oh, okay, never mind. I guess we're done here. Have a nice day, ma'am. They're going to pick you apart. You'll end up taking the fall. I'm not going to let that happen."

"So what do we do?"

"I say we dump the little prick somewhere and stay the hell out of the whole thing."

Dump him?

"Where?"

"I don't know," London said. "Up in the mountains somewhere. We got nothing to lose. Even if we somehow get caught doing it—which we won't—we can still fall back on the story of what really happened."

"Except they might not believe it if they find out we dumped the body," Rave said. "We'll look guilty at that point."

"We have his DNA in your carpet," London said. "We can prove beyond doubt that he got killed in your living room if we need to. You can also prove that you never had any association with him before tonight. Why else would you kill him, if not in self-defense? So if we do get caught by some chance—which we won't—we simply tell the truth about what happened and say we panicked afterwards and did something stupid. By then the gun will be gone and we can tell the police we threw it in a lake or something—we give them a false location and they never find it. That way at least we don't have to face an illegal firearm charge."

Rave chewed on it.

"Plus, once your record shows that you killed someone, even if it's found to be self-defense or justifiable, it'll follow you around for the rest of your life," London said. "That little seed of doubt will always be there. If you ever do something else, they'll figure that you may have gotten away with something the first time, but they'll be real sure it doesn't happen twice."

Rave nodded.

That made sense.

"That's the situation I'm in right now," London said.

"Okay."

"Okay what?"

"Okay, we'll dump him."

London said, "It's going to be light in a couple of hours. Let's get some sleep and figure the rest out tomorrow." She paused and added, "I'll do it. You don't even have to be involved."

Rave exhaled.

"What?" London asked.

"No way. You came here to protect me," Rave said. "If you hadn't been here, I'd be dead right now. So I'm the one who owes you, not the other way around."

"Okay, we'll both do it then."

That was last night.

Now it was morning.

Time to dump the body.

Chapter Eleven
Day Two—April 13
Wednesday Morning

———————————

Teffinger didn't know what to do with Alley, so he brought him up to homicide, found Chief Tanker's office empty, and stuck him in. Then he wrote "Free Cat Inside" on a piece of paper and taped it to the door. An hour later he got notified that the computer geeks got Cameron Leigh's laptop opened.

He was at his desk, drinking coffee and checking out the victim's files, when Alley jumped up and stared at him.

"This isn't going to happen," Teffinger said.

The cat curled up on a manila file.

And closed one eye.

Then the other.

Teffinger almost picked it up and put it back in the chief's office, but noticed a file called Passwords and pulled it up. It had a list of passwords, PINS and lock combinations. The one of most interest was the woman's AOL email address with the password DENVER-VAMP.

He logged on to the net and pulled up the victim's emails.

What he saw he could hardly believe.

Sydney walked into the room and Teffinger waved her over. She made a pit stop at the coffee pot and focused on Alley as she headed over.

"No pets allowed in the office," she said.

"Not funny."

She slurped the coffee.

"You look too happy," she said. "What's wrong?"

"We're in Cameron Leigh's emails. Here's the last one she sent, which happened to be at 8:07 on Sunday night—the night she got killed. Read it."

She did.

It was to someone named Pamela.

The important part of it said, I saw some guy twice today in different locations. I got a creepy feeling that he was following me because the first time I saw him was downtown and then next time was in the parking lot of my grocery store an hour ago. If I turn up dead, be sure they put KILLED BY A SKINHEAD WITH LOTS OF TATTOOS on my gravestone.

Sydney looked at Teffinger.

Stunned.

"You got to love technology," she said.

"Yes you do."

"And karma," she added.

"What do you mean?"

"You adopt Alley and now good luck's coming your way."

"I did not adopt that fur ball," Teffinger said.

"Then why is he on your desk?"

Teffinger ignored her and typed an email to Pamela, whoever she was, asking her to call him. With any luck, she knew more about the skinhead than just this email.

Two minutes later, he was in a conference room with Sydney and Sergeant Katie Baxter, who wore her hair short and her smile big. Alley scooted in just before Teffinger closed the door. Teffinger looked at the cat, said "I'll be right back," and stepped out. Thirty seconds later he returned with a cup of coffee.

There.

Better.

"You're not going to be happy about my latest and greatest plan because it's going to be 99 percent grunt work and 1 percent fun," he said. "But here it is. First, we find out where Cameron Leigh did her grocery shopping. My guess is that it's the King Soopers or Safeway closest to her house. Then we find out if the store has any surveillance tapes from Sunday that show the skinhead."

"Doable," Baxter said.

Teffinger looked at her, nodded, and purposely kept his eyes off her world-class chest.

Which wasn't easy.

"The next part is harder," he said. "She also got followed by Mr. Wonderful quote-unquote downtown. We need to call everyone programmed into her cell phone and see if they know where she went downtown. Then we need to locate all the surveillance cameras that may have shined on her and our skinhead friend, see if they have any tapes, and check 'em."

"Ouch," Sydney said.

"I want this guy's face on the six o'clock news," Teffinger said.

"Six o'clock of what month?" Baxter asked.

"That's a lot of work," Sydney added.

True.

It was.

But the woman would be dead a lot of years.

"I just had another thought," Teffinger added. "This guy may have been hanging around the victim's house. We need to find out if any of the neighbors saw him."

"What about her work?" Baxter questioned.

Teffinger didn't get excited. "She's a teller at the Wells Fargo Bank in Lakewood, on Union, and didn't work on Saturday or Sunday. My gut tells me that she didn't start to get stalked until Sunday, so the bank will be a dead end. We'll keep it on the list, but at the bottom for now." He paused. "That's the plan unless someone has a better one."

No one did.

So they divvied up the work.

On the way out of the room, Sydney said to Baxter, "I've never seen him like this before."

"What do you mean?"

"He actually kept his eyes up where they were supposed to be," Sydney said. "Now he knows what your face looks like."

Baxter laughed.

"Yeah, I noticed that," she said. "I actually reached under my blouse and squeezed myself once to see if the air had come out."

"I can hear you," Teffinger said. "I'm right here."

"We know," Sydney said.

"We just don't care," Baxter added.

They split up.

The fur ball followed in Teffinger's wake down the three flights of stairs to the parking garage.

And ended up riding shotgun.

"This is a one-shot deal," Teffinger said. "Don't get used to it. And don't think I talk to animals, because I don't."

Chapter Twelve
Day Two—April 13
Wednesday Night

———————————

Tripp landed at Denver International Airport just as the sun went down. He grabbed a Westword from a newsstand, rented a nondescript Dodge and checked into a rat-under-the-bed hotel on Colfax, paying cash. He found a high-end escort service in the back of the Westword that seemed promising.

He dialed.

Talked.

And gave a credit card number.

An hour later he was at a wildly insane downtown nightclub called The Church, dancing with an incredibly sexy dark woman who called herself Kanteese.

Tripp liked her smile.

And her body.

And her perfume.

And the way she stayed so close.

Unlike Rozeen, who was cute-beautiful, Kanteese was stately-beautiful—a modern day Sophia Loren. Tripp couldn't figure out her ancestry, but pictured her jogging on a Mediterranean beach.

Greece, maybe.

Or southern Italy.

Unfortunately, he didn't get the opportunity to consummate the relationship, because Jake VanDeventer called shortly after eleven and said his flight from Johannesburg had just landed at DIA.

VanDeventer wanted to meet immediately.

And what VanDeventer wanted, VanDeventer got.

After all, he was paying the bills.

Tripp made Kanteese a deal—he'd give her an extra $500.00 cash now, which she would have earned later this evening, but she would owe him a free hour of first-class sex later and would need to give him her phone number. Otherwise, she could just keep the money he'd given her already and call it even.

She opted for the $500.00.

Tripp took a picture of her with his cell phone, programmed her number in, called, listened to the phone in her purse ring, and smiled. Then he gave her a kiss and headed into the night to meet VanDeventer.

Chapter Thirteen
Day Two—April 13
Wednesday

———————————

Rave and London cruised south on I-25 at two under the speed limit, with the skinhead's body in the trunk and Billie Holiday on the CD player.

They were nervous.

But not overly so.

The biggest thing was to not get pulled over or get a flat or get in an accident. The second biggest thing was to not do something stupid if one of the first biggest things happened.

So far, no problems.

The weather was clear and sunny.

The vehicle—London's dark-blue Camry—had only 5,500 miles

on the odometer and ran great.

They passed Colorado Springs, Pueblo, Trinidad and a bunch of one-store towns, but the population really dwindled after they crossed the line into New Mexico.

Twenty miles later they turned off the highway and headed into a rolling untamed terrain filled with arroyos and sagebrush. Ten miles later—after not seeing a single sign of civilization—they stopped on the asphalt and killed the engine. They put on baseball caps and dark sunglasses and stepped out.

Not a sound came from anywhere.

Two large black birds floated on silent wings high above them.

Not a wisp of air moved.

They could see a long ways down the road in both directions.

Miles.

Many miles.

They were alone.

No question about it.

"What do you think?" London asked.

"Let's do it," Rave said.

They carried the skinhead's body a good fifty yards off the road and dumped it in a deep arroyo. No one would be able to see it from the asphalt in a million years.

When they got back to the car there was still no one in sight.

They turned the vehicle around, being careful to stay on the asphalt and not get the tires in the dirt.

Then they headed back towards the freeway.

And didn't encounter a single vehicle.

They headed north on I-25.

Miles later they made another diversion off the freeway.

And came to another stop.

Rave stayed at the car and kept watch.

London walked into the terrain holding the gun in a plastic bag. They had already wiped their prints off the weapon multiple times while wearing Latex gloves, to be absolutely sure that there were no remnants.

Five minutes later London walked back, waving the empty plastic bag, and said, "Done."

"You didn't touch it, did you?"

London rolled her eyes.

"Are you nuts? I just opened the bag and let it fall into the hole."

"How deep is it?"

"About a foot," London said.

"That should do it," Rave said.

"That'll more than do it."

They turned around and headed back to the highway.

Not encountering a single vehicle.

Then pointed the front end of the Camry towards Denver.

Feeling good.

Singing to Madonna's "Open Your Heart."

If nothing unexpected happened, Rave would make it to her gig at the Old Orleans tonight just in time.

Chapter Fourteen
Day Two—April 13
Wednesday Night

M ost people along the front range knew Jena Vellone as the roving TV 8 reporter with the charismatic personality, the thick blond hair and the scintillating green eyes. Teffinger knew her from the high school days back in

Fort Collins, when she was the ticklish tomboy down the street.

Teffinger was at his desk, alone in homicide, when she called.

"Got a proposition for you," she said.

He raised an eyebrow.

The large industrial clock on the wall, the one with the twitchy second hand, said 8:02, and made Teffinger realize that he had been going nonstop on the Cameron Leigh case since six this morning.

And that his brain was fried.

"What kind of proposition?" he asked.

"There's a blues singer down at the Old Orleans tonight who's supposed to be incredible," Jena said.

"Who?"

"I don't remember her name, some woman," Jena said. "Geneva saw her and says she's really hot. She was even chatting her up on her show this morning. Anyway, I'm going to let you take me to see her. And if you get me drunk enough, I'm going to let you come back to my place afterwards and wrestle me."

Déjà vu.

Teffinger had gotten this proposition before.

Lots of times.

Three or four times a year, in fact.

Always tempting.

But never good timing.

He almost said no but surprised himself and said, "I'll make you a deal. I sort of got stuck with a cat and need a place to put him short-term, until I can find him a home. If you'll take him for a week or so, then I'll get you as drunk as you want tonight."

"Really?"

Yeah.

Really.

Jena got paid well and her 5,000 square foot Cherry Hills ranch reflected it. When Teffinger knocked on the maple entry door, Jena gave him a quick kiss and then focused on the cat. "My God, look at those eyes! It's like a little, furry you!" she said, taking the animal out of Teffinger's hands. "I'm keeping him."

"Really?"

"Absolutely," she said. "I mean, look at him. This is so cool."

"His name's Alley," Teffinger said.

"Alley Cat," she said.

She gave her new pet a can of tuna and a bowl of milk. It turned out that Alley's front claws were clipped, so Jena let him roam the house as she made a makeshift litter box.

Then she took Teffinger's arm and said, "Get me drunk, cowboy."

Thirty minutes later they walked into the Old Orleans and got charged $15 each at the door. Teffinger paid and said, "I expect you to defend me when people call me the cheapest guy on the face of the earth."

"Defend you? I'm the one who's been warning them."

Teffinger had never been here before.

It turned out to be a large dark place with a cozy New Orleans feeling. An extremely tight band played on a stage at the far end, not overbearingly loud, letting the singer do the work—a singer who was giving an incredibly perfect interpretation of "Black Velvet."

Considerably better than the original.

Teffinger couldn't believe the woman's voice.

Soulful.

Lamenting.

Modernly hypnotic.

The room was packed but Teffinger spotted some daylight between a couple of people seated at the bar and squeezed in to order.

A screwdriver for Jena.

A Bud Light for him.

Suddenly he noticed that the person sitting to his right, watching the singer, was a woman.

A black woman.

An exceptionally beautiful black woman.

With light brown skin and an exotic, island look.

She wore white shorts and an aqua tank, with her bellybutton showing. Perfectly-straight, raven-black hair cascaded down her back, almost to her waist. Teffinger swallowed and debated whether he dared make a move. Then he decided he had to.

"The singer's good," he said.

The woman turned.

She had blue eyes.

As soon as Teffinger looked into those eyes, a primal instinct kicked in. This was the woman he'd been searching for. The one he'd been waiting for. He always knew he'd recognize her when he finally met her. And this was her.

No doubt about it.

He never suspected she wouldn't be white.

But she wasn't.

And that was fine.

The woman held his eyes.

And studied him.

"You're already with someone," she said, nodding towards Jena Vellone. The woman had an English accent with a French overlay.

Totally unexpected.

Very sexy.

"She's an old high school friend," Teffinger said.

The woman leaned in close and put her mouth to Teffinger's ear, almost touching, and whispered, "You and your old high school friend have a good time tonight."

Then she stood up and disappeared into the crowd.

Teffinger almost followed, but the bartender was shouting at him.

Setting down drinks.

Wanting money.

He pushed through the crowd, back to Jena Vellone, handed her the OJ and vodka and said, "I need you to do me a favor."

Sure.

What?

"I just met a woman but she ditched me because she thought I was with you," he said.

"You are with me."

"Yeah, I know," Teffinger said, "but she thinks I'm with you romantically."

"Nick—"

"Look," he said. "All I need you to do is tell her that you and I aren't involved."

"I got a better idea," she said. "Why don't you put the little fellow back in his cage, chill out, and just have a nice evening with me."

He held her eyes.

"This is important," he said. "I really need to see if I have a chance with this woman."

"Why didn't you ever go after me like this?"

He shrugged.

"You know why," he said. "You were younger."

"Yeah, back in high school, but not now."

He almost added, "Plus you were Matt's sister," but detected something in her eyes, and said, "You know something—you're right. I came here to get you drunk so let's get going on it." He clinked her glass with his can and took a long swallow.

Good stuff.

Ice cold.

"Get me drunk and wrestle me," she said.

"Right."

Then Jena shook her head and said, "Okay, I'll do this for you."

"You will?"

She nodded.

"But after I get you set up with the woman, you need to spend the rest of the evening with me and get me drunk and wrestle me like you're supposed to."

Teffinger clinked her glass.

"Agreed."

They headed into the crowd.

Chapter Fifteen
Day Two—April 13
Wednesday Night

———————

Tripp sat behind the wheel of the Dodge rental in a lower downtown parking lot near Coors Field, waiting for Jake VanDeventer to show up.

Tripp didn't know a lot about the man.

But did know a few things.

He knew that VanDeventer opened his first gem mine thirty years ago in North Dakota at age fifteen, and mined it at a profit for two years without the help of a single human being. Now, thirty years later, he lived in Johannesburg and owned a large number of insanely successful diamond mines scattered throughout Africa. He had a rugged, tanned face and a lean body that hadn't lost an ounce of strength.

He wasn't a man to be messed with.

With as much money as VanDeventer had, he should be happy.

He wasn't.

Anything but, in fact.

He had his reasons.

Reasons that Tripp couldn't argue with.

Suddenly Vandeventer appeared at the passenger window, opened the door and climbed in.

They shook hands.

And then hugged.

"Good to see you," VanDeventer said.

"Likewise."

"Still no word from Abbott," VanDeventer said. "I had a P.I. friend check around town to see if he was in custody or in a hospital. He isn't, so I'm guessing he's dead."

Tripp was afraid of that.

And pulled up an image of the tattooed skinhead.

Dead.

"No reports of his body showing up though, I assume," Tripp said.

"That's true," VanDeventer said. "My guess is that he went after Rave Lafelle and somehow got himself killed. Then the woman decided to not be associated with him and disposed of the body, or had a friend do it. Who knows?"

Tripp shook his head.

"Abbott was a good guy," he said. "But he wasn't the most careful guy in the world." A pause. "You going to replace him?"

VanDeventer nodded.

"I already have someone in mind."

"Good."

"In the short-term," VanDeventer said, "we need to have a heart-to-heart with our little vampire friend, Rave Lafelle." The man exhaled and said, "So tell me about the Paris woman, Diamanda."

Tripp filled him in on the details of last night and added, "I swear to God she was every bit as strong as me. Have you ever seen a pit bull fight a dog?"

No.

He hadn't.

"Well the pit bull just gets the other dog by the throat and never lets go no matter what," Tripp said. "The other dog can be clawing at his balls or whatever, it doesn't matter, the thing just doesn't let go. Then when the other dog gets tired, the pit bull gets an even deeper bite on the thing's throat. Eventually the other dog just suffocates to death. That's how this Paris vampire was. She got her hands on my neck and pushed her thumbs into my throat and I couldn't get her off to save my life. I actually thought she was going to kill me. The only thing that saved me was that I dropped and did something like a crocodile death roll."

VanDeventer nodded.

"I'm not surprised."

"She was stronger than her bodyguard and he was almost as big as me," Tripp said. "It was freaky."

"Some of them definitely have powers," VanDeventer said. "They're watered down, but they're there."

Tripp exhaled.

"Maybe that's how Abbott ended up dead," VanDeventer added. "Got into more than he could handle."

Tripp nodded

And said, "I tried to get information. But somehow I tripped an alarm and had to get the hell out of there. The only thing I managed to do was grab a laptop from the woman's bedroom."

VanDeventer was shocked.

"I didn't know about that," he said.

"Sorry, I forgot to tell you," Tripp said. "I tried to boot it up but you need a password."

"Where is it?"

"The laptop?"

"Yes."

"In my hotel room. Why?"

"Let's go have a look."

"Now?"

"Yes, now."

Chapter Sixteen
Day Three—April 14
Thursday Morning

R ave woke Thursday morning in a strange bed with someone sleeping next to her—London, the vampire. Then she remembered London's warning last night that other slayers would be arriving in Denver to finish what the skinhead started. "It'll be suicide to stay at your place tonight," London said. "Especially without a gun."

So they made sure no one tailed them after they left the Old Orleans at two in the morning and then checked into a cheap hotel in Lakewood.

Paying cash.

London's treat.

Now, outside, it was daylight, but the curtains were doing a good job of beating it back. Rave looked at her watch.

Good.

She'd slept for a solid eight hours.

She put her arms above her head and stretched. The movement woke London who moaned and said with a scratchy voice, "What time is it?"

"Eleven."

London threw off the sheets, jumped out of bed and headed for the bathroom, naked.

"What's going on?" Rave asked.

"I'm supposed to meet that man for lunch." Two seconds later the shower came on. "I'm leaving the door open so you can use the facilities if you need to."

Actually, Rave did.

But she dressed first.

And waited until London was behind the shower curtain.

There.

Better.

Now she needed coffee.

London emerged ten minutes later, toweling off, totally at ease with being nude in front of another woman. Rave couldn't believe the woman's body. She looked for a flaw and found none. Not an extra pound, not a sag, nothing. The most amazing thing was the woman's ass, perfectly taut and rounded. Rave had never seen an ass like that and probably never would again. London had won the gene lottery, no question about it.

"Have you ever heard of Wong's, on Court Street?" London asked. "That's where I'm supposed to meet this guy."

No.

Rave hadn't.

But she knew where Court Street was.

"It's smack downtown," she said. "You'll be hard pressed to find a parking spot."

"Man—"

"If you want, I can drive and drop you off."

London's face lit up.

"Thanks."

"What's this guy's name?"

"Nick."

"Nick what?"

"I don't know."

"What's he do?"

"I don't know," London said. Then she grinned and said, "Me, I hope."

They screeched to a stop in front of Wong's at 12:03. London jumped out and said, "Remember, a 9mm SIG—two of 'em." Then she was gone. Fifteen minutes later Rave stepped into a gun shop on Colfax and filled out the forms to buy two handguns.

At London's insistence.

Because they couldn't afford to be sitting ducks.

Then she did something she promised London she wouldn't do. She swung by her house and threw stuff in a suitcase—clothes, CDs, shampoo, a hair dryer.

Then got the hell out of there.

No problem.

She pointed the front end of London's vehicle back downtown to find a place to park and wait for London's call. On the way, she noticed something unusual.

A vehicle seemed to be following her.

Doing the exact same speed as her.

Hanging back fifty yards.

Just for grins, Rave took a right on the next side street.

The other car followed.

She shouldn't have gone home.

Why hadn't she been smart enough to listen to London?

Maybe it was just a coincidence.

She made another turn.

Left this time.

The other vehicle followed.

Chapter Seventeen
Day Three—April 14
Thursday Morning

Teffinger didn't get home from Jena's until two in the morning and then got up at six, seriously in need of a truckload of coffee. He should have slept longer but London was already in his head. The big question is whether she would actually show up for lunch today.

Or blow him off.

He was at his desk when Sydney walked into the room shortly after seven. She studied him as she poured coffee, then walked over and took a seat in front of his desk.

"You look like Alley dragged you around all night," she said.

Teffinger grunted.

"Alley got adopted."

Sydney raised an eyebrow.

"By who?"

"Jena Vellone."

Sydney rolled her eyes. "Probably to get in good with you," she said. "That woman would do anything for a plate full of Nick Teffinger, in case you haven't noticed."

Teffinger shrugged.

"Which totally baffles me," Sydney added. "Since she's the most eligible bachelorette in Denver and you're—well, you're you."

Teffinger chuckled.

"It's an enigma," he confessed.

"An enigma wrapped in a mystery," Sydney said.

Teffinger didn't know whether he should venture into the subject he was contemplating, but had to tell someone, if for no other reason than to see how the words sounded out loud. "I met a woman," he said.

Sydney studied him.

And must have recognized the look because she said, "You're in lust." Teffinger didn't deny it. "What's the poor victim's name?"

"Oh, no you don't."

"What do you mean?"

"You know you'll be running a background check on her before that cup is empty," he said.

"So?"

"So, forget it." He sipped coffee and added, "She's Jamaican."

"Jamaican?"

He nodded.

"A black Jamaican, with blue eyes."

Sydney chuckled and said, "You're way out of your league, cowboy. You know that, I hope."

Cameron Leigh—the woman murdered with a wooden stake through her heart—had a friend named Beth Sorenson. Beth's number was programmed into Cameron's cell phone. Sydney called that number twice yesterday, to ask the woman if she knew where Cameron had planned to go "downtown" on Sunday afternoon. The woman never answered so Sydney left messages.

"She called me back at 10:30 last night," Sydney said. "She said Cameron was going to go to a rave in an old brick building off Wazee."

"A rave?"

"Yeah. A gothic rave, apparently."

"What's a rave?"

"You don't know?"

No, he didn't.

So she explained.

"Anyway," she said, "my plan this morning was to walk around the area and check for security cameras."

Teffinger swallowed the rest of his coffee.

"Let's go," he said.

"You're coming with me?"

"I want that skinhead and I want him now," he said.

They filled a thermos.

Then headed out.

Four hours later they were back, with videotapes from a furniture warehouse that had security cameras that shined on an alley that a lot of people used on Sunday to go to a rave.

Teffinger and Sydney watched for a half hour.

And saw no signs of Cameron Leigh.

At least not yet.

But did see plenty of skinheads.

"This is going to be tougher than I thought."

Then he looked at his watch—high noon, exactly.

"Oops."

"What?"

He was already out of his chair and said over his shoulder, "I'm supposed to be at Wong's."

London was sitting in a booth when Teffinger ran into the restaurant at 12:15 out of breath. He slipped into the opposite side and said, "I am so sorry. Thanks for waiting."

She said nothing.

And instead studied him.

"Your eyes are two different colors," she said. "One's blue and one's green. I didn't notice that last night."

"And?"

"And what?

"And does it freak you out?"

She laughed.

"Nothing freaks me out anymore," she said. "I like them, so relax."

They ordered.

Then Teffinger said, "Tell me about you."

She told him about Jamaica.

And Paris.

And South Beach.

She was still a citizen of Jamaica, technically, but had been living in South Beach for the last three years, following the death of her mother. She was in Denver visiting Rave Lafelle, the singer from the club last night.

She had no boyfriend.

Or kids.

And had never been married.

Teffinger wanted to take her, right then, right there. He wanted to sweep everything off the table, throw her on top and rip her shorts off. He wanted to make her scream. He wanted to turn her into a sweaty, out-of-control animal.

But he didn't.

Because there were rules against that at Wong's.

"I'm thinking we should see each other again," Teffinger said.

"Sure."

"I'm thinking tonight," he added.

She didn't hesitate.

"Okay."

"What's your last name?"

"Fontelle."

"London Fontelle?"

"Right."

Nice.

Very nice.

An hour later they parted company and Teffinger hoofed it back to headquarters, feeling sorry for every guy in the world who wasn't him.

Sydney spotted him as soon as he walked in the door.

"Good news," she said.

"How good?"

"I think we got a picture of the skinhead."

Chapter Eighteen
Day Three—April 14
Thursday Morning

———————————

Tripp made several sweeps past Rave Lafelle's house Thursday morning. The woman's VW was parked in the driveway but there were no signs of life inside the house.

It would be too risky to break in.

She'd be prepared for intruders, given the Mathew Abbott fiasco.

Hell, she might be sitting in a closet with a shotgun, just waiting for the next dumb slob to open the door.

Then something unexpected happened.

When he made another pass, the woman actually turned into the driveway driving a dark-blue Camry. She hopped out and ran inside.

Tripp circled around the block.

Then he parked down the street and killed the engine.

Five minutes later the woman emerged, threw a suitcase in the back seat and took off.

Tripp followed.

Hanging back.

Where she wouldn't spot him in a million years.

Then he noticed something strange.

Another car was following her too.

A silver Volvo.

Tripp closed the gap until he got close enough to read the other car's license plate. Then he veered off, stopped and wrote down the number.

Weird.

Later that afternoon, Jake VanDeventer called and said, "Guess whose face is all over the news?"

"Abbott's?"

"Bingo."

"So what's the deal?"

"He's wanted for questioning in connection with Cameron Leigh," VanDeventer said.

"So the cops don't know he's dead?"

"Apparently not."

"Interesting," Tripp said. "Did you get that French laptop open yet?"

"Yes."

"And?"

"And we now know the phone numbers and emails of most of the top models in Paris," VanDeventer said. "Other than that, it's a bust."

Tripp exhaled.

And said, "Damn."

After he hung up, Tripp went for a five-mile jog and questioned whether he had just made a fatal mistake in not telling VanDeventer about the Volvo that had been following Rave Lafelle.

He decided that he made the right decision.

But better not get caught.

He showered.

Then found out who the Volvo was registered to.

Avis.

Chapter Nineteen
Day Three—April 14
Thursday Afternoon

R ave squealed down side streets and busted through red lights until she finally shook the silver Volvo. When she picked up London at Wong's, her hands were shaking.

"Did you get a look at the driver?" London asked.

Rave nodded.

"Sort of, it was a man—he had long hair."

"Blond?"

"Right."

London grinned.

"Parker," she said. "That's so like him, to make a dramatic entrance."

"You know him?"

London nodded.

"He's on our side."

They got caught at a red light.

Three seconds later a silver Volvo pulled up on their left. The driver powered down the passenger side glass and said, "Follow me."

Rave looked at London, who nodded and said, "Do it."

They headed west on the 6th Avenue freeway for twenty miles, all the way through Lakewood to the Golden exit. They turned left and climbed a dangerous road that snaked up the face of Lookout Mountain. The Volvo pulled into a dirt turnoff about three-fourths of the way up and the women pulled in next to it and killed the engine.

They all got out.

From there, a panoramic view opened up for thirty or forty miles. In the valley below—nestled between North Table Mesa and South Table Mesa—lay downtown Golden and the Coors Brewery. Denver seemed small and insignificant, more than twenty miles to the east, followed by flatlands that stretched to DIA and then all the way to Kansas.

While the view was stunning, Rave spent only a heartbeat with it before being pulled in by the man's face. He wasn't anything like she expected.

He looked like a California surfer.

With an incredible face.

White teeth.

A good tan.

A solid, athletic build.

Long thick blondish hair that fell past his shoulders.

About thirty.

No wedding ring.

Dressed in khaki Dockers and a blue cotton shirt.

Very sexy.

She swallowed and wondered if they would end up sleeping together.

He wasted no time getting to the point. "I apologize for getting into Denver so late," he said. "I had some stuff going on and couldn't break away. London has already filled me in on the skinhead you shot. That makes you in this as deep as we are, and because of that I'm going to be able to share some things with you that I probably wouldn't otherwise—emphasis on the some because it's better for you if you don't know too much."

A magpie flew.

High off the valley floor, but below them.

It was peculiar to look down on flapping wings.

"What kind of things?" Rave asked.

"Let me give you some background," Parker said. "First—let's get this out in the open right off the bat—I'm a bloodline descendent of a man named Randolph Gertz, who was reputed to be an immortal vampire back in his day. He got murdered at age twenty-five with a wooden stake through his heart. Then they burned his body to ashes in a bonfire. London, as you already know, is also a bloodline descendent. There are more of us, too."

"How many?"

"That's under constant investigation," he said. "As more and more information has become available on the net, and as more and more historical documents around the world are being archived and translated and made available to the public, the science of genealogy has opened up to proportions never before known, for those who care to dig. While it's still a very arduous and time-consuming endeavor, it's getting increasingly easier to trace bloodlines further and further back into the past. Currently, we have thirty-one living bloodline descendents identified. We've formed something in the nature of an association, if you will."

"An association?"

"Right," he said. "The problem is, over time, the word has gotten out and another group has formed—a group of slayers who are hell bent on eradicating us."

"Why?"

"We're not exactly sure, but we have a couple of theories," Parker said. "One is that they think we'll go crazy and start copycatting our ancestors and start killing people and sucking blood."

"Do you?" Rave questioned.

Parker chuckled at the absurdity of the thought.

"Kill people? No, of course not," he said. "Another theory, perhaps the better one, is that they think we're carriers of immortality—in other words, that there's something latent in our genes that could cause someone else to be immortal even though we obviously aren't. We're not sure, but they could even be trying to capture some of us alive and trying to tap into that immortality."

"That's downright creepy," Rave said.

"Agreed," Parker said. "But here's where we are, right now, today. We have a woman up in Montreal who is doing our genealogy research. We think that the slayers somehow found out who she was. She keeps all of her files locked up in an incredibly sound safe. She called me last week in a panic, convinced that she was being followed and that her life was in imminent danger. We immediately got her to a safe refuge and didn't even allow her to go home. At the time, she had been working on three files that weren't locked up. They were sitting on the desk in her study. Her house was broken into and those files disappeared."

"What does this have to do with me?" Rave asked.

"The first file was a French model named Diamanda," Parker said. "It turns out that she was killed at her estate south of Paris the night before last, on Tuesday. She was beaten badly and then a wooden stake was pounded through her heart."

"You're kidding."

No.

He wasn't.

"It's all over the French newspapers," Parker said. "You can pull the stories off the net. The second file was a Denver woman named Cameron Leigh," Parker said. "She was killed Sunday night."

Rave knew that.

The murder had been in the papers.

And on the news.

But she didn't know the background.

"Was she killed with a wooden stake?"

"We don't know," Parker said. "My suspicion is that she was, but the police are keeping it close to the vest."

Rave said nothing.

"The third file was you," Parker said. "It turns out that you and Cameron Leigh had the same great-great grandfather. I don't know if you knew that or not."

No.

She didn't.

She didn't know anything about her genealogy.

"There must be a mistake."

Parker shook his head.

And said, "I'm sorry this is happening. If I could change your past, I would."

"You shouldn't have dug it up," she said.

"I'm sorry we did," he said. "But we can't undo what's been done. All we can do at this point is deal with what we have."

Rave sank to the ground.

And leaned against the front tire of the Camry.

And bowed her head.

She knew she shouldn't.

She knew she was coming off as weak.

She tried to stop.

But couldn't.

She kept hoping the whole situation would go away. Instead, it kept getting more and more real.

Suddenly Parker was down in the dirt with her.

And had his arm around her shoulders.

And let her lay her head on his chest.

Chapter Twenty
Day Three—April 14
Thursday Afternoon

———————————

T he security tapes from the furniture warehouse showed a tattooed skinhead following Cameron Leigh to the rave and then, three hours later, from it. Each time he hung twenty steps behind. Whereas most people wore black, he wore white. Teffinger got his face on every news station in Denver as soon as he could. So far, however, no one had called with information on the guy. Nor had Teffinger been able to match the face to any databases.

He hung around his desk.

Wadding up paper and throwing it into the snake plant.

Waiting.

Getting nothing.

Then he got the clearest pictures of the man's tattoos that he could and faxed them to every tattoo shop in Denver to see if anyone recognized them.

And waited some more.

And got more nothing.

Piles and piles of nothing.

Then the phone rang.

"Nick, it's me." The voice belonged to Dr. Leigh Sandt, the FBI profiler. "I checked around for you to see if anyone else got killed with a wooden stake. Nada for the U.S., but get this—the exact same thing just happened in Paris, to a model named Diamanda."

"When?"

"Tuesday evening."

"Tuesday as in two days ago?"

"Bingo," she said. "It's the front page story in every French newspaper."

Teffinger chewed on it.

"I need to get in touch with whoever is in charge over there," he said.

"Get a pencil," she said.

She gave him a name and number.

He wrote them down.

"Do you speak French?" she questioned.

"No, just that one line from the song."

"What song?"

"Voulez-vous coucher avec moi, ce soir."

She chuckled. "How come that doesn't surprise me?"

Teffinger was just about to call his French counterpart when his cell phone rang. It was Geneva Vellone, the radio half of the Vellone sisters, a 27-year-old fireball who had an insanely popular morning show on FM 104 called Hot Talk.

Teffinger listened to it a few times.

And found it a little too over-the-top for his taste.

In high school, Jena Vellone was the baby sister of Matt Vellone, Teffinger's best friend. Jena was three years younger, a tomboy, and always hung around whenever Teffinger was over. She was cute enough that Teffinger always had a bit of a crush on her, but nothing ever became of it.

Except that Jena would start wrestling fights every now and then, and wouldn't stop until she got pinned and tickled.

Geneva was the third of the Vellone siblings.

Three years younger than Jena.

Six years younger than Teffinger.

He didn't pay much attention to her back in the older days, but they turned into flirting-buddies four or five years ago.

"Where's Jena?" Geneva asked.

Teffinger didn't know.

"You were with her last night, right?"

"Yeah. Why?"

"She was scheduled to do an interview a half hour ago and didn't show up," Geneva said. "The station's in a panic—and mad. Jena isn't answering any of her phones. The girl needs to get herself in gear, and I'm talking about right now, this second."

"Did you go over to her house?" Teffinger asked.

"Not yet."

"Try that," he said. "She got pretty trashed last night."

"She did?"

"She's probably still sleeping it off."

The line went dead.

Teffinger called his French counterpart and got informed by an assistant that the man was up to his eyeballs in a murder investigation. Teffinger explained that he had a similar case in Denver, meaning a woman stabbed through the heart with a wooden stake, and thought that the cases might be connected.

"We'll let him know."

"Be sure he calls me," Teffinger said.

"Sure."

"We think that the suspect is a skinhead with lots of tattoos," Teffinger added.

A pause.

"Do you have a picture of him?"

Teffinger did.

And emailed it.

Forty-five minutes later, Geneva Vellone called. "Jena's not here," she said. "Her bedroom's trashed and there's blood on the sheets."

Teffinger stood up and headed for the door.

"Stay there and don't touch anything," he said. "I'm coming over."

As he bounded down the stairs, he had a sinking feeling in his gut. He tucked Jena into bed last night, drunk; and kissed her on the cheek before he left. But he definitely didn't activate her security system when he left. Now, thinking back on it, he couldn't remember if he locked the front door on his way out.

Man—

If something happened to her, and it was his fault, he'd never forgive himself.

Chapter Twenty-One
Day Three—April 14
Thursday Afternoon

L auren Long had more money than she could spend in ten lifetimes, but liked to dress like she had none. Right now, Lauren—the 22-year-old daughter of oilman Peter Long—walked down the 16th Street Mall in the heart of downtown Denver, wearing torn jeans and a faded Aerosmith T-shirt ripped off at the bottom so people could see her abs.

Those incredible, tight abs.

Finely honed from a ridiculously strict diet and insane workouts directed by Lauren's personal trainer five days a week at the Denver Athletic Club. Abs that were nicely bronzed from sitting out by the pool while she listened to hip-hop and talked to the girls about what club to do next.

She was richer than the peons around her.

And cuter.

And in better shape.

And more popular.

Right now, with a summa cum laude degree from Brown under her belt, she owned the world.

She crossed California Street and continued down the mall under a warm Colorado sky. A hotdog vendor sat next to a cart on a nylon director's chair, bored, stuck in that transition period between lunch and supper. Lauren Long looked at him for a half-second, maybe less, just long enough to register that he wasn't part of her world.

The hip world.

The in world.

She kept walking.

Tripp followed.

Ten steps behind.

Watching her body swing.

Chapter Twenty-Two
Day Three—April 14
Thursday Afternoon

———————

After the meeting with Parker on Lookout Mountain, Rave sat silently in the passenger seat of the Camry while London drove back to Denver.

Choices were upon her.

Ugly choices.

She could either run, change her name, give up her identity and existence, and then spend the rest of her life hoping that she had gone deep enough to get off the slayers' radar.

Or she could keep the status quo.

The former meant abandoning her life as a singer.

The latter meant that sooner or later she'd be grabbed from behind, taken to some godforsaken place and killed with a wooden stake through her heart.

Not good.

"How many slayers are there?" she questioned.

London looked over.

And shrugged.

"One less, with the skinhead gone," she said.

"I'm serious," Rave said. "How many more?"

"We don't know exactly."

"I don't want any of this," Rave said. "I just want to be free to live my life."

London looked over.

With a serious expression.

"Look," she said. "Parker and I have already talked about this. We already decided that they've given us no choice but to grow teeth and bite back, if we ever get the chance. The problem is that we've never gotten the chance so far because we never knew where they were going to strike next. Things are different now. We know they're after you."

True.

"So we sort of have a fork in the road," London said. "At least as far as you're concerned. You can either disappear and run and hope they never find you, or you can just stay here in Denver and see what happens."

"What does that mean?"

"It means, see if me and Parker can get them before they get you."

Rave thought about it.

"Meaning I'm bait."

London focused on the road.

And said nothing.

"If I were you, I'd just run," London said. "It's the safer bet."

"The problem is that I can't ever make it as a singer without being on stage," Rave said. "Even if I change my name and appearance and stay hidden for the next two years, once I surface again they'll spot me."

True.

Then Rave said, "Okay."

"Okay what?"

"Okay, I'll be the bait."

London nodded and said, "You don't have to do anything when it comes time. Me and Parker will do all the work."

Rave exhaled.

"I'm going to defend myself if it comes to it," she said. "That's my right."

London nodded.

Yes it was.

"And I'm not going to let anyone hurt you either," Rave added. "I at least owe you that much for saving my life."

"You don't owe me anything," London said.

Rave nodded, but added, "Just because I'm doing this doesn't mean I'm not scared."

"You and me both."

They powered up a Madonna CD and then cranked up the volume as they rolled east on the 6th Avenue freeway towards downtown.

"Material Girl."

"Like A Virgin."

"La Isla Bonita."

Suddenly they were hungry and decided to splurge because—who knows?—it might be their last meal. Then, at the last minute, they pulled into Wendy's instead.

And felt good about saving the money.

Chapter Twenty-Three
Day Three—April 14
Thursday Afternoon

_____

As Teffinger headed south on I-25, he noticed something ironic just after he passed Colorado Boulevard—a billboard displaying Jena Vellone's smiling face, next to "Another TV8 Winner" and the station's logo. He pulled up the memory of Jena calling him a month ago, bubbling with excitement because she was going to get some type of award for excellence in TV journalism.

At an elegant dinner reception.

Everyone who was someone was going to be there.

She wanted Teffinger to be her escort.

"Sure," he said.

"Really?"

"Yeah, I'm proud of you."

"You don't even know what it's for."

"I don't need to."

Then he had to cancel at the last minute.

And now wished he hadn't.

Twenty minutes later he pulled into Jena Vellone's cobblestone driveway and parked behind a red Viper. Geneva bounded out the front door wearing black shorts, a red tank and a spa tan.

She looked serious and walked fast.

She hugged him tight as soon as he stepped out.

"It's worse than I thought," she said. "Someone took her, I know it."

"Let's not jump—"

"All her stuff is here, Nick—her car, her keys, her purse," Geneva said. "That's the killer; there's no way she would go anywhere without her purse—not in a million years."

True, Teffinger thought.

Except for a jog or something.

The entry consisted of an oversized oak door, very fancy, with glass on each side and above, encased in a modern architectural enclave. "Was the door open when you got here?" Teffinger asked as they approached.

"No," Geneva said. "It was closed but it wasn't locked."

Not good.

That's what Teffinger was afraid of.

"So you could just turn the knob and go in?" he asked.

"Right," she said.

Teffinger thought about telling her that he was to blame, but decided to see if there was another explanation first. He put on a pair of latex gloves and handed a second pair to Geneva. Then he opened the front door, touching the knob only on the very tip, and headed in.

Alley pranced over and Teffinger picked him up.

Everything looked normal.

To the left, the house opened into a large vaulted space that led all the way to a designer kitchen. Teffinger walked straight towards the back, to the master bedroom.

As soon as Teffinger saw the bed, he flashed back to last night, when he brought Jena home from Old Orleans. She was sloppy drunk. He got her out of the Tundra and let her lean on him until they got to the front door. She slumped down while he fumbled around in her purse and found the keys. He opened the door, slung Jena's purse over his shoulder and then picked the woman up in his arms and carried her into the house.

He headed straight for the master bedroom and laid her on the bed.

She spread her legs and pulled her sundress up.

Exposing a black thong.

Incredibly sexy.

"Come here," she said.

He actually considered it for a heartbeat.

But couldn't, not with her trashed like that.

"Tomorrow," he said. By the time he took her shoes off and tucked her in, she had already passed out. He kissed her on the cheek, headed out the front door, swung it shut as he stepped through, and went home.

That was last night.

Now she was missing.

Jena's purse sat on top of an expensive cherry dresser, exactly where Teffinger tossed it last night. And now, unlike last night, there was blood on the sheets.

Teffinger checked the bathroom.

No blood there.

Not a drop.

If Jena had gone there, fallen, and smashed her face on the counter or the tile floor, the evidence would be there—but it wasn't. Nor was there blood on the doorframe, or nightstand, or anywhere else.

It was only on the sheets.

And not centralized by the pillow, as if she got a nosebleed.

It was scattered.

As if someone had punched her.

And she had struggled.

He checked the route from Jena's bedroom to the front door and found blood drippings that he hadn't noticed before, as if someone had carried her out of the house while she was bleeding. He inspected all the doors and windows and found them locked and without any evidence of tampering or break-in. The white sundress that Jena wore last night—the one she still had on when Teffinger tucked her in—was nowhere to be found.

Teffinger looked at Geneva.

And exhaled.

"This is my fault," he said. "I left her here last night and didn't lock the front door on my way out. I tucked her in and left and just swung the door shut on my way out. I guess I was tired but, man, that was just so stupid—"

Geneva stared at him.

Then she said, "If someone was set on taking her, it wouldn't matter if the door was locked or not."

"Yeah, but—"

"Stop it," she said. "This isn't your fault."

"It is," he insisted.

"Here's the thing," she said. "Jena's gone and we need to find her, right now, this second. So get your act together. This isn't about you. It's about her."

Chapter Twenty-Four
Day Three—April 14
Thursday Afternoon

———————————

Tripp was on a bench on the sunny side of the 16th Street Mall in the middle of downtown Denver, watching the skirts stroll by and waiting for Lauren Long to come out of the Hard Rock Café, when his phone rang.

He looked at the incoming number.

Jake VanDeventer.

Boss man.

"Got a complication," VanDeventer said. "I'm heading to the airport as we speak."

"Why? What's going on?"

"One of my mines had a cave-in."

"Ouch."

"Seven people are trapped," VanDeventer added. "I'll be back as soon as I can."

"When do you think that will be?"

"That'll depend on how the rescue goes," VanDeventer said. "If things go fast and go good, I'll hardly be gone at all. If things turn ugly, there's no telling."

"So what do you want me to do in the meantime?"

"Keep Rave Lafelle in your sights," VanDeventer said. "If she bolts out of town, follow her and then rope her in for a little heart-to-heart. If she doesn't bolt, then proceed as if the vampires are in town and are using her as bait."

"Screw 'em."

"Don't be a hero," the man emphasized. "In fact, if she's rubbing elbows with them, that's not necessarily a bad thing. That means she's learning stuff. That'll just make her all the more valuable, when the time comes."

True.

Very true.

Lauren Long brought her pretty little face out of the Hard Rock Café twenty minutes later and came within five feet of Tripp as she crossed to the sunny side of the street. He wasn't sure, because the woman wore sunglasses, but thought that she may have thrown him a glance as she passed.

No problem.

He'd be extra careful.

She headed north.

Probably en route to Larimer Square or LoDo.

Tripp followed.

Feeling good.

The woman's swing looked just as appetizing as before, but now she had trouble walking in a straight line; maybe because she had a little powder up the nose.

Two blocks later, the woman stopped and studied something in the window. Tripp hung back and assessed the situation. Then the woman grabbed a man walking past, handed him her cell phone and stuck a pose. The man pointed the phone at her, obviously taking a picture.

She said Thanks and kept walking.

Tripp followed.

Suddenly a sinking feeling grabbed him.

Had the woman spotted him?

Had she asked the man to actually take a picture of Tripp instead of her?

Had she already emailed it to someone with a text message?—
This man is following me.

He broke off.

And walked the other way.

Chapter Twenty-Five
Day Three—April 14
Thursday Evening

———————————

The VW sat in the driveway. Rave walked around nervously inside the house, occasionally adjusting the windows and repositioning the curtains, making it apparent that she was home in case anyone was watching. If she was going to be prey, she needed the predator to see her.

Parker sat on the floor in the bedroom.

Leaning against the wall with his legs stretched out.

Hidden.

Waiting.

On the floor next to him sat a large survival knife.

And a baseball bat.

Both purchased with cash this afternoon. Rave would feel better if he had a gun, but when she mentioned it, Parker just laughed and told her not to worry about it. He occasionally flipped the knife in the air and caught it by the handle. Billie Holiday came from the CD player, barely audible so it didn't become a communications barrier.

Rave flopped down on the couch and lit a joint.

Parker must have smelled it because he said, "That's not a good idea."

"Probably not," she said.

And then took another drag.

The world softened.

A layer of stress peeled off and floated away.

She wasn't sure she should approach the subject on her mind but decided to just go for it. "So are you and London sleeping together?"

"Why?"

"No reason," she said. "Just curious."

"No."

"Not now? Or not ever?"

"Both."

Rave exhaled.

"And no to your next question too," Parker added.

"Which question is that?"

"Whether I have a girlfriend."

She chuckled.

"Well someone's a little full of himself," she said.

"Are you saying you weren't going to ask?"

"I don't know if I was or not," she said.

"How about you?" he asked.

"No and no."

"Good."

"Good?"

"Yeah, good," Parker said.

She finished the joint and looked at her watch—seven o'clock. "I should probably start getting ready," she said, referring to the evening gig at the Old Orleans.

"I want you to get ready exactly as you always do," Parker said.

"Exactly?"

Right.

"But you're in the room."

"Forget I'm here," he said.

She swallowed, pushed herself off the couch and walked into the bedroom. She stopped next to the bed, pulled the T-shirt over her head and tossed it on the covers. Then she reached behind her back, unclasped her bra and threw it on top of the T-shirt.

Next her socks came off.

Then her jeans.

Then her panties.

She walked over to the closet, opened the door and sifted through her wardrobe, feeling sexy and looking for something to match her mood. She chose a short black dress with a plunging neckline, pulled it off the hanger and laid it on the bed. She pulled a white thong from the top dresser drawer and tossed it on top of the dress.

Then she walked into the bathroom.

Left the door open.

Adjusted the shower temperature.

And stepped in.

Parker could see her from where he sat. The shower doors were clear glass. She'd be partially distorted by the water, but not much.

She put her head under the spray until her hair was soaked.

Then shampooed.

Imagining how she looked with her arms up and her breasts stretched high.

She had a good body.

She knew that.

But was it good enough for Parker?

With the shampoo still in her hair, she grabbed the bar of soap and worked it over her body.

Wishing that the door would suddenly open.

And that Parker would step inside.

Chapter Twenty-Six
Day Three—April 14
Thursday Evening

Technically, Teffinger didn't have jurisdiction to investigate Jena Vellone's disappearance, so he and Geneva filed a missing-person report with Cherry Hills P.D. and asked for permission to run a "parallel" investigation, meaning that Teffinger would take the lead and keep them in the loop. At first they were hesitant, since Teffinger had been the last person to see Jena safe and alive. But Teffinger's chief called and staked his personal reputation on the fact that Teffinger wasn't involved in any way, form or shape.

That tipped the scales.

Of course, Teffinger still couldn't take possession of physical evidence, so Cherry Hills took the bloody sheets. They'd use the CBI to run a DNA analysis and determine if the blood belonged to Jena, a third-party, or a combination of the two.

None of Jena's neighbors saw anything.

Or knew anything.

The prints lifted from Jena's house didn't trigger any database matches. Trace evidence got collected, but nothing that could identify the perpetrator.

Squat.

Squat.

Squat.

Rule out robbery, though.

Lots of good stuff in plain sight didn't get taken.

Whoever came in wanted Jena.

Not her things.

Jena's emails, computer files and personal effects didn't point towards stalkers or weirdos in her life. Plus, that's the kind of thing she would have told either Teffinger or Geneva about in any event.

No ransom calls came in.

Teffinger was alone in homicide, wondering what to do next, when darkness fell on the city. He looked at the coffee pot—usually his friend—and determined that his hands were already shaking too much.

Not good.

He grabbed his sport coat, walked down the stairwell to the parking garage and headed home.

On the way his cell phone rang.

And London's voice came through.

"I thought we were going to get together tonight," she said.

"Tomorrow might be better," he warned. "I'm not very good company right now."

She didn't care.

"We can just hang out at your house if you don't feel like doing anything." He gave her directions and then tried to remember if his house was a minor or major disaster area.

Major, he decided.

And stepped on the gas.

London showed up just as the streetlights kicked on. She wore a sleeveless white dress, short enough that it would lift up to her cheeks if she reached above her head. Teffinger couldn't remember ever seeing a woman so beautiful. She handed him a bottle of white wine and said, "This is in case you decide to get me drunk."

"Actually, that sounds like a pretty good plan," he said. "You want to grab a glass? They're in that top cabinet right there."

She walked over.

Then gave him a sideways look. "You better turn your head," she said.

"Towards you or away?" he said.

She chuckled.

Then waited until he looked away.

"Did you wear that dress for me?" Teffinger asked.

"Actually it's for me," she said. "Otherwise I'd be nude."

He made a concerned face.

"We certainly don't want that," he said.

Alley walked into the room.

London picked him up and said, "He's like a little, furry you."

"Or I'm like a big him," Teffinger said. "It's a raging debate."

Teffinger lived in a split-level ranch near the top of Green Mountain, third house from the end, on a cul-de-sac. The mountain slanted down to the back of his property, leaving almost no backyard. But he built a redwood deck off the side of the mountain that was higher than his roofline. Up there, at night, you could see the city lights all the way from Boulder to the Tech Center.

That's where he took London, after getting her a sweater.

She was impressed but said, "I'll bet it's even better from the top of the mountain."

"True," Teffinger said.

"Show me."

"It's a half hour hike," he said. "In the daylight."

"Are you scared?"

He chuckled.

"Okay, but remember, you asked for it."

He stuffed a blanket, three cans of Bud and the bottle of wine into a small backpack and then led London up the draw towards the transmission tower at the top of Green Mountain. Each step brought them closer to the barking of coyotes.

"Remember, if they attack, you don't have to be able to run faster than them," he said. "You only have to be able to run faster than me."

"I heard that joke before, except with bears."

"It works with anything that has teeth."

"I see."

"I tried it once with chickens," he said. "It didn't work."

"Because they don't have teeth."

"There you go."

When they got to the top and settled down on the blanket with drinks in hand, the trip was worth it. It seemed like they were in an airplane, coming in for a night landing.

They laid on their backs and looked at the stars.

Teffinger knew this was the point where he was supposed to roll over and take her, but he couldn't get Jena Vellone out of his head. Wherever she was, Teffinger was to blame. Not fully, but at least partially.

Chapter Twenty-Seven
Day Three—April 14
Thursday Afternoon

After breaking off from Lauren Long, Tripp headed back to his car, which was parked on the south edge of downtown not far from the library, two rows over from where the woman had parked. Cotton clouds floated in from the mountains, typical for an April afternoon in Denver. The temperature was nice.

Tripp felt good.

But being around all the women downtown had made him horny. Maybe he should call that escort—the one he partied with at The Church on Tuesday—and collect what she owed him.

That sounded good.

But a fresh woman sounded even better.

Lauren Long would be perfect.

But he dared not take her today.

She'd be incredibly fun, once the time came. As soon as she disappeared, the activity would be deafening. Mr. Daddy Big-Shot would launch an army to find his precious little baby. That was the beauty of the thing. It reminded Tripp of when he was a kid and spotted a pile of ants on the sidewalk, thousands of them, all in one spot for some stupid reason, just asking to be stepped on. As soon as he did that, every single little black spec went into a panic, scampering this way and that way as fast as possible. But not a bit of it did any good. Nothing could undo what had already been done.

That's what Lauren Long would be like.

After he took her.

He walked south.

Coming up on the library and the art museum.

The Denver Public Library was pretty cool from an architectural viewpoint. It looked like several different buildings joined together, which could have turned out terrible, but didn't. The Denver Art Museum, on the other hand, was a disaster. It was a silver titanium abstract shape with non-vertical walls that came to triangular points. It looked like a Picasso cube on acid that had fallen out of the sky, which could have turned out cool, but didn't.

The parking lot came into view.

One more block and he'd be there.

Suddenly footsteps approached from behind.

Tripp turned to see two men. They were tall, muscular, and walking fast. They both stared directly into his eyes as they approached, like predators.

Vampires?

He could take either one of them by themselves, but wouldn't have a chance against both at the same time.

"Hold up buddy," one of them said.

Tripp stopped and turned all the way around.

Facing them.

His heart racing.

"Why were you following Lauren Long?"

Then it made sense.

They must be the woman's bodyguards.

They must have been walking behind her, giving the woman space, and spotted Tripp.

He turned and said over his shoulder, "I don't know what you're talking about."

He turned away and continued walking.

Then one of them said, "Hey, wait a minute, one more thing."

When Tripp turned, the man was already swinging at his face. Then Tripp's head exploded in colors, he fell, and his forehead bounced off the concrete.

Seriously hurt.

Disoriented.

"We're not going to be as friendly next time. Do you understand?"

A minute later he was muscling himself into a standing position when a woman ran over.

"I saw what those two men did!" she said. "I got a picture of them with my cell phone."

Chapter Twenty-Eight
Day Three—April 14
Thursday Night

———————————

At the Old Orleans, the stress made Rave drink more than she should, but it didn't affect the performance. If anything, it loosened her up and let her get further out on the edge.

The people noticed.

And hollered and hooted to prove it.

The place was dark and packed with sexual tension.

Perfect.

Well, not totally perfect.

Parker wasn't there.

His theory was that the slayers wouldn't make a move in public, so she was safe inside the club. And it would be better if Parker wasn't seen in Rave's vicinity any more than necessary. So he hung around outside the club, in the shadows, watching the entrance. If Rave spotted anyone conspicuous inside—say a man by himself, not drinking, studying her every move—she was supposed to call and describe the guy. So far, however, that hadn't happened.

She was belting out a spirited version of Bob Dylan's "Like a Rolling Stone" when she spotted a familiar face at the bar.

A man about forty-five.

Bald.

Designer sunglasses.

Immaculately dressed.

Flamboyantly gay, even at a distance and in a crowd.

Tim Pepper.

Her manager.

He waved, clearly getting a kick out of the surprise on her face. Then he leaned to the person next to him, a nice woman about forty, and said something in her ear.

Three songs later, during the break, Rave went over and joined them. Pepper already had a screwdriver waiting for her.

"Thanks," she said, draining half the glass in one gulp.

She looked at the woman, then back at Pepper and said, "Who's your lady-friend?"

"Amanda Pierce," he said.

The woman held her hand out to shake.

But she looked friendly, so Rave gave her a hug instead.

"She's with Storm," Pepper said. Then he just looked at her, letting the implications hang.

"Storm as in Las Vegas?"

Pepper nodded.

Then he said, "Oh, by the way, I forgot to tell you that you're on audition tonight."

"What—"

She smacked him on the arm.

"You should have told me."

She would have dressed better.

She would have sung better.

She would have drunk less.

"Was on audition," the woman said. "When I came here, the big question was whether you were as good as your portfolio and whether we should book you for a month. Now I'm thinking that your first stint needs to be six months, minimum. Be warned that we'll want exclusion options for Vegas bookings for an extended period, so our competition can't grab you after we turn you into a household name."

A household name?

Rave must have had a deer-in-headlights expression because Pepper laughed.

Then he hugged her.

"Welcome to the big time, darling."

Rave looked at the woman—Amanda Pierce—who nodded and said, "The next step is for you to come to Vegas and meet some people," she said.

"When?"

"No rush, in the next couple of weeks."

Cool.

Way cool.

Pepper said, "We're going to need to make your sound bigger. I'm thinking something like adding a keyboard player and a couple of female background singers."

"Got to have plenty of sex on stage," the woman added.

When the club closed, Rave followed Parker back to her place. He parked down the street and then ran through the backyard shadows until he got to her house. He entered the back door to be sure everything was okay.

It was.

He pulled the curtain aside a few inches and motioned for her to come in.

She did.

Then what she hoped would happen did happen. Parker put his arms around her waist, pulled her stomach to his with incredible strength, and locked her into position.

He kissed her.

With a passion that she'd never experienced before.

A passion that made her tremble.

And want to give him every fiber of her being.

Chapter Twenty-Nine
Day Four—April 15
Friday Morning

———————————

Teffinger got up before dawn Friday morning, jogged three miles, and then encountered something strange when he got back—the sweet aroma of coffee. He followed the scent to the kitchen and found London, dressed only in a T-shirt, pouring pancake batter into a hot frying pan.

"I'm guessing you like pancakes since you got them," she said.

She wore no makeup.

And had her hair pulled into a ponytail.

So unpretentious.

So real.

"Sorry about last night," he said, referring to the fact that he didn't make a move on her under the stars, or back at the house afterwards, or even in the bed when she talked him into letting her give him a backrub.

"It's okay," she said.

Teffinger walked over and kissed her on the back of the neck.

She didn't turn around but said, "You're such a tease."

"Trust me," he said. "I'm not trying to be. I'm in a total reactive mode. I'm reacting to Jena Vellone disappearing, I'm reacting to finding you, I'm reacting to the fact that I have a picture of a skinhead who pounded a wooden stake into a woman's heart and I still can't catch him—"

"Finding me?" she asked.

"Right."

"Does that mean you've been looking for me?"

Teffinger wrapped his arms around her from behind, clasped his hands on her stomach and pulled her in tight. Then he nibbled on the back of her neck.

"Ordinarily this is where I would come up with some smart-ass answer," he said. "But the truth is yes, I have been looking for you."

"You mean, looking for someone—"

Teffinger headed for the shower and said over his shoulder, "I want you to move to Denver. I won't be able to handle a bunch of miles between us. I'm not that kind of guy."

"I just met you yesterday," she said. "You expect me to pack up my whole life and move just because you think it would be a neat idea?"

Teffinger chuckled and said, "I'll take that as a yes."

Then he stepped into the bathroom and closed the door.

He stripped.

Then got the shower temperature adjusted.

And stepped inside.

Two minutes later the lights mysteriously went off.

And London stepped under the spray with him.

"Okay, why not?" she said.

"Why not, what?"

She smacked him on the arm and said, "Don't be a smart-ass."

"When I said Denver, I meant my place," Teffinger said. "Just so we're on the same page."

"Okay, your place." Then she got serious and said, "Are you sure?"

He didn't hesitate.

"Positive."

"Positive positive? Or—oh my God I hope she doesn't snore—

positive?"

"Positive positive," he said.

She put her arms around his neck and pushed her breasts onto his chest. "Now that that's settled, show me if I made a mistake or not."

Teffinger got her heated up in the shower.

Then led her to the bed.

Soaking wet.

Where he took his time with her.

And she with him.

Teffinger got to work before everyone else and had one thing and one thing only on his mind—finding Jena Vellone. The problem was, he didn't have a single lead.

Nothing.

He called everyone who knew Jena, to see if she'd complained to them about strangers or bumps in the night or anything else that would possibly explain what had happened.

No one knew squat.

But forgave him for waking them up.

When Sydney showed up at 7:30, Teffinger said, "I'm starting to get the feeling that it was just a random, spur-of-the-moment thing, in which case whoever targeted her probably did it at the club that night. Maybe someone hit on her when I was talking to London, and Jena never mentioned it to me."

Sydney took a slurp of coffee and asked, "So how are you getting along with this London woman?"

"She's going to move in," Teffinger said.

Sydney scrunched her face.

"Are you nuts? You just met her—"

"She's nice," he said.

She shook her head in disbelief.

"None of the rest of the universe moves as fast as you do, Teffinger," she said. "Did you ever stop and think that maybe there's a reason for that?"

He shrugged.

"Their loss."

"What are you going to do in a month when you two have a fight?" she questioned. "What are you going to say? Oops, I made a mistake, go ahead and move back out now."

"Here's the thing," Teffinger said. "There aren't any guarantees no matter how you do it. Right now, I want to see her every day, every minute, every chance I get. You only get so much life. You got to live it."

She rolled her eyes.

"Teffinger, you fall in love way too easily and it always comes back to bite you in the ass," she said. "What I don't understand is why you can't figure that out and just slow down for once in your life."

He shrugged.

"Just because I don't know what I'm doing doesn't mean I'm wrong," he said.

She laughed.

"That doesn't even make sense."

"Yeah, well, just because it doesn't make sense doesn't mean I don't know what I'm doing."

They headed down to the Old Orleans, expecting the place to be locked, especially since Teffinger used up all his good luck for the morning by getting the Stone's "The Last Time" on the ride over. Surprisingly, however, the back door was open and someone was inside, waiting for the morning beer trucks.

They asked if the club had any surveillance cameras.

Thirty minutes later they were back at headquarters.

Sliding the first tape from Tuesday night into a VCR player.

As soon as it kicked up on the monitor, Teffinger hit pause and said, "I'll be right back," and headed towards the door.

He returned with two cups of coffee.

And handed one to Sydney.

Then he noticed that hers didn't have cream.

So he switched.

Then punched play.

Chapter Thirty
Day Four—April 15
Friday Morning

Tripp crawled out of the seedy hotel bed mid-morning, took a long piss and then studied his face in the bathroom mirror as the shower warmed up. The swelling—compliments of Lauren Long's bodyguards—had almost completely subsided and the color was closer to normal.

Good.

At least he wouldn't be walking around today looking like Frankenstein.

Last night had been interesting.

Dressed in all things black, at two in the morning, he hugged the deepest shadows of a Ponderosa Pine in Rave Lafelle's backyard, waiting for the vampire to return. Then something unexpected happened. Someone came out of the neighbor's yard, jogged past Tripp—not more than ten feet away—and used a key to enter the vampire's back door. Ten seconds later headlights came down the street and pulled into the driveway. Shortly after that, the vampire went into the house.

Tripp crept on cat feet to a back window.

And saw nothing.

Then moved to a side window.

And saw two shapes making love on the couch in the dark.

Heated love.

Ordinarily, he would have busted in. But if he got hit in the face again, in the same place, the pain might disable him.

They might get the upper edge.

Plus, he had to assume they had guns.

In fact, the whole sex-on-the-couch thing could be a setup to get him to come in thinking he had the upper edge. Then they'd both turn, with guns in hand, and fill him full of holes.

Something he wasn't found of.

So he decided to not go in.

Instead, he watched.

The vampire had a doable body.

Ample tits.

A nice ass.

A flat stomach.

The man was built like a lifeguard, totally ripped, so strong in fact that Tripp wasn't sure that he'd be able to take him in a fair fight, even though Tripp was a good two or three inches taller.

He watched for as long as he dared.

Then crept back into the shadows.

And headed down the street to check out a hunch.

Sure enough, a silver Volvo was parked about six houses down.

Exhausted, he went back to the motel and jerked off.

That was last night.

Now it was morning.

Breakfast was a bagel and three cups of coffee at Einstein Bros.

Then he drove around the fringes of the city, in the old warehouse districts on the north side of LoDo, and looked for an abandoned building. Some of them had been converted into lofts but there were still a number of vacant structures hanging FOR SALE signs.

One in particular looked interesting.

A six-story brick building with plywood behind the glass.

He parked in the alley behind it, muscled up to the bottom of a rusty fire escape, and walked up. The door at every landing was locked.

Good.

Street people hadn't infiltrated it.

From the top of the fire escape, Tripp muscled his way onto the roof, and found the access door unlocked. He entered the building and checked every floor.

It was definitely abandoned.

And would do nicely.

Chapter Thirty-One
Day Four—April 15
Friday Morning

Following a gig, Rave usually slept until at least noon the next day. But Friday she woke mid-morning with a disturbing mix of Vegas, Parker and vampire slayers bouncing in her head. Parker was already up and reading the paper when she walked into the kitchen. The coffee pot was half full.

"Good news," he said. "We have a reinforcement coming in."

"We do?"

He nodded.

"Forrest. You're going to like him."

She poured coffee in a cup, took a heaven-sent slurp and said, "When?"

Parker looked at his watch.

"A little over two hours," he said.

"Is he flying in?"

Parker nodded.

"Are you going to pick him up?"

"We're going to pick him up," he said. "I have something I want to tell you on the way."

"Tell me now."

He grinned and went back to reading the paper.

"What, you're not going to tell me?" she asked.

He kept reading the paper and said, "Apparently not."

She set the coffee down, stood in front of him, straddled his lap and brought her mouth down to his, an inch away. "Now are you going to tell me?" she asked.

He shook his head.

Then she kissed him.

"How about now?"

"Nope."

"You're so mean," she said.

He kissed her and said, "That was in the fine print when you signed up."

She stood and said, "Who said I signed up?"

They were halfway to DIA, driving east on I-70 under a strong Colorado sun, when Parker finally told her what he had to tell her.

"I mentioned before about the woman we have in Montreal who does our genealogy research," he said.

True.

Rave remembered.

"She called me this morning," Parker said. "She came across a rather remarkable discovery."

"Like what?"

"It turns out that you're a descendent of two separate and distinct vampires," Parker said. "Their bloodlines intersected, or crossed, or merged, or whatever you want to call it. So far, you're the only person in the world that we know about with that kind of pedigree."

Rave chuckled.

Nervously.

"You're messing with me, right?"

He shook his head.

"I'm actually jealous," he said. "This makes you a queen or something."

"I don't want to be a queen or something."

Parker laughed.

"This doesn't mean I'm going to start being nice to you," he said. "Just because you're royalty."

She punched him in the arm.

Then got serious.

"Do me a favor, will you?" she asked.

He nodded.

Sure.

"Don't tell anyone."

"Really?"

"Really," she said. "I need to get this whole part of my life gone, not get further in."

Okay.

No problem.

But he added, "Not many people in this world get to be queen of something, you know."

"Well, if it actually was in this world—that would be a different story."

He chuckled.

"Understood."

Forrest was standing outside at passenger pickup, two steps in from the curb where maniac drivers couldn't run him over, when Parker pulled up, killed the engine and told Rave, "That's him in the blue shirt." Rave liked the man immediately. He was older than Parker—about forty—and had an Indiana Jones aura to him. She half expected him to pull out a bullwhip and snatch a handbag out of someone's grip just for the hell of it.

"Be careful of this guy," Forrest told her, nodding towards Parker. "He doesn't drink beer. He only drinks those mixed drinks. I even saw him get something once that had one of those little umbrellas in it. It was embarrassing to be in the same state."

"So what do you drink?"

"Me?"

She nodded.

"Milk," he said.

She laughed

"In a dirty glass, like a man." Then he got serious and looked at Parker. "She's too pretty to let anything happen to her. Good thing you called me."

Chapter Thirty-Two
Day Four—April 15
Friday Morning

———————————

The surveillance tapes from the Old Orleans didn't help. Teffinger had been with Jena most of the evening. The few times he left her alone, no one came over and put a move on her. Nor did the tapes show anyone stalking or studying her. When the monitor turned blue, Teffinger broke a pencil in half. And frowned.

"Now what?" Sydney asked.

"I don't know."

Suddenly the chief—F. F. Tanker aka Double-F—walked into the room with every wrinkle in his 60-year-old face creased. Teffinger sensed trouble. Tanker politely scooted Sydney out, closed the door and said, "This Jena Vellone thing is getting huge press. And I'm not just talking about her own TV station, I'm talking about all of them."

Teffinger hadn't been following the news.

But it didn't surprise him.

"Questions are being raised as to why you're on the case," the chief said.

"Screw 'em."

"My thoughts exactly," Tanker said. "But here's the problem. A Denver detective spends the evening with the victim. He takes her home, drunk. She then disappears. Instead of being the prime suspect, he's the prime investigator on the case. That's a conflict of interest, at the least, and maybe something worse."

Teffinger nodded.

Understanding the talk.

But he said, "There's nobody in this world as motivated to find her as I am."

Tanker nodded and said, "Or as capable."

Teffinger grunted.

"Let me get right to the bottom line," Tanker said. "The mayor doesn't want an appearance of impropriety and has asked me to take you off the case."

Teffinger smacked his hand on the table.

"That's not going to happen."

"Hold on," Tanker said. "I'm in a delicate situation here. I need to do what the mayor says. But I'm not going to put Jena Vellone at further risk by doing something stupid, either. So here's the deal. Officially and publicly, you're off the case. Between you and me, you're still on it. You just can't let anyone know."

Teffinger stood and paced.

"That's going to slow me down," he said. "I can't spend my time worrying about staying out of sight just because some dumb reporters are asking stupid questions."

Tanker nodded and said, "It sucks. But that's the best we can do."

Teffinger headed for the door.

Tanker said, "I'm putting myself out on a limb for you."

Teffinger turned and said, "I appreciate that. I'm just pissed. This is the last thing I need right now."

"Understood."

Teffinger turned the doorknob and almost opened the door, but paused and said, "Between you and me, if you had taken me off the case completely, I would have quit and kept going on my own."

Tanker cocked his head.

"There you go again," he said.

"What?"

"Telling me stuff I already know."

Teffinger knew that was a compliment.

And that he should acknowledge it as such.

But all he could say was, "It's my fault she's gone." Then he raked his fingers through his hair and said, "I'm going to need Sydney."

"Can she keep her mouth shut?"

"Yes."

"Your call, then. Just be sure that all this doesn't come back to bite me in the ass."

"It won't."

"I have enough bite marks back there already."

Teffinger chuckled.

Then headed out of the room.

Teffinger needed to stretch his legs and blow off steam, so he took Sydney for a walk to the 16th Street Mall, explained the situation and bought her a hotdog and diet Pepsi from a street vendor.

They were on a bench in the sun, chewing, when Teffinger's phone rang. It turned out to be Jean-Paul Quisanatte, the Paris detective in charge of the case of the model who got a wooden stake pounded into her heart. Teffinger brought him up to speed on the Cameron Leigh case.

"I looked at the picture of the guy you emailed," Jean-Paul said. "How tall would you say he is?"

Teffinger reflected back to the warehouse tapes.

"Five-ten."

"That's what I thought," Jean-Paul said. "I don't think he's our guy. Diamanda's bodyguard was six-three and built. Someone beat him to death with their bare hands. I don't think your man could have done that."

"I didn't know the guy was so big," Teffinger said.

"Well he is. A black belt, too."

Chapter Thirty-Three
Day Four—April 15
Friday Afternoon

———————————

Tripp decided to capture Rave Lafelle alive and do it tonight, after her gig, if possible. In preparation, he pushed a cart through the Lakewood King Soopers and filled it with non-perishable items that didn't need to be refrigerated or cooked.

Fruit.

Granola bars.

Canned soup.

Bread.

Tuna fish.

Cookies.

Bottled water.

Juice.

The food went into the trunk of the Dodge. For a brief moment he thought about moving it into the old brick warehouse now, but decided it would be safer to wait until after dark. Then he stopped at Ace Hardware and bought some more necessities.

Rope.

Flashlights.

Chain.

Locks.

He swung by Rave Lafelle's house mid-afternoon and saw something he didn't expect, namely a dark-blue Camry backing out of the driveway, with a raven haired beauty behind the wheel.

A black woman who looked like an island girl.

Very sexy.

She led him to the base of Green Mountain and then wove up twisty streets until the asphalt didn't go much higher. She disappeared up a street called South DeFrame Way that snaked up a draw and looked like a dead-end. Tripp hung back and waited. When the vehicle didn't come back after ten minutes, he turned the radio off and drove up.

The Camry was parked in the driveway of a green split-level ranch, third house from the end, on the left, backing to the side of the mountain.

Tripp drove past, used the turnaround at the end, and then headed back down.

He shielded his face with his hand.

And kept his nose pointed straight.

At the stop sign, he turned right and then right again at the next one, and found himself heading up another draw, but one with no houses built yet. He parked the Dodge on the shoulder and walked up the side of the mountain about a hundred yards to a ridge that looked down on the split-level.

He smiled.

If it was dark, he could walk straight down to the house.

No one inside would have a clue he was coming.

Suddenly his cell phone rang.

He checked the incoming number and decided he better answer.

"What's going on at your end?" Jake VanDeventer asked.

"No opportunities have come up yet," Tripp said. "She had a singing gig last night and then a boyfriend stayed over."

"Okay."

"Maybe tonight."

"Play it safe," VanDeventer said. "I don't want another Abbott on my hands."

Tripp chuckled.

As if there was any comparison.

"How are things going at the mine?"

"You don't want to know."

Chapter Thirty-Four
Day Four—April 15
Friday Afternoon

Forrest had a last name—Jones—which was ironic, given his resemblance to Indiana. He took the backseat of the Volvo and was already spitting out ideas before DIA got in their rearview mirror.

He wore jeans, tennis shoes and a blue T-shirt.

Strong arms stuck out.

"We need to set a trap," Forrest said. "No offense, Parker, but hiding in the house while Rave walks around pretending to be alone isn't going to cut it. The problem is, that's a normal routine. We need to assume that they've already spotted you and they know that you'll be guarding all her normal routines. What we need to do is stage an upset condition, preferably something that takes you out of the loop. They'll figure that Rave's alone and that this is their chance. What they don't know, however, is that I'll be hiding in the wings."

Parker looked at Rave and said, "I think you already figured out that I'm the pretty one and he's the brains."

She laughed.

Then Parker asked, "Do you have something specific in mind?"

Forrest patted him on the back.

"In fact I do," he said. Then to Rave, "It's going to be a little risky, on your part."

She exhaled.

"How risky?"

Half an hour later, they dropped her off at the 16th Street Mall in downtown Denver. She walked on the sunny side of the street under a blue Colorado sky and occasionally stopped and pointed her nose into a store window to see if anyone behind her came to a similar halt. No one did, at least that she noticed, not that that meant much.

The city buzzed.

Full of energy.

Loaded with people poised on the edge of the weekend.

Business people.

Young people.

Street vendors.

Cops on horseback.

Of course, the mall was closed to street traffic, except for the free shuttle buses that ran up and down the ten block stretch. The sidewalk tables at the Paramount Café were completely filled, mostly with business-types munching on snacks and kicking off the FAC. Rave scouted the faces, didn't see the ones she was looking for, and headed inside. Suddenly someone tapped her on the shoulder.

Tim Pepper.

Manager extraordinaire.

"Good thing I'm not a rattlesnake," he said. "You'd be dead right now."

He led her outside.

Where she had just looked and not seen them.

The woman from Storm—Amanda Pierce—waved as they walked over. A half-filled cocktail sat in front of her, clearly not her first. She stood and hugged Rave.

"There's our star."

"Shooting star," Pepper said.

As soon as Rave sat down, a waitress appeared and set a screwdriver on the table. She took a sip and suddenly felt incredibly good.

Warm sun.

Alcohol.

On the verge of Vegas.

"Amanda and I have been working out the details," Pepper said in that incredibly gay voice of his. "The contract's going to go to you alone, not the band. The band guys are good enough to come with you, if they want, but they'll have to do it in the capacity of hired musicians, not as a band. They'll get paid well—a lot more than they're making now—but they won't have contract rights like you will."

"They don't really bring anything special to the party," Amanda said. "They're interchangeable with fifty others just like them. You're the star, so you get the contract."

Pepper nodded.

"If they don't want to come," he said, "we've got replacements waiting in the wings."

"But they can come if they want, right?" Rave asked.

Pepper nodded.

"It'll be their choice."

Okay.

Fair enough.

"Next topic," Pepper said. "Amanda wants us to get your CD out ASAP. She has ties to a label called Bang Bang. Have you ever heard of them?"

No.

She hadn't.

Amanda patted Rave's hand and said, "They're out of Chicago. They're smaller, but totally up-and-coming, with deep money and even deeper connections. I already sent them your demo tape and they wet their pants."

Really?

Yes, really.

"They want you to come to Chicago and lay down a few tracks to get a better feel for you," Amanda said. "But that's just a formality. You're already in."

"You're kidding?"

No.

She wasn't.

Pepper jumped in and said, "Which brings us to our next issue, namely material. We have six good tracks right now, including the three you wrote. That brings us halfway there. Bang Bang has been sitting on a number of hits, just waiting for the right voice."

"Meaning you," Amanda said.

"If that's true, we have everything we need for our first CD, right now. We can start recording next week."

"Next week?"

Pepper chuckled and said, "You should see your face."

She could imagine.

"This is happening so fast."

Pepper put a serious expression on his face and said, "It's going to be incredibly rewarding but it's going to be a hell of a lot of work, too. So get yourself ready for it."

Chapter Thirty-Five
Day Four—April 15
Friday Afternoon

Mid-afternoon, Teffinger went to Jena Vellone's house to scout around and see if he had overlooked something. If he had, it wasn't lighting up in neon. She had been gone almost a day and a half now.

Not good.

Someone obviously had a motive.

Who?

And what?

Suddenly his cell phone rang and Geneva's voice came through. "What's all this talk about you being off the case?"

"Where did you hear that?"

"The 104 news, twenty seconds ago."

Not good.

"Where are you?"

"Jena's."

"I'm heading over."

Fifteen minutes later a red Viper pulled into the cobblestone driveway and Geneva stepped out, wearing jean shorts, a black T-shirt and a baseball cap with a ponytail pulled through the back. She hugged Teffinger and said, "This is nuts. I don't understand what's going on."

Before Teffinger could answer, his cell phone rang.

It turned out to be Tanker, the chief.

"We have a development," he said. "Now don't get pissed or take this personally, but the Cherry Hills P.D. wants your Tundra to see if Jena's blood is in it."

"Give me a break," Teffinger said.

"You'd do the same thing in their shoes," Tanker said. "It's standard procedure."

True.

But it still sucked.

"They're in the spotlight," the chief added. "They have no choice. They won't find anything and then we'll be one step closer to having them off your back."

They won't find anything.

The words resonated in Teffinger's head.

Then he realized why.

"Oh, man—," he said.

"What?"

"They will find something," he said. "Well, let me rephrase it, they may find something."

"What do you mean?"

"Jena was seriously drunk that night," Teffinger said. "She had the radio cranked up and was swinging her head and singing. All of a sudden she said, Ouch, and got still. When I looked over, she was holding her hand to her nose, and it was bleeding."

"So her blood is in your truck?"

"I don't know," Teffinger said. "It wasn't bad and I handed her a bunch of Kleenexes right away. But she may have touched something while her fingers were wet. I just don't know."

"Where are you?"

"Jena's house."

Silence.

"I just thought of something else and it's not good," Teffinger added. "She put the Kleenexes on the floor. I'll bet you dollars to donuts there's blood on the mat."

"Where are the Kleenexes?"

"Gone—I threw them out at a gas station."

Silence.

"Okay, here's the plan. Bring your truck down to headquarters," Tanker said. "And above all, don't clean it or throw the mats away. I'd rather have them find blood in there than find it wiped down or tampered with."

Teffinger hung up and looked at Geneva.

"Good news," he said. "They're zeroing in on a suspect."

Her face lit up.

"Who?"

"Me."

Teffinger explained why he had been taken off the case. At first, Geneva was horrified, but then calmed down when Teffinger assured her that he wouldn't back off.

Not in a million years.

"You feel like helping me?" he asked.

"Yes."

Abso-freaking-lutely.

"Okay," he said. "We're going to walk around the neighborhood and see if any of the houses around here have security cameras pointed at the street. If they do, you'll knock on the door, explain that you're Jena's sister, and ask if they have any tapes from Tuesday evening through Wednesday daybreak. If they do, see if they'll make you a copy. Don't take the originals, though, no matter what. They're evidence and we can't afford to break the chain of custody."

"I thought you already talked to the neighbors," she said.

He nodded.

"We did, but only the closer ones," he said. "Now it's time to widen the circle."

Chapter Thirty-Six
Day Four—April 15
Friday Afternoon

The mysterioius exotic black woman had Tripp's full attention. So much, in fact, that he seriously thought about having his fun with her instead of Lauren Long. Sure, the manhunt wouldn't be anywhere near as exciting, but that would be offset by the quality of the private time with the woman.

At the abandoned warehouse, he parked in the alley, looked around and saw no one.

Yeah, baby.

Luckily, the back of the building faced the back of a similar one directly across the alley.

Both were windowless.

Both were abandoned.

Both were tucked away from prying eyes.

Tripp bounded up the fire escape with a flashlight wedged in his back pocket, stood on the top railing, muscled up to the roof, entered the building, found it still wonderfully and perfectly abandoned, and took the stairs two at a time down to the ground floor. He pushed the bar on the fire door and it opened, almost directly at the Dodge. He propped it open, brought in the food and goodies, and then closed it.

There.

Good.

He carried everything up to the top floor. Then he used rope to secure the fire bar of that door in a "push" position, so that the door could be pulled open from the outside. He fastened a chain and lock so that the door could only be pulled open from the outside far enough to reach the lock with a key but not far enough for anyone to squeeze in. That way, later he'd be able to enter easily, without climbing onto the roof.

The building was primarily a gutted, empty shell.

A few eclectic things remained here and there.

Nothing worth anything.

Tripp did manage to spot an old broom and swept up an area near the back wall that had plenty of places to attach rope and chain for his precious little victim-to-be.

Whoever she might be.

Maybe Lauren Long.

Maybe the vampire.

Maybe the exotic woman.

Maybe a combination.

Or all of them, even.

Under a perfect cerelean sky, Tripp headed back to Green Mountain. He needed to get the license plate number of the exotic woman's vehicle.

And figure out who she was.

When he got there, though, the driveway was empty.

He slowed enough to get the house number.

Then did a little research.

It turned out to belong to someone named Nick Teffinger.

The name seemed vaguely familiar.

But Tripp couldn't place it.

Chapter Thirty-Seven
Day Four—April 15
Friday Afternoon

For a few brief moments on the 16th Street Mall, with the sun on her face and a screwdriver in her gut and Tim Pepper's gay exuberance bubbling out, Rave actually forgot all about vampires and slayers and everything else except her impending stardom.

She could make it happen.

Storm.

The CD.

The household name.

Everything.

Of that she was certain.

All she had to do now, to get her life perfect, was get this slayer stuff behind her. And, it turned out, Forrest Jones had a pretty good plan how to do exactly that.

That afternoon, they swung by the gun shop and picked up Rave's two new 9mm SIGs. From there, they drove west on the 6th Avenue Freeway through Lakewood, turned left on Colfax and then made another left on Rooney Road. The asphalt twisted through rolling open fields at the base of the foothills.

There were no houses.

Or shops.

Or streetlights.

Or anything.

Just undeveloped, barren land.

Suddenly Forrest said, "Stop."

Parker pulled to the side of the road and killed the engine.

The three of them got out.

The plan was simple—deceptively simple. Tonight, after the gig at the Old Orleans, Rave would come out the front door after most of the crowd had left and would walk briskly to her VW, agitated. Just as she was getting in, Parker would run out of the club after her.

They'd have an argument.

Loud.

Angry.

She'd slap him.

Get in the car.

And squeal off.

Hopefully the slayer would be there, somewhere in the night, sitting in his car and keeping an eye on Rave's vehicle to see if an opportunity presented itself.

He'd watch the whole little charade.

And then follow her.

Knowing she was alone.

Unguarded.

Not paying attention.

She'd drive west on 6th Avenue, through Lakewood, first to Colfax and then to Rooney Road. Once she was out in the middle of nowhere, she would suddenly pull over to the side of the road, get out and open the hood, as if she had engine trouble.

The slayer would pull up behind her.

Ostensibly to help.

But with intent.

Intent to knock Rave to the ground and pound a stake in her

heart. Or intent to get her in his car and take her somewhere. There was no telling.

But what he wouldn't know is that Forrest Jones would be hiding in the dark.

Waiting for him.

That was the plan. Now, out here in the middle of Rooney Road, Forrest scouted around and liked what he saw.

"Okay," he said. "This is the place. You stop right here. See that little gully over there? I'll be in that. As soon as the slayer pulls up, I'll sneak up from behind. I should be able to get over here before he even gets his door open. It'll be pitch black. He won't have a clue. As soon as he says something to indicate he's the slayer, instead of just some poor slob passing by, I'll make my move."

Rave nodded.

"If you get a vibe before I do, shout, Stop!" Forrest said. "That'll be my cue to get to you as fast as I can."

"Okay."

"The timing is critical," Forrest said. "I don't know how fast he's going to try to make a move once he steps out. We don't want to waste a second we don't have. As soon as it starts going down, I want you to run."

"Okay."

"I mean it," Forrest emphasized. "Don't get involved, don't watch, and don't help. I'll be a lot more effective knowing you're not around to be taken hostage."

"What exactly are you going to do—kill him?"

Forrest picked up a stone and threw it.

"Actually, I'm going to have a chat with him, if I can."

"About what?"

"About who the other slayers are," he said. "And about why they're after us."

Rave frowned.

"What are you going to do if he won't talk?"

Forrest kicked a stone and said, "We'll see how it plays out."

He looked at Parker and said, "Give Rave a five minute head start and then follow her out here." To both of them, "Drive at exactly the speed limits. That way we'll keep a five minute spread between the two of you, more or less. The traffic lights will jack us around some." To Parker, "The main thing is that you don't run up this guy's tail and spook him."

Parker nodded.

Forrest focused on Rave and said, "You're going to be on your own from the time you leave the club until the time you get here, and also when the guy pulls up and steps out. Can you handle that?"

"No, but I will."

He grunted.

"I'll have my gun in the car," she added, referring to the SIG.

"Fine," he said. "Just don't let him see it. And no drugs or alcohol tonight, for obvious reasons. Have the bartender make you fake drinks just in case the guy ends up in the club."

She nodded.

He must have seen something on her face because he added, "I mean it, stay sober."

"Okay."

"That's important."

"Okay, I said."

Three seagulls flew overhead. "Is there water around here somewhere?" Parker questioned.

Rave looked at him and knew she needed to get some quality time alone with him before tonight, just in case she never got the chance again.

She pointed south.

"Bear Creek Lake's over that hill," she said.

Chapter Thirty-Eight
Day Four—April 15
Friday Afternoon

———————

Teffinger's brilliant idea about finding houses in Jena Vellone's neighborhood that had security cameras pointed at the street turned out to be a bust. He and Geneva walked the area for over an hour and didn't spot a single one.

Now what?

They were hoofing it back to Jena's when Teffinger's cell phone rang and London's incredibly sexy voice came through. "You don't have a litter box," she said.

True.

Then he realized why she must have brought it up.

"Don't tell me that cat crapped in the house."

She chuckled and said, "No. He was smart enough to sit by the door and cry. As soon as I let him out he ran straight for the dirt. Anyway, I swung by PetSmart and got a litter box, and some cat food, and a scratching post, and this really cute little bed."

"So the cat moved in?" Teffinger asked. She laughed.

"I guess that's one way to look at it."

When he hung up, Geneva asked, "Who was that?"

"London."

"London? What kind of name is London?"

Teffinger shrugged.

"I don't know," he said. "Why? Don't you like it?"

"Yeah, it's fine," she said. "It's just sort of weird for a person, since it's a city and everything."

"You mean, unlike Geneva?"

She chuckled.

"Got me."

"Yes I did," he said. "Anyway, she's living with me."

"Living with you? Since when?"

He shrugged. "Since this morning, I guess."

"You guess?"

"Right."

She rolled her eyes.

"I can't even believe you sometimes."

He searched for a smart reply, but his thoughts diverted to the conversation he had earlier today with the Paris detective—who said that the skinhead wasn't strong enough to commit the murders over there. If that was true, then maybe Teffinger was going after the wrong man. Or, if he was going after the right man, then there were two perpetrators committing almost identical crimes thousands of miles apart. Either way, he needed to give a lot more thought to the Cameron Leigh case.

But not right now.

Because she was already dead.

Whereas Jena Vellone hopefully wasn't.

"So now what?" Geneva asked.

"This is a long shot," he said. "But we have some footage from the club I took Jena to. Why don't you watch it and see if you recognize anyone in the crowd?"

"Fine. When?"

Before Teffinger could answer his phone rang and the chief's voice came through. "I thought you were going to bring your truck down—"

Oops.

"I didn't forget," he said. "I'm heading there right now."

"Good. I got people here chewing my ass."

Teffinger hung up, looked at Geneva and said, "You better follow me in your car since I might not be able to bring you back."

Chapter Thirty-Nine
Day Four—April 15
Friday Night

Tripp was a balloon expanded to its limit, ready to pop. Rave Lafelle's rusty VW was parked on the street, a block from the club. Tripp sat behind the wheel of the Dodge, a half-block down, pointed the same direction as hers, keeping an eye in his rearview mirror. The club closed at two. Now it was ten after. The vampire ought to be coming out any time now.

Then she did.

Walking briskly.

Alone.

Looking agitated.

She was almost at her vehicle when a man bounded out of the club and ran after her. Judging by his build and size, he was the same man who screwed her on the couch the other night.

The boyfriend or whatever he was.

They exchanged words.

Heated words.

Angry words.

Then the vampire slapped him.

The man raised his hand and almost hit her back.

But didn't.

Then the woman got in the vehicle and squealed out.

Tripp cranked over the engine and followed.

So nice.

He already knew what he'd do.

As soon as she pulled into her driveway, he'd slam to a stop behind her, leave the engine running, and do whatever it took to get her in the trunk.

Whatever it took.

Short of killing her.

Then he'd take her to the warehouse.

Unfortunately, something unexpected happened. She didn't exit at Kipling like she should have. Instead she kept heading west. Where the hell was she going?

Not to worry.

Just keep the same plan.

Grab her fast, as soon as she stopped.

She turned left on Colfax and then left again on another road a mile or so later. Tripp didn't catch the name. The sign went by too fast. But it was a dark road that winded away from the lights.

Tripp dropped back.

The last thing he needed was to spook her.

Where was she going?

A girlfriend's?

There were no other headlights.

Coming or going.

Then something totally unexpected happened.

The vampire pulled over to the side of the road and stopped. There was nothing Tripp could do. He had no choice but to continue going in that direction and pass her.

He approached.

Getting closer and closer.

Then he saw a wonderful sight.

A perfect sight.

She was standing in front of the vehicle.

The hood was up.

Tripp looked in his rearview mirror.

He saw no cars.

He looked ahead.

And saw no cars.

They were the only two out here in the middle of nowhere. Life didn't get any better than this. He pulled up behind her, left the engine running, punched the trunk release button, stepped out and walked towards her.

"Car problems?" he asked in his kindest voice.

Chapter Forty
Day Four—April 15
Friday Night

————————

With four screwdrivers in her gut and two joints in her lungs, Rave wished that she had taken Forrest Jones' advice and stayed sober.

But she hadn't and that was that.

When the gig was over, she stepped into the Denver nightscape and headed for the VW, just like she was supposed to. Parker ran over just like he was supposed to.

And they argued.

Just like they were supposed to.

With one exception.

It was real.

"You're stoned!" Parker said. "You screwed it all up—"

She pushed past him.

"I'm fine."

"This is a no go," he said.

"The hell it is."

He grabbed her arm.

But she twisted away and slapped him.

He almost hit her back.

She ducked in the car, pushed the lock down before Parker could get his hand on the handle, and squealed off. She watched him in the rearview mirror, waving his arms for her to stop, frantic.

"Love you," she said.

And kept going.

She took the 6th Avenue freeway west to Colfax and then to Rooney Road, speeding. The city lights disappeared and blackness took over.

Game time.

Her heart raced.

A solitary car followed.

A ways back.

Him.

She could feel his eyes.

She pictured him twisting a wooden stake in his fingers as he drove.

She got to the place she was supposed to stop. She slowed, but was too scared to actually pull over.

Then she did.

She left the engine running and the headlights on.

And stepped out.

She opened the hood as if she had engine trouble.

Just like she was supposed to.

And waited.

The other car continued to approach. At first, it was just a pair of headlights. Now those headlights punched out glimpses of terrain. Then the sound came—first, the humming of the tires; and then the purring of the engine. Finally it was all the way there. She held her breath and prayed for it to pass. It didn't. Instead it pulled behind her and stopped. A touch of dirt kicked up and flickered in front of the headlights. A strong man stepped out and said, "Car problems?"

At that moment she realized something.

The gun.

She had forgotten to grab it.

It was still under the passenger seat.

Okay—

Just be cool.

Forrest wouldn't let anything happen to her.

The man was next to her now, illuminated by the headlights. He was big, well over six feet. He must have seen a look of fear on her face because he said, "I'm not going to hurt you." He smiled and added, "Rave."

Rave?

He knew her name!

He was definitely the slayer!

"Stop!" she shouted.

Forrest's cue.

She looked towards the back of the car, where Forrest would charge from.

But he didn't come.

Not in the next second.

Or the one after that.

Or the one after that.

Then she realized that she had stopped at the wrong place.

Chapter Forty-One
Day Four—April 15
Friday Night

———————

The stress of not finding Jena made Teffinger prop up with too much coffee during the day, so much so that even now, at nine o'clock at night, his nervous system still sparked like a downed power line. He drank a Bud Light in three long gulps to counterbalance it. Then he pulled another one out of the fridge, looked at London and said, "You feel like taking a walk?"

She did.

So they headed out the front door and put one streetlight after another in their wake. They were ten minutes into it when Teffinger said, "Jeez, I just realized it's Friday night. You're probably used to doing something fun—"

She hooked her arm through his.

"Trust me, there's nowhere I'd rather be."

"I'll make it up to you," he said.

"There's nothing to make up.""Tomorrow," he said.

"Relax, Nick. I'm not here to be entertained," she said. "I'm here because we're starting something. Right?"

He squeezed her.

"Yeah."

"Okay, then."

He hesitated and then said, "I need to give you a heads-up on something. The press has been spotlighting Jena Vellone, which has forced everything to be strictly by the book. The problem is, when you look at it strictly by the book, I was the last person to see her alive, meaning that I'm automatically a person of interest."

"That's wrong."

"Yeah, well, unfortunately the truth doesn't matter," Teffinger said. "They pulled me off the case today. Then they took my truck this afternoon and processed it. They found some drops of blood and are going to have them analyzed. My suspicion is that the blood is Jena's, but it's there only because she got a nosebleed that night when I was driving her home. Anyway, once the press finds out that Jena's blood is in my truck, they're going to get real interested in me."

"Screw 'em."

Teffinger grunted.

"I could care less about the whole thing," he said. "Except that it's totally messing up my investigation."

"If I can do anything, let me know," she said.

He nodded.

Maybe he would.

"I just didn't want you to get blindsided by it." He drank the rest of the beer, crushed the can with his foot and then shoved it in his back pocket. "The whole thing will blow over eventually," he said, "but I didn't want you to get overly excited about it in the short-term."

They walked in silence.

Then Teffinger said, "I got the weirdest case. Someone pounded a wooden stake into a woman's heart as if she was a vampire. I thought I had it solved, but now I'm not so sure."

"What do you mean?"

"I was pretty sure a skinhead did it and even got his picture all over the news," he said. "But it turns out that there was a similar murder in Paris—a model named Diamanda. The strange part, though, is that she had a bodyguard who got beaten to death. My skinhead wouldn't have been strong enough to do it. Meaning that I either have the wrong man, or I have the right man but there are two or more people doing the same thing."

"Bizarre," London said.

Teffinger nodded.

"What was the woman's name?"

"You mean my woman?"

"Right."

"Cameron Leigh," Teffinger said. Then he chuckled and added, "Here's something even more eerie. She had a whole wall full of vampire books in her house. And we found a vial of human blood in her purse."

London looked startled.

More than Teffinger expected.

"Human blood?"

"Right."

"Hers?"

"No."

"Whose?"

"We don't know yet."

"Someone she killed?"

"We don't know," Teffinger said.

"Are you sure it wasn't animal blood?"

"Positive," he said. "There are distinct characteristics that are easily identifiable in the lab."

"Well I will say one thing, you have an exciting life."

"Actually it's pretty tedious," Teffinger said. "It just sounds exciting when I speed it up. Oh, by the way, all this stuff is off the record. Don't repeat it to anyone."

"Or what? You going to spank me?"

Teffinger chuckled.

"No, I'm going to do that anyway."

When they got home, Teffinger grabbed another beer and plopped down on the couch. Suddenly the lights went out and the room slipped into darkness, broken only by a few peripheral rays of illumination thrown from a distant streetlight.

London walked over through the dark.

Barely discernible.

But visible enough for Teffinger to tell that she was naked.

Incredibly naked.

Hypnotically naked.

She laid across his lap.

Face down.

And wiggled her ass.

Then she said, "Okay, let's see what you got."

He chuckled.

"Be careful," he said. "I'm not as straight-laced as you might think."

"Go ahead then."

He put his hand on her ass and was amazed, yet again, at how taut it was.

Then he gave her a few light taps.

"That's it?" she asked. "What's the matter? Haven't you ever done anything kinky before?"

"Of course I have."

"What?"

"I had a girlfriend once who liked to be tied up," he said. "Does that count?"

London wiggled her ass.

"In what position?"

"Spread-eagle on the bed."

"Nice," she said. "And what did you do to her, when she was all helpless and under your control and spread-eagle on the bed?"

"I teased her."

"You teased her?

"Right."

"How?"

"I'd feel her all over and bring her to the verge of an orgasm but wouldn't let her come," he said. "Then I'd start all over. I'd make her beg and beg for it but wouldn't let her come until I felt like it."

London wiggled.

"I want you to do that to me."

Teffinger grunted.

"Right now," she said. "Do you have rope?"

He did.

Ten minutes later he had her secured to the bed.

He worked her over slowly, getting acquainted with her body, finding the sensitive spots, the ticklish spots, the responsive spots.

He turned her into an animal.

Out of control.

Pulling at her bonds.

Wanting and needing only one thing.

But not getting it.

Not until he was good and ready.

Then, after an eternity, he gave in.

Twice.

Then he untied her.

She immediately pushed him on his back and said, "Your turn."

Chapter Forty-Two
Day Four—April 15
Friday Night

—————————

Rave tried to escape down the dark lonely road but it did no good. Tripp was fast and always had been. He closed the gap in no time and punched her in the back from behind. She hit the ground face first and made a terrible noise. Her face dripped blood as Tripp grabbed her by the hair and pulled her to her feet.

"Don't fight me!" he warned.

The words must have registered because the intensity went out of her body. Tripp kept an iron fist in her hair and yanked her towards the car.

She went.

Resigned to her fate.

With her fingers on her face.

Trying to feel how much damage there was.

Then something happened.

Tripp thought he heard a voice.

Hollering.

A long way down the road.

But heading this direction.

He froze and concentrated on it.

Yes.

A voice.

A man's voice.

Shouting something.

Rave?

Was that what he was saying?

The vampire must have heard it too because she suddenly dug her feet in and tried to pull her hair out of his grip. Tripp didn't need that. He clasped harder and yanked. The woman screamed and dropped to the ground. He tried to pull her up by her hair but she wouldn't budge.

"Get up!"

"Screw you!"

The words snapped something in Tripp's brain. He let go of her hair and punched her in the head as hard as he could. All movement in her body immediately stopped. He might have killed her.

He didn't know.

And didn't care.

The voice was getting closer by the second. Tripp looked up the road and was astonished to actually be able to see the man now.

Charging.

"Rave!"

Tripp kicked the woman in the ribs.

Wind came out of her lungs.

But she didn't move.

Tripp had time to get away. He could hop in his car, this second, and be gone by the time the man reached him. But he wouldn't have time to get the woman in the trunk first.

Screw that.

He ducked behind the car and then snuck into the blackness.

When the other man came, he spotted Rave on the asphalt and rolled her over to see if she was dead.

That's when Tripp attacked from behind.

Chapter Forty-Three
Day Four—April 15
Friday Night

_____

When Rave regained consciousness she knew she didn't have time for the pain. Forrest Jones and the slayer were beating each other to death in the middle of the road not more than thirty feet away.

Do something!

Now!

Hurry!

Her body didn't want to move, but she forced herself into a standing position and leaned against the car to keep from falling over.

Blood ran out of her mouth.

She wiped the back of her hand across it.

Then remembered the gun.

Under the front seat.

She got it, released the safety and then pointed it at the men with her finger on the trigger.

They didn't see her.

They didn't know.

She pointed it into the air and pulled the trigger.

It exploded more violently than she thought.

And the kickback was fierce.

So much so that the weapon recoiled out of her grip and fell to the asphalt with a cold steel thud. She scrambled for it as fast as she could, desperate to get it back in control.

Then she had it again.

And pointed it at the men who were locked together.

The slayer was behind Forrest Jones, with his arms wrapped around his head.

"Put it down or I'll snap his neck!"

Forrest struggled.

Helplessly.

Hardly able to move.

His face was a bloody mess and there was something seriously wrong with his breathing, as if his ribs were cracked.

"Let him go!" Rave warned.

"I will," the man said. "Just put the gun on the ground and step back."

"Don't do it!" Forrest shouted.

The slayer released one arm from around Forrest's neck just long enough to punch him in the side of the head.

"Let him go!" Rave shouted.

"Drop the gun."

She didn't move.

Not knowing what to do.

A second went by.

Then another.

Then another.

Then Forrest said, "Shoot him."

The slayer punched him again in the head.

"Shoot him, I said!"

Rave knew he was right.

She knew that if the slayer got the gun, then he'd kill them both.

Their only way out was for him to die.

Forrest couldn't do it.

So she had to.

It was their only chance.

"Let him go and I'll let you walk away," she said.

And meant it.

The slayer laughed.

As if it was a trick to get him to stand up so he'd be a better target.

"I'm going to count to five," he said. "Then he dies."

She took aim directly at his face, which was right next to Forrest's.

"I'll shoot," she warned.

"One—put the gun down."

"Let him go!"

"Two."

She tightened her finger on the trigger.

"Three."

"Shoot!" Forrest said.

The man didn't move.

Forrest didn't move.

She didn't move.

"Four," the slayer said. "Last chance. Put the gun down."

She thought about it for a split second.

Then pulled the trigger.

Chapter Forty-Four
Day Four—April 15
Friday Night

———————————

Flesh exploded as soon as Rave pulled the trigger. Both men fell backwards. Rave stared, transfixed. Not knowing which one she hit. Then the man farthest back began to climb out from under the other one.

The slayer!

The slayer was moving!

His face was covered with blood and torn flesh.

The sight repulsed Rave and gave her hope at the same time.

She stepped closer.

And couldn't believe what she saw.

Forrest Jones' face was blown in; totally and unquestionably disintegrated.

She had hit him!

Not the slayer!

The blood and guts on the slayer's face were splatter.

Vomit shot into Rave's mouth.

She tried to gag it down but it came out.

Then she turned and ran.

She ran so fast that her lungs burned. She didn't look back.

Get away.

Get away.

Get away.

Then she realized something.

Something bad.

The gun was no longer in her hand.

What happened to it?

Did she drop it?

Did she throw it?

She couldn't remember.

And ran even faster.

Then she veered off the road, into the field—straight into the darkness. The weeds and dirt and rocks slowed her down and twisted her ankles, but she didn't fall and didn't stop. This was her only hope.

Run.

Run until she couldn't run another step.

Chapter Forty-Five
Day Five—April 16
Saturday Morning

Teffinger rolled over in bed as soon as the first rays of dawn entered the bedroom Saturday morning. He was still tired but couldn't close his eyes again knowing that Jena Vellone was out there somewhere in the world. He popped in his contacts, threw on sweatpants and bounded out the front door for a jog before doing anything else, to keep at least some measure of fitness going.

On the way, he wondered what to do next.

To find Jena.

But didn't come up with any brilliant ideas.

Or non-brilliant ones.

So far, he didn't have a clue as to why anyone would take her.

None of Jena's friends knew anything.

Including Jena's sister, Geneva, who reviewed the Old Orleans tapes yesterday but didn't recognize anyone in the crowd.

Geneva.

Wait a minute.

Maybe this whole thing wasn't about Jena at all. Maybe it was about Geneva. Could someone have taken Jena as a way to make Geneva suffer?

Or Teffinger, for that matter?

Had some maniac come out of his past with intent to torture him by screwing with the people in his life?

No.

That couldn't be it.

It was too far-fetched.

Wasn't it?

But Geneva might be a different story. She was attractive, out-spoken, opinionated, fearless and liberal to a fault. No doubt her high-octane, well-caffeinated, live-and-let-live, sexually liberated talk show had alienated more than one listener. How much hate mail did she get? Was anyone crazy enough to kill her sister to make her suffer?

It didn't make sense.

But it made as much sense as anything else.

When teffinger got home from his jog, London was still sleeping. However, she was up and in the kitchen when he came out of the shower—sitting on a barstool at the counter, reading the Rocky Mountain News and sipping coffee.

Teffinger kissed her on the back of the neck.

"Umm," she said.

He filled a cup of coffee and said, "This Jena Vellone case is so weird that it's starting to make me have strange thoughts."

She lifted her eyes from the paper.

"How so?"

"Jena and I have been friends for years," he said. "I'm starting to wonder if someone took her, not to get her, but to get me."

London didn't seem impressed.

"That seems awfully indirect," she said.

"True," he said. "But here's the extension of that thought. If someone took her, to get me, they might take you next, to get me even more."

London laughed.

"God, you have an imagination."

"Just be careful, is all I'm saying."

"I will."

"Promise?"

She nodded and handed him her cup. "Could you fill that, as long as you're up?"

He could.

"So what's the agenda today?" she asked.

He frowned.

"If I had my way, we'd take the '67 for a ride up Clear Creek Canyon," he said, referring to his 1967 Vette. "Unfortunately, I'm not going to get my way until I get Jena Vellone resolved. I'm sorry, but—"

She cut him off.

"Nick, I'm right here and I'm not going anywhere," she said. "You do what you have to do. We'll have lots of time to concentrate on us, later."

"You sure?"

"Positive."

Ten minutes later he was in a 4Runner—a rental until Cherry Hills returned the Tundra—eating a bowl of cereal as he drove to headquarters. On the way, he called Geneva. She answered even though she had clearly been sleeping.

"I had a thought that maybe someone took Jena not to hurt her, but to hurt someone else who cared for her, someone like me or you."

"Me?"

"Right," Teffinger said.

He asked her lots of questions designed to find out if she had any enemies. As far as she knew, she didn't. Nor had she done anything recently that she could think of that would generate any serious ill will against her.

"Do you ever get any hate mail?" Teffinger asked.

"You mean emails? At the radio station?"

"Yes."

"Everyone in entertainment gets that crap," she said. "It's part of the job."

"Do any stick out in your mind as really threatening?"

She laughed.

"Teffinger, I don't waste my time reading that junk."

"You don't?"

"Hell no," she said. "We have people that pull all that stuff out."

"Do they save them?"

"I don't know."

"Do me a favor and find out," he said. "If they save them, get me everything you got from the last year."

"Are you serious?"

"Yes."

After he hung up, he wondered if he really was serious or whether he was just creating motion so he could delude himself into thinking that he was actually doing Jena some good.

Sydney's car wasn't at headquarters when Teffinger pulled in. He didn't know if she planned to come in today or not. He bypassed the elevator and hiked up the stairs two at a time to the third floor. On the way, Geneva's statement resonated in his thoughts.

Everyone in entertainment gets that crap.

As soon as he got to his desk—even before starting the coffee pot—he called Sydney.

She answered, groggy.

Teffinger was waking up the whole world.

"Hey, sorry to wake you," he said. "Are you coming in today?"

"Sure, if you want."

"Do me a favor," he said. "Contact channel 8 and see if Jena received any emails of a threatening or hateful nature. That's a place we haven't looked yet."

"Okay."

"Love you," he said.

She grunted.

"I'll take that as a threat."

Chapter Forty-Six
Day Five—April 16
Saturday Morning

———————

Tripp slept in Saturday morning and would have slept even longer except that Jake VanDeventer called from Johannesburg to get an update on what happened last night, if anything.

Tripp took a piss while explaining how he'd been set up.

How a fight ensued.

And how the female vampire—Rave Lafelle—tried to shoot him

but hit the other guy in the face instead. "Now here's the important part," he said. "The guy looked like Indiana Jones."

"You're kidding me? It was him?"

"In the flesh," Tripp said.

"Well I'll be damned."

"True but not relevant," Tripp said.

"That is so sweet," VanDeventer said.

"I thought you'd be happy," Tripp said.

"There isn't even a word for what I am right now," VanDeventer said. "So where is he now? Out there on the road?"

No.

He wasn't.

"I decided it was best to not leave him there," Tripp said, "since my blood was all over the ground. So I put him in the trunk of my car and drove down the road until I spotted a car, which I figured was his because it was all by itself out there in the middle of nowhere. I checked, and it was his all right. Then I switched him over to it and drove back to the city and pulled into a dark abandoned area by some railroad tracks. I pulled him out, onto the ground, and hammered a wooden stake into his heart. Then I walked about three miles, called a cab from a 7-Eleven, and had it drop me off a couple of miles from my car. Then I walked back to my car, zigzagged through town to be sure I wasn't being followed, and went back to my hotel room."

"Good job," VanDeventer said.

"Oh, there's something I forgot to tell you," Tripp said. "The guy didn't have any ID on him, but I did find something of interest in his pants pocket."

"What's that?"

"A vial of blood."

"That little freak," VanDeventer said.

"Yeah, the world's a better place this morning, that's for sure."

"What did you do with the vial?"

"I just left it in his pants," Tripp said. "Let the police worry about it."

"Good call. You wiped your prints off, I assume."

"Better than that," Tripp said. "I wore latex gloves the whole time."

"Nice."

"Oh, one more thing," Tripp said. "The woman dropped her gun at the scene. I figured it might come in handy later, so I took it."

"Come in handy how?"

"Blackmail her with it, if we have to," Tripp said.

He expected praise.

But got silence.

"I'm not sure if it's a good idea for you to have possession of it," VanDeventer said. "If the police find you with it—"

"Possession?"

Tripp laughed.

"I'm not stupid," he said. "I stashed it. The important thing is that the woman thinks that I have it; that and the fact that I can have it, if I choose to."

"That's better," VanDeventer said. "You had me worried for a second."

"You should know me better by now," Tripp said.

After he hung up, Tripp jacked off and then went back to sleep. He got up two hours later and bought a bottle of carpet shampoo, a bucket, a sponge and bottled water at Home Depot. Then he drove to Washington Park, found a nice secluded parking spot, and cleaned the trunk of the Dodge repeatedly until he was positive that not a trace of evidence remained.

Then he went for a walk.

Under a nice Colorado sky.

Chapter Forty-Seven
Day Five—April 16
Saturday Morning

R ave got pulled out of a fitful sleep when the doorbell
rang and Parker jumped out of bed to check. She looked
at the clock—10:15 a.m.—and pictured two cops standing on the front steps. Then Parker shouted, "It's London." She
pushed out of bed, used the facilities and studied the damage to her
face while the shower warmed up.

She was lucky to be alive.

Very lucky.

And she owed it all to Forrest Jones.

The man she shot in the face.

Parker tried to convince her last night that Forrest's death wasn't
her fault. "He was already beat. If you turned the gun over, you'd
both be dead right now. Your only option was to shoot. If you hadn't
pulled the trigger when you did, Forrest would have gotten his neck
snapped a heartbeat later. All you did when you pulled the trigger
was give him a chance. That's what he wanted you to do." He paused
and added, "Forrest was my best friend in the world. If anyone was
going to blame you, it would be me. If he was here right now, he'd
have no problem with what you did."

Those words might be true.

As far as they went.

But there was a lot more to the story.

She violated her directions to stay sober.

Because of that, she pulled over at the wrong place.

And because of that, Forrest had to run a long way to get to her; and lost the element of surprise. When he finally did get to her, he was totally exhausted. He fought as well as he could, but the fight started lopsided and quickly got worse. So it was true that he was already beaten when Rave had to decide whether to pull the trigger, but he was already beaten because she had forced him into that situation.

He was dead because of her.

That was a fact.

And it would never change.

She should have listened to Parker outside the club when he told her to abort.

Everything was her fault.

She stepped into the shower and stuck her head under the spray. The hot water on her scalp felt good. Her ankle felt less twisted this morning, too. Luckily she veered off the road last night when she ran. Otherwise, the guy would have killed her.

He followed.

And tried to find her.

Coming within ten feet.

As she laid there in the weeds holding her breath.

He stood there.

Looking around.

Listening.

Then he ran back to the cars and drove away, taking Forrest's body with him. Why he did that was still a mystery.

Parker showed up a minute later.

And got her calmed down enough to drive.

They searched for her gun but couldn't find it.

Then they came home.

And stayed awake until dawn, waiting for slayers.

But none came.

When Rave got out of the shower, London had scrambled eggs and hot coffee waiting for her.

She also had news.

"I've been waiting for Nick to volunteer something about the Cameron Leigh case," she said. "Last night he did. He told me two very interesting things. First, she died with a wooden stake through the heart."

"I knew it!" Parker said. "Those freaks."

"The other interesting thing is this," London said. "They found a vial of blood in her purse."

Parker looked at Rave and said, "It's probably time you knew a few more things. Some of us have an affinity for the taste of blood. So what we do is exchange blood between one another. The blood that Cameron had was probably mine; although it could have been Forrest's or a number of other persons, too."

Rave didn't quite understand.

"What do you mean, you exchange blood?"

"We make a slight cut, just deep enough to bleed, and then drain the blood into a vial," he said. "Then we exchange those vials among one another. Not everyone participates, but some of us do."

"Meaning that you do?"

He nodded.

"I didn't want to tell you before, because it's sort of freaky," he said. "I didn't know if you'd understand or not."

She didn't understand.

But didn't care at this point, either.

"What are we going to do?" she asked.

Chapter Forty-Eight
Day Five—April 16
Saturday Morning

Teffinger was alone in homicide when his phone rang and the voice of Barb Winters came through. She was the proud owner of new breast implants, a new wardrobe and a few new male callers.

"Got some job security for you," she said, meaning a body.

Teffinger stood up, realized his coffee was lukewarm and dumped it in the snake plant.

"I'm totally slammed," he said. "Call Baxter. "You're going to want this one," Winters said.

"Why?"

"Because the guy has a wooden stake sticking out of his heart," she said. "As if he was a vampire or something." She chuckled and added, "If you want, I can call around to the hotels and see if Van Hellsing is checked in anywhere."

"It's a guy?" Teffinger asked.

"That's what they say."

On the way to the scene, Teffinger passed a billboard of Jena Vellone; someone had climbed up there with a can of red spray and painted HELP ME, as if Jena was speaking the words.

An image flashed.

Him, walking out of Jena's house, swinging the door shut on his way out—not checking to be sure it was locked. Too busy thinking about London.

And now there was another vampire slaying.

As if he had time.

He poured coffee from a thermos into a disposable cup, steering with his knees. Ten minutes later he arrived at a place that would have been dark and deserted last night, on the north edge of town, next to a BNSF railroad spur. Sydney, bless her heart, had already beaten him there. Teffinger left the coffee in the 4Runner, put on gloves and walked over to the body.

The man had a wooden stake sticking out of his heart.

But more than that, someone had shot him in the face.

And even more than that, someone had beaten him with a vengeance.

A news helicopter hovered above, washing the air with a deep rumble. Teffinger looked at it and said, "There's no keeping this one under wraps."

Sydney nodded.

And said, "I don't think our skinhead could have done this."

Teffinger agreed.

The victim had a solid build.

And muscular arms.

"What the hell is going on?" he asked.

"I don't know, but maybe this will get the press off Jena Vellone," she said.

Two minutes later, Paul Kwak pulled up in a white van, walked over scratching his truck-driver's gut, and said, "This guy is seriously dead."

Teffinger grunted.

"This is connected to Cameron Leigh," he said. "So give me your best work."

"Good thing for you I didn't get drunk last night," Kwak said. "Hey, by the way, guess what I saw on the way over here?"

Teffinger didn't know.

"A split-window, just like mine except red," he said, referring to his 1963 Corvette.

Teffinger raised an eyebrow.

"Really?"

"Yeah," Kwak said. "It's really weird to see them on the streets. I always said I'd never have a trailer queen, but I got to admit, I'm getting more and more reluctant to get in traffic."

"Too many idiots," Teffinger said.

"Right," Kwak said. "And that's not even counting me and you."

Teffinger chuckled.

Then they processed the scene.

It didn't hold many surprises, but did have one. They found a vial of blood in the victim's front pants pocket. Teffinger dropped it into an evidence bag and said to Kwak, "I'll bet it's the same as Cameron Leigh's."

Kwak cocked his head.

"How much?"

"Huh?"

"How much do you want to bet?"

Teffinger didn't care.

Then Kwak said, "Okay, here's the deal. If it matches the stuff we found in Cameron Leigh's purse, you win and I have to buy you a box of Krispy Kremes. If it doesn't, though, you have to get in the elevator on the third floor and take it all the way down to the parking garage."

Sydney laughed.

"He'd never do that."

Teffinger knew she was right.

But knew he'd win, too.

"That's nothing," Teffinger said. "You got a deal."

Then Jena came back into his thoughts.

And the red spray paint.

HELP ME.

"I have to go," he said.

On the drive back to headquarters, he had a strange thought. Could the person who sprayed the billboard be the same person who took Jena?

Was it his way of saying she was still alive?

Was he playing a game?

Was he actually talking to Teffinger?

Chapter Forty-Nine
Day Five—April 16
Saturday Morning

Tripp took a cab to Avis and rented a black hardtop Jeep Wrangler with tinted windows. He didn't turn the Dodge in, though. That was still parked at the hotel. It wouldn't hurt to have two different vehicles at this point. Just as he was finishing up the paperwork, a TV monitor in the waiting room caught his eye—a news report about a crime scene investigation in progress down by some railroad tracks.

Tripp watched.

And did something that he forgot to do last night.

Namely, write down the license plate number of the vampire's vehicle. He nodded at the TV and said, "Thanks for the good work."

Suddenly a man appeared on the screen.

Incredibly good looking.

But that's not what made Tripp catch his breath.

It was the man's eyes that did that.

And not because they were two different colors.

But because they looked like Tripp's own eyes.

When he was on the hunt.

The man turned out to be Nick Teffinger. Tripp recognized the name but couldn't place it. Then he remembered. Nick Teffinger owned the house in Green Mountain—the one that the island girl went to after leaving Rave Lafelle's house yesterday.

Interesting.

Teffinger looked tough.

He'd be some work if it ever came to a life-or-death fistfight. But Tripp had beaten stronger men than Teffinger before—lots of 'em. That's not to imply that he didn't get his share of damage and pain.

He did.

But he was always as good as new in a week.

An athletic black woman hugged Teffinger's side throughout the news report; attentive to his every word and gesture. She was young, but wore a serious face and looked like she knew what she was doing. A detective, no doubt.

Yummy.

For a moment, Tripp pictured her at the warehouse—captured. He chuckled. Teffinger would go nuts. That would be even more fun than taking Lauren Long. Or even better yet, what if he took both the detective and the island girl?

Now that was an idea.

So many options.

So little time.

Chapter Fifty
Day Five—April 16
Saturday Morning

———————

Rave spent the morning frantically teetering on whether or not to walk out the front door, right now this minute, and disappear into the world. Forget the singing career. Forget Parker. Resurface at some point down the road when everything had cooled off. Since this whole thing started a mere five days ago, she had already shot two men in the face.

Before that she hadn't hurt a fly.

She'd loose Parker if she walked.

And her dreams.

But at least she'd be alive to lament the loss.

Then, suddenly, she stopped all such thoughts when she looked at Parker. Not because she loved him and couldn't stand the thought of life without him, but because she realized that he was in this too; a strong man, granted, but just as vulnerable as she was in his own way.

London too, for that matter.

They were here right now.

Putting their lives on the line for her.

It was only right to do the same thing in return.

Okay.

The debate was over.

The decision was made.

She'd play it out until the end.

Whatever the end might be.

She wouldn't run.

Then something totally unexpected happened. Four men showed up at her front door; the members of her band—Jason White, Randy Mortimer, Bruce Jensen and Ronnie Zang.

They didn't look happy and Rave sensed trouble. "We need to talk," White said.

He was the lead guitarist.

The smartest of the bunch.

The most aggressive, too.

A hippie-type complete with red bandanna and hair halfway down his back.

"We just found out from Tim Pepper about this Vegas deal," he said. "He said the contract would be going to you and that we'd be hired musicians. I thought we were a band."

"We are a band."

"Then how come we're not on the contract?"

Rave shrugged.

"Tim says you'll be making good money," she said.

"Not as good as you, apparently."

"I don't know how it will all break down," she said. "We're on our way—all of us. We're all going to make a lot of money, we're going to be on stage doing what we want. I don't understand what the problem is."

"The problem is that you can dump us anytime you want," White said. "Quite frankly, that doesn't sit well. We either need to do this as a group, meaning all of us in it together, or not at all."

Rave frowned.

"What does that mean?"

"It means that we're either on the contract or we're out of the whole thing, starting right this minute."

"What do you mean—right this minute?"

"Exactly what I said."

"What about the gig tonight?" Rave questioned.

"Screw the gig."

"What are you saying? That you're not going to show up?"

"That's right."

"But we made a commitment," she said.

"Screw the commitment," White said. "This is nut-cutting time. The future starts now, one way or the other. It's your decision."

She stared out the window.

Not needing this right now.

"I need to talk to Tim," she said.

They stood up.

"You do that," White said. "You have one hour."

When they left, Rave stepped into the backyard and called Tim Pepper. His decision was immediate. "We can't have people around who threaten to leave you high and dry on the spur of the moment. It's immature and unstable. It's better that we found this out now instead of down the road."

"So they're out?"

"Damn right they're out," Pepper said. "We gave them an incredible opportunity and all they did was get greedy. Quite frankly, I'm not sure they had the stage presence we were looking for anyway."

"So what about tonight?"

"I'll put something together," Pepper said. "Are you available for a rehearsal this afternoon?"

Yes, she was.

If necessary.

"I'll call White and give him the news," Pepper said. "If they show up to harass you, call the police."

Chapter Fifty-One
Day Five—April 16
Saturday Morning

———————————

Teffinger swung by Jena Vellone's billboard—the one with the spray paint. HELP ME. A fixed vertical ladder went up about thirty feet and ended at a narrow walkway that ran along the base of the display. The bottom of the ladder was ten feet off the ground, no doubt to keep kids from getting up and killing themselves. Teffinger pulled the 4Runner underneath, stepped onto the bumper and then muscled up to the ladder.

Yuck.

Every particle of rust in the universe was there.

Plus half the world's pigeon droppings.

Teffinger tried to keep his clothes from brushing against it but didn't have much luck. When he got to the top and poked his head above the walkway, he noticed that it didn't have a guardrail.

Of course.

Because that would have made his life too easy.

Then he saw what he hoped to see, namely a can of spray paint sitting on the walkway, about ten steps over. He got up, put his back against the face of the billboard, and then edged sideways one careful step at a time until he was directly by the can.

It was red paint.

Good.

This wasn't for nothing.

It was no doubt the one used to spray HELP ME.

The best maneuver at this point would be to pick it up by the bottom edge and then carry it down. But he pictured himself doing a half gainer to the ground as soon as his back came off the billboard. So he kicked the can off the edge and then concentrated on not killing himself as he made his way back to the ladder.

Geneva called as Teffinger was driving to headquarters.

"I rounded up all my hate mail," she said. "There was a lot more than I thought." She chuckled and added, "That means I'm doing something right."

"Good," Teffinger said.

Then he came up with a plan.

He coaxed Sydney into calling TV 8 to get the locations of every single one of Jena Vellone's billboards throughout the city. Then he picked up Geneva, let her ride shotgun, and had her read her hate mail to him as they drove from one billboard to the next. After she read each one, he told her to put it in either pile A, B or C, with A being the highest priority for follow-up.

On south Broadway he found another billboard with HELP ME in spray paint—blue this time, but the same handwriting.

"Bingo," he said.

"I can't believe it," Geneva said.

"This guy wants to be sure we see it," Teffinger said. "I'll bet we find five more before the day's over."

"And I thought you were just hallucinating."

"Not all the time," he said.

He pulled the 4Runner under the ladder, just like before.

They got out and Teffinger frowned.

"What?" Geneva asked.

"I'm not real fond of heights."

The expression on his face must have seriously highlighted his words because Geneva studied him and said, "I'll go."

"Really?"

"Yeah."

Teffinger almost said, Fine, but instead said, "You're wearing a dress."

Which was true.

A white sundress.

Thigh high.

"I know that," she said.

"Well, that's going to be revealing."

"I'm wearing panties," she said. "It's not like I'm naked under there."

That might be true, but Teffinger couldn't let her do it. So he muscled onto the ladder and then climbed up to the walkway.

Unbelievable.

There it was.

The can.

Sitting there nonchalantly ten steps over.

Teffinger put his back against the surface of the display area and edged sideways, inch by inch.

"You should see your face," Geneva shouted from below.

"Glad I amuse you," he said.

"Be careful," she said. "A turtle just passed you."

"Just for that, you get the next one," he said. "I don't care if you are wearing a dress."

It turned out that there actually was a next one, on a Santa Fe billboard near Evans; same handwriting and same words—HELP ME—but purple paint this time. Teffinger didn't let Geneva go up even though she said she would.

So he exhaled.

And headed up once again.

To retrieve yet a third can.

Then Geneva said, "I'm starved. I'll buy you lunch for being such a gentleman."

"Okay to the lunch," he said. "But stop calling me names."

Chapter Fifty-Two
Day Five—April 16
Saturday Afternoon

———————————

The license plate of the vampire's vehicle was registered to Hertz. Tripp called the company from a payphone and said he was Detective Alan Green with Denver homicide. The rental had been found next to a homicide victim, who he assumed was the person who rented the car. He wanted to know the name of the man who rented the vehicle, to verify the connection.

They told him.

"Forrest Jones, 29832 Shaker Heights Boulevard, Shaker Heights, Ohio," the man said. "You want a phone number?"

"Shoot," Tripp said.

The man shot.

Tripp wrote it down.

"Thanks," he said. "We'll be in touch."

"Do you want us to fax you the paperwork?"

"Hold off on that," Tripp said. "We'll need to get the originals anyway."

"Is the car okay?"

"We have some blood in the interior that we'll need to cut out and preserve for evidence," Tripp said.

"Ouch."

"Sorry about that."

After he hung up, Tripp called Jake VanDeventer in Johannes-burg. "The vampire's name is Forrest Jones," he said. "He's from Shaker Heights, Ohio."

"Where's that?"

"I think it's near Cleveland."

"Excellent work," VanDeventer said.

"You want me to head out there?" Tripp asked. He didn't have to explain why. They both knew it was to get into the man's computers and files and phone records and whatever else he could find, to get the names of other vampires.

He expected the man to say yes.

And swallowed when the man paused.

"No," VanDeventer said. "I'll go. You stick with Rave Lafelle."

"So you're done at the mine?"

"As done as I'll ever be," VanDeventer said.

"That doesn't sound good."

"We lost three men," VanDeventer said.

"That's not good."

"No, but it could have been worse."

"You know, it would probably be better if I went to Ohio and you came to Denver," Tripp said. "Things are hot for me here. A changing of the guard would probably be good."

A pause.

VanDeventer was chewing on it.

Tripp held his breath.

"No, just stay there," the man said.

"Okay."

He exhaled.

"By the way," VanDeventer said. "I made a sizeable deposit into your Cayman account this morning for the good work you did on our Indiana Jones friend."

"How sizable?"

VanDeventer chuckled.

"Sizeable enough to show my appreciation," he said. "As soon as I'm done in Ohio, I'll be out to join you."

"Good."

"Probably sometime tomorrow," VanDeventer added.

Chapter Fifty-Three
Day Five—April 16
Saturday Afternoon

_____

London and Parker's presence at Rave's house didn't bring the same peace of mind as before. They didn't have a new plan. Parker was unfocused and on edge. London was preoccupied. The whole world was off-key. And now Rave's band had walked.

Not good.

Billie Holiday's voice wove through the house.

Nice.

But not as magical as it should be.

"Maybe I'm not really a bloodline descendent," Rave said. "You said that the woman in Montreal was working on my file, which is why it was on the desk."

Parker nodded.

Correct.

"Well if she was working on it, that means she wasn't done," Rave said. "I mean, in the end either I'm connected to someone or I'm not. Until there's proof of a connection, there's always the possibility that the connection isn't there, right?"

"Unfortunately, your genealogy is clear," Parker said.

"But—"

"I admit that sometimes the traces aren't a hundred percent certain," he said. "The research is primarily based on old documents, both public and private. Sometimes those documents are subject to interpretation or trustworthiness. In your case, however, the connection is undisputable. Let me show you something."

He booted up a laptop, got on the net, logged onto an encrypted website and entered a series of passwords on different screens.

"This is more secure than having the information in a computer at a house or office that the slayers can find and take," he explained. "Only a few people know the passwords and they're not written down anywhere. Okay, here. Look at this."

"What is it?"

"This is Cameron Leigh's genealogy."

Rave expected to see a simple diagram, something in the nature of a family tree with names stuck on branches. Instead, she saw something more in the nature of a lengthy thesis, very detailed, analyzing a large number of old documents.

"This isn't what I expected," she said.

"It's a historical investigation," Parker said. "Very complex."

"I see that."

"Sometimes there are breaks in the chain," Parker added. "When that happens, you have to fill them in with the best inferences and speculations that you can, using the information that's available. In that case, there's a certain amount of subjectivity, deduction and extrapolation that gets laid in."

"So nothing's a hundred percent certain," Rave said.

"That's not correct," he said. "Some cases are a hundred percent certain. Cameron Leigh is a classic example. If you were to read this word for word, you'd see that each and every link in the bloodline is well established. Yours is the same way."

"Can I see mine?" Rave asked.

"It never got formally written up, but you're looking at it, to a point," Parker said. "Your genealogy is the same as Cameron Leigh's, to the great-great grandfather."

She frowned.

"Maybe this is wrong," Rave said. "Maybe we should double-check everything and see if there's a break in the chain. If there is, then maybe we can get the slayers off my back."

Parker looked sympathetic.

"What?" she questioned.

"First, there is no break in the chain," he said. "Second, the slayers wouldn't believe a word of what we said at this point, even if we had a way to communicate with them, which we don't. And third, they wouldn't care even if they did believe it. The skinhead died in your house. And you participated in the plan last night to lure them into a trap. At this point, you're on their radar screen and that's the way it's going to be."

She exhaled.

He was right.

"You really know how to cheer a girl up," she said.

He hugged her.

"We'll get through this," he said. "I promise."

Tim Pepper called ten minutes later. "Good news. There's a brand new group that just got formed in Denver called Friday's Child. Have you ever heard of them?"

No.

She hadn't.

"They're supposed to be pretty good," Pepper said. "They're going to back you up tonight. Can you come to the club at three for a rehearsal?"

She could.

"Did you talk to White?" she asked.

"Yes."

"And?"

"And he hung up on me."

Chapter Fifty-Four
Day Five—April 16
Saturday Afternoon

Back at headquarters, Teffinger called his counterpart in Paris—Jean-Paul Quisanatte—to let him know about the second vampire-like murder. "That skinhead that I told you about before couldn't have done it," Teffinger said. "The victim had good arms. He wasn't the kind to go down easy."

"Could be my guy, then," Jean-Paul said.

"How are you coming along on that?"

"Between you and me and the Rive Gauche, we aren't," Jean-Paul said.

Teffinger recognized the frustration.

"Look," Teffinger said, "if your guy and my guy are one and the same, it would really be nice to have the airline manifests of people who flew from Paris to the U.S. in the relevant timeframe."

Silence.

Then Jean-Paul said, "Are you giving me work to do?"

"No—"

"Too bad, because I was going to say thanks."

"Well in that case, I guess I am."

"I'll get on it," Jean-Paul said. "But the guy could have hopped on a train and flown out of London or Rome or wherever he wanted. So we're basically looking for people who flew from anywhere in Europe to anywhere in the United States."

"Understood."

"We'll start with Paris," Jean-Paul said. "Have you ever been here?"

"To Paris?"

"Right."

"No," Teffinger said. "I've been to Iowa, though. I heard they're pretty similar."

Jean-Paul laughed.

"I'll be in touch," he said.

He headed to the coffee and found two pots, one decaf and one regular. He held his hand out to see how bad it shook, decided that he had injected enough caffeine into his blood for one day, and reached for the decaf.

It turned out to be lukewarm.

Someone had turned the burner off.

He dumped it in the sink and filled up with regular.

Nice and hot.

The lab called and said, "Those three paint cans—no prints available."

"Thanks," Teffinger said.

The result didn't surprise him.

The cans were oily with spray residue, counterproductive to printing.

Then he called the fbi profiler, Dr. Leigh Sandt, and told her about the Jena Vellone case, including the fact that someone sprayed HELP ME on three billboards. "I'm starting to wonder if some kind of game player took her," Teffinger said. "I half expect to drive by one of them in a day or two and find HELP ME crossed out. Down below it will be, NEVER MIND. TOO LATE."

"If that's your theory, then stake them out," Leigh said.

Teffinger had already thought about that.

"Even if we put aside the manpower problems," he said, "I want this guy before the fact, not after."

A pause.

"You never know," Leigh said. "Maybe the next message will be HURRY."

Teffinger hadn't thought of that.

"Am I totally off base on this, or what?"

"It's thin, I have to admit that, but that doesn't necessarily mean you're totally off base," Leigh said. "We both know there's no short-age of sickos out there who like to play games. I'm wondering if there's any significance to the different colors. Why didn't he use the same color everywhere? I mean, put yourself in his shoes. There he is at the store. He pulls a can of red paint off the shelf and sticks it into a basket. Why not just grab two more at that point? Why scout around and get different colors. What were the other colors again?"

"Blue and purple," Teffinger said.

"So red, blue and purple," Leigh said.

"Right. That doesn't mean anything to me."

"Me either," Leigh said. "Unless he wants to send you on a wild goose chase to the stores to see if you can find who bought those three particular colors. It could be his way of putting you on a tread-mill."

Teffinger grunted.

"If that's the case, I'll probably end up finding that he paid cash," Teffinger said.

"Exactly," Leigh said. "Another thought is—the colors might be the same as a flag or coat of arms or something. Or maybe the initials stand for something—RBP or BPR or whatever. You don't know the order they got painted, I assume."

Teffinger sipped coffee.

And said, "Correct."

"There's another possibility, too," Leigh said.

"What's that?"

"The guy might have nothing whatsoever to do with the woman's disappearance," she said. "He might be nothing more than someone who has adored her from afar for years and views this as an opportunity to get noticed by her, after the fact. The way he sees it, if she shows up alive, he'll send her an email that says, By the way, I'm the one who put HELP ME on the billboards. So glad you're okay. In his mind, then she'll say, That was so sweet. No one else went to such a bother. Why don't you let me take you out to lunch to say thank you?"

Teffinger scratched his head.

"I just realized something," he said.

"What?"

"Whenever I call you to get things clearer, you make them muddier."

She chuckled.

"Or it might be something even more innocent," she said. "It might be nothing more than some teenager who thinks the whole thing is funny. A woman disappears and then her billboard talks. Chuckle, chuckle."

"Do you have time to check around and see if there are any other billboard cases floating around out there?"

"No—"

Ouch.

"—But I will."

"I owe you one," Teffinger said.

"One?"

"Okay, another one. I didn't know you were keeping score."

"I'm not," Leigh said. "I ran out of fingers and toes."

As soon as Teffinger hung up, he realized he forgot to tell Leigh about the second vampire murder. He almost dialed her back but decided to wait until the next time they talked.

Okay.

Now what?

He refilled his cup, walked down the hall and found Chief Tanker at his desk, with every crease in his 60-year-old face wrinkled.

"Problems?" Teffinger asked.

Tanker looked up. "Always," he said.

"I'm chasing a wild theory on the Jena Vellone case and want to get some manpower to stake out some billboards," Teffinger said. Then he explained.

Afterwards, the Chief said, "If it was anyone but you asking for this, the answer would be no."

Teffinger stood up.

"Thanks," he said. "I owe you one."

"One? What kind of a math system are you using?"

Chapter Fifty-Five
Day Five—April 16
Saturday Afternoon

———————

Tripp parked the Wrangler at the side of the hotel, stepped out and headed towards the back entrance with the key in hand. He hadn't taken more than ten steps when two large men appeared from out of nowhere. One of the men got up close and stuck a gun in his side.

"Do something to make me use this," the man said.

Tripp recognized him immediately.

Lauren Long's bodyguard.

Tripp stopped walking and said, "What do you want?"

"You're taking a ride."

Tripp looked around to see if someone was around to call the cops if he shouted out. The parking lot was empty.

"Walk!" the man said.

Tripp did.

Ten seconds later he was in the back seat of a black Lincoln with deeply tinted windows, pulling out of the parking lot.

"Where we going?" he asked.

"Shut your mouth."

They ended up at the far corner of a Target parking lot, parked with the engine off. Two minutes later a white Chevy sedan pulled up. The driver got out, opened the front door of the Lincoln and scooted in. He was about fifty, on the smaller side, but with a no-nonsense demeanor.

He turned and looked Tripp directly in the eyes.

"Do you know who I am?" he asked.

Tripp did.

But said, "No."

"I'm Lauren Long's father," the man said. "I'm going to ask you a question. It's one simple question. Now, before I ask it, I want you to understand something. You're either going to tell the truth or you're going to lie. If you lie, there's going to be a lot of pain in your life—the kind of pain that comes from pliers and matches and needles in your eyes. Do you understand the kind of pain that I'm trying to explain to you?"

Tripp looked for something in the man's face to indicate that he was exaggerating.

And found nothing.

"Yes," he said.

"You fully understand?"

"Yes."

"You need to tell me the truth, but it's your decision to make," the man said. "If you lie, the pain will start and there won't be anything in the world you can do after that to make it stop."

Tripp felt the need to relieve himself.

The man looked at him and asked, "Now, are you ready for the question?"

"Yes."

"Why were you following my daughter?"

Tripp almost denied it immediately.

He almost said, "I wasn't following her."

But he choked the words back.

Not because it was a lie.

But because it was an obvious lie.

"I parked in a parking lot and started walking downtown," Tripp said. "There was a woman in front of me. I liked her and wondered if there was some way I could meet her. So I hung around behind her a little bit and then finally figured she was out of my league. I headed back to my car and then these two gentlemen showed up. That's all there is to it."

He swallowed.

The man stared at him.

Processing it.

Searching Tripp's face for lies.

"I'm gong to make you a deal," the man said. "You're going to get your face out of Denver, right now, and never come back again. And I'm going to let you live. If you don't leave, or if you ever—and

I mean ever—come back, I'm going to take that as all the proof I need that you're lying to me. Then we're going to be knee deep in that pain we've been talking about. Do you understand?"

Tripp nodded.

"Say it!"

"I understand."

The man looked at the driver and said, "Be sure he does." Then he opened the door, stepped out, looked at Tripp and said, "If I ever think, for any reason, that you intend—or did at any point in time intend—to harm a single hair of my daughter's head, things are going to go very badly for you. Have a nice day."

The door slammed.

The driver cranked over the engine.

And pulled out.

Chapter Fifty-Six
Day Five—April 16
Saturday Afternoon

They used the Old Orleans stage for the three o'clock rehearsal. Friday's Child started off too loud for Rave's style, but they kept turning the knobs to the left until Tim Pepper smiled and said, "Yeah, right there." They were loose and edgy, like a garage band. All four of them could sing; and not only that, they laid in killer backgrounds without even trying.

The sound was like nothing Rave had ever heard before.

They rehearsed for two hours.

Long enough to get enough material for tonight.

Short enough to not fry their vocal cords.

Afterwards, Rave told Pepper, "That's the sound I've always had in my head."

He agreed.

"I'm sitting here listening and it's like I'm watching the birth of a whole new sound," he said. "I still can't believe it. I mean, it's rough, but—I don't know—maybe that's why it's so good."

"We need to bring them to Vegas," Rave said.

Pepper nodded.

"Let's see how the gig goes tonight and how the crowd reacts," he said. "If things go the way I think they will, we'll talk to them afterwards."

Yeah.

Oh, yeah.

Then she got serious and looked at Pepper.

"I really am going to make it, aren't I?"

He hugged her.

"Three months from now, radios across the country will be burning up with your songs. The world better get ready, because here comes Rave Lafelle. Just don't dump me when you get a call from the big boys."

She squeezed his hand.

"Never in a million years," she said. "In fact, write up something for me to sign."

Chapter Fifty-Seven
Day Five—April 16
Saturday Evening

———————————

I t was almost five o'clock when Teffinger's phone rang and the voice of Dr. Leigh Sandt came through. "I'm still looking for more billboard connections," she said, "but I came across something I thought you'd want to know about right away."

Teffinger stood up.

"Go ahead," he said.

"This happened in May of last year. It turns out that there was a female radio DJ in Chicago by the name of Kennedy Pinehurst," she said. "She had a morning talk show and her face was on a lot of windy city billboards. One day she vanished. They found her two weeks later in an old abandoned warehouse on the edge of the city. She was hanging upside down from her ankles, totally naked, with her wrists tethered to the floor, in sort of an upside down spread-eagle position. Her throat was slit, deep, with something sharp like a razorblade or carpet cutter. It turned out that she had been dead for about a week, meaning she was killed about one week after she disappeared."

Teffinger pictured Jena Vellone in that position.

With blood oozing out of her neck, dripping down her face, and making a bigger and bigger puddle beneath her.

He caught his breath.

And forced himself to concentrate.

"Was there any writing on the billboards?"

"Negative," Leigh said.

Teffinger didn't care.

There were too many similarities to ignore.

"I assume they never caught the guy," he said.

"You assume right."

"Any suspects?"

"No," she said. "I spoke briefly with the detective in charge, a man by the name of Thomas Stone. I told him that you'd probably give him a call. You got a pencil handy?"

He did.

He did indeed.

Teffinger was zigzagging to I-25 six minutes later when Geneva called and wanted to know if he had done any follow-up on her hate mail. He told her about the Chicago case and said, "I'm on my way to the airport right now."

"I'm coming with you," she said.

He almost said no but then said, "The plane leaves in two hours."

"Did you get tickets?"

"Didn't have time," he said. "I'm just hoping to get lucky. If it's filled, I'm just going to wait for the next one."

"What airline?"

"United."

"I'll meet you at their ticket counter."

"If you're there, you're there," he said. "But I can't be waiting around."

"I'll be there."

Teffinger hung up and then realized that he had forgotten to tell Leigh thanks.

So he called and told her.

Two hours later, he was in a 727, seat 29C, putting his armrests into a death grip as the plane taxied down the runway at an ever increasing speed.

Geneva looked at him and said, "You should see your face."

He closed his eyes and concentrated on breathing.

"This thing's too heavy to fly," he said.

She chuckled.

"You're such a baby sometimes," she said.

Suddenly the aircraft lifted.

Teffinger waited for the inevitable crash.

But it didn't happen.

Not in one second.

Or five.

Or ten.

His grip should have gotten lighter; but he only squeezed tighter.

"Do you know who invented the airplane?" he asked.

"The Wright brothers—"

"Wrong," he said. "The same people who invented the elevator."

She laughed.

"The world's in a big conspiracy to mess with you," she said.

"Exactly."

The plane landed without crashing. But then they found out that a convention had just about sucked up every room in the city. They finally found one room—a last minute cancellation with a king-sized bed—at the Swissotel on Wacker Drive, and decided to take it. It was almost eleven by the time they got checked in and unpacked. Teffinger should have been exhausted, but caffeine still grated on his nerves and he was anxious about what he would or wouldn't learn tomorrow.

So when Geneva asked if he wanted to go out somewhere and get a drink, he said, "You're reading my mind."

She chuckled and said, "It's small print, just for your information."

"Not funny."

"A little funny," she said.

"Okay, a little," he admitted.

They asked a cabbie where the action was. He dropped them off on Oak Street, where they had a pick. They wandered into a country-western bar with a foot-stomping band and a let's-get-drunk atmosphere.

After a couple of drinks they headed to the dance floor to see if they could line dance.

They could.

Then the band suddenly slowed it up. Teffinger turned to head back to the bar but Geneva put her arms around his neck and said, "I'm scared, Nick. I need you to hold me."

He thought of London.

And said, "That's probably not a good idea."

But Geneva wouldn't let go.

He felt her tremble.

And realized she was on the verge of sobbing.

So he slow danced with her.

He let her hold him.

And rest her head on his chest.

And feel protected.

Afterwards she squeezed his hand, looked at him somewhat embarrassed, and said, "Thank you for that."

"It's the least I can do," he said. "And that's what I always do."

She groaned.

"Bad, even for you."

"Actually not bad, for me."

They took a cab to the hotel, curled up on separate sides of the bed and closed their eyes.

"No spooning," she said.

He chuckled and said, "You too."

Then they went to sleep.

Chapter Fifty-Eight
Day Five—April 16
Saturday Afternoon

Lauren Long's bodyguards headed west on the 6th Avenue freeway towards the mountains. The driver watched the road. The other one watched Tripp, who sat in the back, docile, not as quick as a trigger finger.

No one talked.

Tripp knew they were taking him somewhere to jack him up, but didn't know how bad it would be. As he saw it, there were two options. He could let them beat him, then check out of the hotel, return the rentals, fly out of Denver, return under one of his aliases tomorrow, and try to stay off their radar screen while he concentrated on Rave Lafelle. Or he could do something a little more in keeping with his basic nature.

They passed Golden.

Then headed north on Highway 93, parallel to the foothills.

Two miles later they headed west down a deserted gravel road.

That road ended at a trailhead near the base of a mountain.

No cars were there.

Or people.

A gunshot from there wouldn't be heard anywhere else in the world.

Tripp untied the shoelace of his right shoe.

They pulled to a stop. The driver killed the engine, opened the door and stepped out. He looked around, scouting for witnesses. Then he opened Tripp's door and said, "Let's get this over with."

By the time Tripp climbed out, the other bodyguard—the one with the gun—had come over to that side of the car.

"How bad is this going to be?" Tripp asked.

"That depends on you."

Tripp nodded.

"I won't resist," he said.

"That's smart."

Tripp bent down to tie his shoe. At first, one of the men started to say something, but broke off when he saw what Tripp was doing. As Tripp stood up, he grabbed a handful of dirt and threw it at the man with the gun.

Two minutes later, Tripp was breathing hard and deep.

Exhausted.

So weak that he bent forward with his hands on his knees to steady himself.

The bodyguards laid on the ground.

Both of them.

Bloody.

Unmoving.

Dead.

Tripp walked over to the Lincoln, sat down in the dirt and leaned against the back wheel. He found a rock by his hand, picked it up and threw it at the closest body. The man's eyes were open and the rock hit him directly in the right eye and bounced off.

The eye moved but didn't close.

"Feel good?" Tripp muttered.

He found a blanket in the trunk of the Lincoln and spread it out on the driver's seat to prevent any migration of his blood or hair into the interior.

He grabbed the cell phones.

And guns.

Then cranked over the engine and got the hell out of there.

No cars came down the road as he left.

Overhead, the sky was blue.

Very nice.

A couple of magpies flapped across the open space.

He turned on the radio, flicked the stations and stopped when he got to Beyonce's "Crazy in Love."

Chapter Fifty-Nine
Day Five—April 16
Saturday Night

———————

At the Old Orleans on Saturday night, Rave resisted the urge to roll smokes in the dressing room during breaks. Instead, she concentrated on not screwing up on stage. Of course, the inevitable mistakes came—she stayed with the main chorus while Friday's Child went into the bridge—things like that. But the crowd didn't care because there were too many moments when the sound wasn't just good, it was dead on.

Crazy dead on.

Magical, almost.

Something was being born.

Everyone in the club could not only feel it, but felt lucky to have accidentally stumbled in on the very night when it was happening. Including Tim Pepper, who sat at the bar giving Rave big grins and thumbs up, and buying drinks for London as if they were gay soul mates.

Rave wished Parker could be here to witness it.

But he was outside.

Somewhere in the shadows.

Standing guard; watching for slayers; poised to run inside and save her if the need arose.

Her hero.

She'd reward him well later, when they were alone.

Then, halfway through the night, something happened.

She didn't want this to ever end.

And suddenly had a desire to live forever.

To be immortal.

When the gig ended, she was too terrified to go home. She now understood the slayers better. Their viciousness and drive had become clearer.

More real.

More deadly.

More immediate.

Until now, she had viewed the whole situation as something vague and distant, as if the people who got killed had somehow inexplicably done something to justify it, something that Rave hadn't done. But now she realized she had been lying to herself. Just being a bloodline descendent was enough to bring on everything that was headed her way. Being good, or naive, or unthreatening didn't matter.

She called Parker from the dressing room after the last song.

They hooked up and he drove.

London came with them.

They zigzagged north through the city and ended up pulling into the parking lot of a low budget hotel off I-76, somewhere in Brighton. Parker killed the engine and they watched for vehicles that may have followed.

None appeared.

London didn't want to be a bother and tried to talk them into letting her take her own room, but Parker said they shouldn't split forces. So they ended up in a single room with two double beds.

Rave rolled a joint.

And everything softened.

Then something unexpected happened.

Parker looked at London and asked, "Do you think she's ready?"

She shrugged.

"If she isn't by now—"

Parker laid down on his back on the bed and then pricked the inside of his lower arm with something.

Blood came.

Not a lot.

Just a few drops at a time.

He looked directly into Rave's eyes.

"Go ahead," he said.

She knew what he meant.

She also knew that if she did it, then this would be a turning point in her life—a turning point that would not only bring her closer to Parker, but would bring her further into the strange world in which he lived.

She didn't care about his world.

She wanted him too much to care about it.

She kneeled at the side of the bed.

Then put her mouth to his arm.

Like he wanted.

And maybe like she wanted.

And sucked his blood.

She thought it would taste terrible but it was actually sweet. If she didn't know what it was, she would think it was some kind of liquid candy. Parker ran his fingers through her hair. Then London's face appeared next to hers. And she moved over while London sucked.

They took turns.

For some time.

Then London took her turn on the bed.

While Rave and Parker tasted her blood.

Then rave said, "My turn." She laid down on her back in the middle of the bed and held her arms out to her sides.

"Are you sure?" Parker asked.

She nodded.

"Positive," she said. "Do it."

Chapter Sixty
Day Six—April 17
Sunday Morning

In spite of the late hours on Oak Street last night, Teffinger got up before dawn Sunday morning, took the stairwell to street level, and pushed through the revolving doors of the hotel into the Chicago nightscape. A stiff lake breeze blew trash and paper down the street. He jogged in the same direction, not in the mood to deal with wind in his face quite yet.

The city hardly moved.

It was dead.

Teffinger hugged the river and the bridges as much as he could and used his artist's eye to study the way the lights bounced off the water.

He needed to set up an easel again.

And smell turpentine.

It had been too long.

So long in fact that he'd end up painting two or three duds before he got his eye back to where it needed to be to crank out something commercial. Maybe someday, if his life ever slowed down, he'd find time to really get into it. That's the only way he'd ever find out what his boundaries were.

London didn't know yet that he painted.

What he needed to do was take her down to the gallery in Cherry Creek, nonchalantly point to one of his paintings on the wall as if he'd never seen it before, and ask what she thought of it.

Chicago detective Thomas Stone turned out to be a small wiry man with a receding hairline, a big moustache and darting nervous eyes that never met Teffinger's for more than a second at a time. He didn't put on an attitude about coming into work on a Sunday morning, which meant that he hunted when the hunt was there. For that reason alone, Teffinger liked him.

Plus, the man had coffee and donuts waiting when Teffinger and Geneva showed up at the appointed hour, 8:00 a.m.

"So, how many billboards would you say had the picture of Kennedy Pinehurst on them before she disappeared?" Teffinger asked.

The man shrugged.

"That never became an issue," he said. "Definitely some, though. She was a big deal around these parts."

"How about her hate mail?" Teffinger asked. "Did you pull that?"

Stone nodded.

"That was one of our theories," he said. "A wacky listener."

"What I'd like to do is have Geneva go through them and see if any of them are similar to the ones she received," Teffinger said.

Stone paused—no doubt because Geneva was a civilian. "She'll keep everything confidential."

"I will," Geneva said.

"And your theory is—what?"

"That my missing person—Jena Vellone—may have been taken not because someone wanted her so much, but more as a method of hurting Geneva, who is her sister. Did I mention that?"

No.

He hadn't.

"Tell you what I'm going to do," Stone said. "I'm going to leave you two in the room with the file and close the door. We can't have a civilian looking at it. But if she does, how would I know?"

Teffinger nodded.

"Thanks."

Teffinger and Geneva spent hours, and pots of coffee, going through every piece of paper in the Kennedy Pinehurst investigation file.

Stone had done everything a good detective should.

The file was thorough and exhaustive.

A few things emerged.

The victim—Kennedy Pinehurst—had a morning talk show similar in format, subject, audience and tone to Geneva's. Also, both women were single, clubbers, and a little on the wild side.

"It's almost like she's my twin," Geneva said at one point.

Teffinger didn't disagree.

Then something caught his eye.

Namely the interview notes of the victim's sister—Amanda Pinehurst—who reported that she saw a man once who might have been following her and Kennedy two or three days before Kennedy disappeared. At the time, Amanda hadn't thought much about it, other than the man caught her eye for some reason. Looking back on it, though, maybe it meant something.

"Bingo," Teffinger said.

"What?"

"We have a witness."

Geneva read the interview notes.

And said, "I don't see what you're excited about. She already said she doesn't remember what the guy looked like. Plus, we have no indication that the man she saw had anything at all to do with Kennedy's disappearance."

Teffinger jotted down the woman's address.

They reviewed the rest of the file, didn't find anything of relevance, and thanked Stone for his cooperation; especially for coming in on a Sunday morning.

Back outside on the streets, Teffinger said, "Come on, we're taking a field trip."

Amanda Pinehurst lived in a townhouse on the west side of Chicago. Teffinger and Geneva took a cab, told the cabbie to wait, knocked on the woman's door unannounced, and got lucky enough to find her home. She was dressed down, about thirty, with a shy daughter about three or four years old who stayed behind her leg.

Teffinger explained the situation.

And wanted to know if she could give them any more information about the man who she suspected might have been following her and Kennedy that day.

"Like I told Detective Stone," she said, "all I can remember is that it was a man. That's it. I don't remember if he was big or small, dark or light, or anything else. And I don't even know if he was following us. All I remember is seeing him and getting a eerie feeling for a second or two. The whole thing could just be a figment of my imagination."

"If you saw him again, could you pick him out of a lineup?"

She laughed.

"No."

"You sure?"

"Positive," she said. "I've already told all of this to Detective Stone."

Outside, walking back to the cab, Teffinger said, "Oh well. We had to try."

"She's lying," Geneva said.

Teffinger stopped in his tracks.

And studied her.

"What do you mean?"

"I can tell," Geneva said.

"How?"

"By the way she looked at me," Geneva said. "There was guilt in her eyes."

"Guilt? What are you talking about?"

"She felt guilty for not helping me help my sister," Geneva said. "The same way she didn't help her sister. Correction, make that, couldn't help her sister."

"Huh? Why wouldn't she, or couldn't she, help her sister?"

Geneva shrugged, and said, "I'm guessing at this point, obviously. But if I had to come up with some kind of an explanation, I'd say that the man threatened to kill her daughter if she talked."

Teffinger considered it.

"That's an awfully big speculation," he said.

"Feel free to create a smaller one if you want," Geneva said. "But one thing I know for sure—there was guilt in her eyes. That much I'm positive about. When she looked at me it was as if she was saying, I'm sorry."

Chapter Sixty-One
Day Six—April 17
Sunday Morning

———————

Tripp woke Sunday morning in a strange bedroom, slightly hung over. Next to him was a redhead, lying face down with her arms folded under her pillow, breathing deep and steady, still sound asleep from a wild night of grinding—first on the dance floor and then in the bed. A white sheet covered the lower half of her naked body.

The uncovered part was just as nice as Tripp remembered.

He tried to recall her name.

Brandy?

Brenda?

No—Brittany.

That was it, Brittany.

You're a good one, Brittany.

He rolled onto his back and put his hands under his head, glad that yesterday was over. After he taught the two bodyguards a lesson about messing with the wrong man, he dumped the Lincoln on a side street near 20th and Broadway, made his way back to the hotel, picked up the Wrangler and a few necessities from his room, and checked into the Table Mountain Inn in Golden for a three-day stay.

Under the name Pierce Roberts.

Then he rented a red Mustang coupe from Enterprise, also under the name Pierce Roberts, and bought some expensive new clothes. That evening he went clubbing downtown at The Church, where he walked up to Brandy, leaned in, and nibbled on her ear before she even knew he was there.

No, not Brandy.

Brittany—who turned out to be an HR manager at a mid-sized law firm, an incredibly skilled lover, and a genuinely nice person.

Anyway, that was yesterday.

Now it was morning.

He got the shower warmed up, stepped in and lathered up. In a way, he lamented losing the opportunity to make a possible move on Rave Lafelle last night. But, if the truth be told, he needed a little time off. The whole thing with the bodyguards must have put more stress on him than he realized.

Suddenly the shower door opened and the redhead stepped in.

"Brittany," he said.

"You remembered," she said.

"How could I not?"

She took the soap out of his hand and lathered his cock and balls. Her touch felt so incredibly perfect that Tripp sprang to attention almost immediately. She knew exactly what she was doing and continued doing it until he came in her hand.

"That's for knowing my name," she said.

Tripp kissed her and asked, "What do you usually do on Sundays?"

"I don't know," she said. "Sometimes I take a hike in the mountains, if the weather's nice."

A hike.

Perfect.

"Let's do that," Tripp said. "You want to?"

"Really?"

"Sure, why not?"

She shrugged.

"I just thought you'd be leaving—"

"Let's go somewhere for breakfast first," he said. "I'm in the mood for pancakes."

She grinned.

And rubbed her breasts on his chest.

"I know a place where they smother 'em under so many straw-berries that you can't even tell they're there."

Excellent.

Maybe with some links on the side.

And a truckload of coffee.

Screw the diet for a day.

They were winding up Bear Creek canyon to a place called Lair O' The Bear when Tripp's cell phone rang. He looked at the incoming number.

Jake VanDeventer.

Probably calling to report on what he found last night, if anything, at the house of the dead vampire, Forrest Jones, in Ohio.

Before Tripp could answer, Brittany put her hand on his thigh and said, "I'm thinking bad thoughts."

"How so?"

"I'm thinking I'm going to have to pull you off the trail some-where and spend a little time on my knees."

Tripp stuck the phone back in his pocket without answering.

"You are bad, aren't you?" he said.

She moved her hand up to his crotch.

"It's your fault," she said, "walking around with this body and all."

Tripp pictured her kneeling before him, somewhere off the beaten path, away from prying eyes, behind a boulder or something, with a bright blue Colorado sky overhead and an occasional bird flapping past on silent wings. But he suddenly felt guilty and said, "You don't have to do that."

"Have to?" she said. "You don't know me very well, do you?"

He chuckled.

"I'm serious," he said. "Let's just have a nice walk."

She studied him.

"Really?"

"Sure."

"Okay."

A few minutes later a visual image of the island woman from the cul-de-sac on Green Mountain entered his head, an image in which she had been captured and taken to the top floor of the warehouse.

Chapter Sixty-Two
Day Six—April 17
Sunday Morning

Rave felt different when she woke Sunday—strangely different, wonderfully different, disturbingly different, beautifully different. Part of it came from the gig last night—so incredible, so close to what she'd always pictured in her mind. But, if she was honest with herself, most of it came from the bloodsucking.

It had changed her.

She was closer to Parker now.

London too, for that matter.

She didn't believe in vampires, or voodoo, or anything occult or supernatural. On the other hand, if she did have a dormant gene of ancient and mysterious origin inside her, and if it was to awaken, she would expect the feeling to be much like the one she had now.

Weird.

She pushed her sleepy body out of bed. Parker moved slightly but didn't wake up. London was in the other bed, sleeping naked on top of the covers, more perfect than a human being had a right to be. Rave pulled a sheet over her. Clearly Parker and London weren't lovers and probably never had been. But they had a connection and a deep intimacy nonetheless.

A vampire union.

A vampire intimacy.

Would Rave experience the same type of bond with other blood-line descendents? People she didn't even know yet? It wouldn't surprise her. She had unquestionably experienced a strong tie to Forrest from moment one.

She warmed up the shower, stepped inside and closed her eyes under the spray.

The feeling inside her turned to words.

Words she had never heard before.

Words about a mysterious love.

Then the words became more and more lyrical.

It took several moments to realize that she had actually written a song. It had never happened like this before. All of the other times had been while she sat at the keyboard—starting with chords, laying a melody on top, and then fitting words to the melody.

She wrote the words down as soon as she got out of the shower.

Nice.

Very nice.

She needed to get to a keyboard and figure out the chords.

Right now.

This minute.

Parker and London still hadn't moved and didn't look like they would for some time, so Rave grabbed Parker's car keys and headed south on I-76, towards home. With any luck, she'd be back before they even woke up. The sun was unusually bright this morning. Parker's sunglasses were in the console.

Rave put them on.

There, better.

Much better.

On the way she called Tim Pepper, pulling him out of sleep, but needing to know what happened last night after she left. "It's all set," Pepper told her. "They're coming to Vegas, they'll do the studio work, the whole bit."

"Really?"

Yeah, really.

"They love you," he added.

"I wrote a song this morning," she said. "Well, half a song. I still have to figure out the chords."

"I'm thinking we'll want a rehearsal this afternoon," Pepper said. "If everyone's available, we'll work it up then and see if we have a keeper."

Cool.

Way cool.

She licked her lips and could still taste Parker's blood.

London's too.

As soon as she hung up, her phone rang and Parker's voice came through, frantic. "Where are you?" he asked. She explained that she was almost home. "Are you nuts? Turn around and get back here."

An exit approached.

She almost pulled off.

But didn't and said, "I'll only be there a half hour or so."

"No!"

"I'll be okay. When I get back, I want to know more about vampires. I feel different this morning," she said. "It's really weird."

"Rave!"

She pulled into her driveway five minutes later and killed the engine. She was already out of the car, walking to the front door, when she noticed that it was open.

Wide open.

She stopped and listened.

She heard nothing.

Her heart raced.

She knew she should run back to the car and drive away immediately, before it was too late, but she couldn't stop herself from taking one step after the other towards the house. She prepared herself to find the interior trashed.

What she found was worse.

Infinitely worse.

A dead body.

Chapter Sixty-Three
Day Six—April 17
Sunday Afternoon

———————

On the flight back to Denver, Teffinger kept getting a nagging feeling that he had seen or heard something recently that had a tie to Chicago, besides Kennedy Pinehurst. But he couldn't pull it up to save his life and had no reason to suspect it to be relevant, even if he could.

Geneva sat next to him.

Exhausted.

Solemn.

Then she said something he didn't expect. "When I get on the show tomorrow morning, I'm going to make a plea to the guy to take me and give up Jena. To exchange me for her, is what I'm saying."

Teffinger shook his head disapprovingly.

"I understand your frustration, but all that'll do is bring out every whacko in the city," he said.

She said nothing.

And stuck her face in a magazine.

"I don't have time to baby-sit whackos," Teffinger added.

Geneva exhaled, looked at him and said, "She's been gone since Wednesday night."

"I know that."

"That's three days."

"I know."

"If she's still alive, we're running out of time," she said.

"Which means we can't fill it up with whackos."

Two minutes later she asked, "So what's the plan when we get to Denver?"

Good question.

"Stone is going to send me electronic copies of all the hate mail that Kennedy got," he said. "Then we'll cross-reference them to yours and see if you both got something from the same email address or the same computer."

She frowned.

She already read all of Kennedy's hate mail and saw nothing of relevance.

"What else?" she asked.

He thought about it.

"See if you can get the email address of Kennedy's sister, Amanda," he said. "Send her some pictures of Jena; humanize her, make Amanda see that she's a human being who needs her help. Bond with her; the more we can play on her emotions, the more likely it is that she'll give us information, assuming you're correct and that she actually has some."

Geneva frowned.

"I'll try," she said. "But if she wouldn't help her own sister, I doubt that she'll go out of her way for mine."

"Probably, but you never know," Teffinger said. "Maybe she regrets now what she did and will take an opportunity to make amends." Then Geneva got a distant look in her eye. "What?"

"Well, so far we've only concentrated on hate mail," she said. "But what if the guy sent something positive and flattering? Then he never got a response and felt jilted—"

Teffinger shrugged.

"It's possible," he agreed, but there was no enthusiasm in his voice. "I'm backing off my theory that someone took Jena to punish me, mostly because I don't know Kennedy Pinehurst or anyone else in Chicago. But I'm finding it more and more interesting that both you and Kennedy have so much overlap."

"It's scary," Geneva said.

"Isn't it?"

Teffinger closed his eyes. Then he remembered he was flying, and not only opened them but also listened for abnormal sounds, the kind that meant the wings were about to fall off.

He heard none.

If he was correct that the killer didn't take Jena to get to him, then that meant London was safe.

London.

She'd been a good sport so far.

Not complaining about being in the shadow of the hunt for Jena Vellone; content to be ignored; willing to be second priority.

As soon as they started the descent into Denver, the winds kicked up and the FASTEN SEATBELT signs came on. Teffinger did his best to not appear affected, but must not have done a very good job because Geneva pried his fingers off the armrest and held his hand.

After a long twitchy approach, they touched down without dying. Teffinger wiped sweat off his face with the back of his sleeve.

Geneva said, "Had a little chop up there."

"Really?" Teffinger said. "I wasn't paying that much attention."

When they got to the gate and the aircraft stopped moving, everyone stood up at the exact same second and started dragging stuff from the overhead bins. Teffinger stayed in his seat. He waited until everyone left, then got up and walked down the aisle at his normal pace.

Geneva was waiting for him when he got out.

"Come on," he said.

"Where we going?"

"Cameron Leigh's house."

Chapter Sixty-Four
Day Six—April 17
Sunday Afternoon

———————————

The Lair O' The Bear turned out to be a well-worn Rocky Mountain trail system in a rugged mountain valley next to Bear Creek, given to incredible views, pine scent and a flawless Colorado sky. Tripp and Brittany were a half hour into the hike, working up a sweat, when Tripp's cell phone rang. He looked at the incoming number.

Jake VanDeventer.

"This is business," he told Brittany. "Do you mind?"

No she didn't.

Of course not.

He sat down on a boulder and answered.

"We have a problem," VanDeventer said.

"How so?"

"I had an encounter while scouting around in the vampire's house," VanDeventer said. He didn't need to define the vampire. They both knew he was talking about Forrest Jones, the vampire who set a trap for Tripp on Rooney Road; the one who got his face shot by the other vampire, Rave Lafelle; the one who Tripp later dumped near the railroad tracks and pounded a stake into his heart.

"What kind of encounter?" Tripp asked.

"I was in the guy's bedroom scouting around with a flashlight when someone opened the front door and the lights downstairs came on," VanDeventer said. "I didn't have time to get out of the house so I ducked into the master closet. The person coughed every now and then and I could tell it was a woman. She never talked to anyone so I figured she was alone."

"A girlfriend?" Trent asked.

"No, worse," VanDeventer said. "A detective. My guess is that Denver called the locals and asked if they would check the guy's house for anything that might explain why he ended up dead out in Colorado. Anyway, I was hoping that she wouldn't bother with the closet. Just in case, however, I pulled a shirt off a hanger and wrapped it around my face. Later, unfortunately, the door opened. I punched the woman in the face before she even knew what was happening. But something bad happened."

"What?"

"She got a hand on the shirt as she went down and pulled it off my face," VanDeventer said. "So she might have gotten a look at me."

"You think?"

"It's possible," VanDeventer said. "If she did, it was only for a fraction of a second; and it was while she was in pain and dropping to the floor. So my gut feeling is that no clear images entered her brain. But I just don't know."

"Then what happened?"

"The punch knocked her out," VanDeventer said. "I left and headed back to my hotel room. This morning I walked over to Greyhound and paid cash for a ticket to Cincinnati. That's where I'm calling from right now."

Okay.

"I don't see it as a big deal," Tripp said. "You didn't kill her, after all."

"Here's the problem," VanDeventer said. "This guy gets killed in Denver. The next day, someone's snooping around in his house. The locals are going to tell Denver about it and Denver's going to think that the snooper—me—is either the killer or is connected to the killer. That means that if this local detective got a good enough look at me to work with a sketch artist, the Denver cops will get it and will be looking for me."

Tripp picked up a stone and threw it.

"I still don't see it as a big deal," he said.

VanDeventer wasn't in Denver when the vampire got killed. He was in Johannesburg.

And could prove it if he ever had to.

"So now what?" Tripp asked.

"I'm getting on a plane to Denver in two hours," VanDeventer said. "But I'm going to need to keep a really low profile once I get there, meaning no credit cards, rentals, or that kind of thing."

"No problem," Tripp said. "I'll pick you up at the airport. Give me the flight number and TOA."

When Tripp hung up, Brittany asked, "Do you have to go?"

He kissed her.

"Not right this second," he said. "I still have the afternoon free."

"Good."

Yes.

Actually it was.

Very good in fact.

"I need to warn you about something," he said.

"What?"

"This is nice," he said.

"And how is that a warning?"

"Because you're getting me addicted," he said. "I'm going to need more."

She put her arms around his neck and pressed her stomach to his. "More, huh?" she asked. "How much more?"

Tripp kissed her.

"Lots more," he said.

"Good, because that's exactly how much I have."

Chapter Sixty-Five
Day Six—April 17
Sunday Morning

———————

When Rave first saw the body lying face down on the floor in the middle of her living room, she registered it as just that and nothing more—a dead body. On further examination, she recognized it as the dead body of Jason White, the lead guitarist. She walked over, dropped to her knees and looked for a knife in his chest or a bullet in his head.

She saw no wounds.

Then, without warning, the body moved.

Not much.

Hardly any.

But more than it would if it was dead.

The smell of Tequila came from it.

She stood up and surveyed the damage to her house. The piano was totally, a hundred percent trashed. The keyboard cover had been ripped off and thrown across the room. The ivories were cracked and smashed. The sharps had been knocked off and were now the color of cracked wood instead of black. Rave walked over and pressed a key down.

It sounded fine.

The strings hadn't been broken.

That's more than she could say for the CD player and receiver. They were irretrievably smashed to pieces on the floor—same with the speakers. The furniture hadn't been worth much to start with, but now wasn't even worth that. The sofa and chair had been sliced repeatedly with a knife. The legs were knocked off the coffee table and both end tables. In the kitchen, food that should be in the refrigerator was now splattered on the floor, walls and ceiling.

Mustard.

Ketchup.

Milk.

Bananas.

Leftover spaghetti.

The bedroom hadn't escaped attack either. The sheets had been pulled off the bed and thrown into the corner. The pillow and mattress had been stabbed repeatedly.

Suddenly she heard a vehicle in the driveway.

She pulled the curtain to the side and looked out.

Parker and London stepped out of a cab.

Parker ran through the front door, saw that Rave was in no danger from slayers, and went straight to the body.

"That's the lead guitarist from my band," Rave said. "He's alive. From what I can figure, he got pissed about being replaced, trashed the place and then passed out." She looked at Parker. "He smells like Tequila, but is probably jacked up on a lot more than that. What do we do with him? I don't want any cops here."

Parker knew why.

This is where Rave shot the skinhead slayer in the face.

Self-defense, but still—

Parker nudged the man in the ribs.

The man recoiled and moaned.

"He's not going to die, so we don't need to take him to a hospital. I'll dump him somewhere." Parker covered the man with a blanket, carried him outside to the trunk of the Volvo, took off, and then returned forty-five minutes later.

"Where did you take him?" Rave asked.

"I went up Clear Creek Canyon until I found a turnoff with no one around," Parker said. "I pulled him out and set him on the ground; without the blanket, of course."

"Did anyone see you?"

"No."

"Did you beat him up or anything?"

Parker shook his head.

"If you want me to later, I'll be more than happy to," he said. "But I can't hit an unconscious man."

"No, I don't want you to," Rave said. "This whole thing is partly my fault."

"That's not true," Parker said. "The guy's a first-class jerk and that's all there is to it. He probably would have beaten you to a pulp if he caught you home last night."

Rave frowned.

She had already thought of that.

As they cleaned the place, Rave said, "The fact that my little friend didn't end up dead might mean that the slayers have left Denver." She looked at Parker. "Wouldn't they have killed him if they came here looking for me and found him instead?"

Parker considered it.

"That depends," he said.

"On what?"

"On whether they knew who he was or not," he said. "If they didn't know who he was, then they probably would have taken him for a vampire and acted accordingly, meaning he'd be dead right now. If they knew who he was, on the other hand, they probably wouldn't bother with him."

Rave was confused.

"How would they possibly know who he was?"

"They could have seen him in the club."

Rave shivered.

She always knew that they could have been lurking somewhere in the crowd.

But never wanted to actually believe it.

"Maybe they just gave up and went back to wherever they came from," Rave said.

Parker frowned.

"Not likely," he said. "But that's fine because I've been working on a new plan."

Chapter Sixty-Six
Day Six—April 17
Sunday Evening

———————————

The earth felt good under Teffinger's feet. The wind blew with a vengeance through the airport's west parking garage; the same wind that almost swatted Teffinger out of the sky not more than twenty minutes ago. Now he could care less. He hunted around for the Tundra longer than he should have before realizing that the Cherry Hills police had it. Then he spotted the 4Runner, pointed and said, "There it is."

Inside, before Teffinger could even crank over the engine, Geneva said, "I'm starved. Feed me."

"Feed you?" he asked.

"Right."

"Is that what you just said? Feed you?"

"Right."

"Meaning you expect me to pay?"

"Right."

"You know I'm the cheapest guy on the face of the earth, right?" She nodded.

"Everyone knows that," she said.

"And you still expect me to feed you?"

"Right."

"Now you have my curiosity way up," he said. "Why would I do that?"

She rolled her eyes.

"So I'll never tell anyone that I had to hold your hand."

"You didn't have to," he said. "You just did it."

"You're quibbling over semantics, Teffinger," she said. "Do we have a deal or not?"

They did.

Fifteen minutes later Teffinger pulled off I-70, drove past a Texas Roadhouse and pulled into a Quiznos.

They ate in the car, not wanting to waste time, heading to the house of the dead vampire—Cameron Leigh. Just as they got inside the city limits, Teffinger received a call from the FBI profiler, Dr. Leigh Sandt.

"How'd Chicago go?" she asked.

"It's too early to tell."

"I just found out something interesting," she said. "There was another billboard case. You might actually not be crazy this time."

He knew he should laugh but was too excited.

"Where?"

"San Francisco."

San Francisco?

That meant flying.

Teffinger pushed the feeling down and said, "Details."

She gave them.

As soon as he hung up, Teffinger told Geneva the news and asked, "Do you feel like going to San Francisco?"

She receded in thought.

And looked like she was about to say yes.

But said, "I can't. I have to be on the air tomorrow at six."

Two minutes later, London called.

She missed him.

Would he be home tonight?

"Do you feel like going to San Francisco?" he asked.

"Are you serious?"

He was.

"Do me a favor," he said. "See when the absolute next flight to San Francisco is and get tickets." He pulled his wallet out and gave her a credit card number. "Call me as soon as you get the tickets and let me know when the flight leaves. I'm going to drop Geneva off and then head home."

Five minutes later London called and said, "I have us booked on a 9:45 flight."

"Tonight or the morning?"

"Tonight."

Heavy black storm cells raked across the scariest sky Teffinger had every seen.

He swallowed and said, "Good."

Chapter Sixty-Seven
Day Six—April 17
Sunday Afternoon

————————

When Rave showed up at the Old Orleans in the early afternoon to rehearse with Friday's Child, Tim Pepper greeted her with a busted up face. His right eye was almost swollen shut and his lower lip was puffed up. Rave felt his pain and hugged him long and tight to prove it. Then she said, "Don't tell me. Our guitar-playing friend."

Pepper nodded.

"He was waiting for me when I came out of the club last night," Pepper said. "Apparently he wasn't too thrilled about the way things turned out."

"He's a nut case," Rave said. "It's better that we found out now."

Then she told him how he trashed her house.

"Did you file a police report?" she asked.

"No," Pepper said. "I just want him out of my life. Hopefully, that was it."

"If he bothers you again, let me know," Rave said. "I have a friend who will have a talk with him."

Friday's Child hadn't shown up yet, so Rave sat down at a battered old upright piano in the corner and worked out the chords for the melody that came to her in the shower this morning. Pepper sat on the edge of the stage with his legs dangling. Then he clapped, dropped down to his feet and walked over.

"That, my dear, is your first single."

She studied him.

To see if he was messing with her.

He wasn't.

"You think?"

"No," he said. "I know."

When Friday's Child showed up a few minutes later, they immediately set to work on the new song. Within an hour they had Pepper grinning from ear to ear.

"Now I know how Brian Epstein felt," he said.

Parker picked her up after the rehearsal and said, "You don't have a gig tonight, right?"

"Right."

Not tonight.

Or tomorrow night either.

"Good," he said.

"Why?"

"I want to take you on a little trip."

"A little trip to where?"

"New York."

"New York?"

"Right," he said. "Have you ever been there?"

No.

She hadn't.

"What's in New York?" she asked.

He kissed her and said, "Me—the real me. I want you to know who I am so you can decide whether you want to be with me or not."

"I already know that, Parker," she said.

"Reserve your judgment until after tonight," he said.

"Why? What's going to happen tonight?"

"You're going to meet some more vampires."

Three hours later they lifted off a DIA runway into a violent, turbulent sky. Rave didn't care about the sky. There were no slayers up there.

That was the main thing.

Plus she was with Parker.

And had the new song.

"My life is all peaks and valleys," she said. "There's nothing in between anymore." She squeezed Parker's hand. "Whatever happens tonight isn't going to change the way I feel about you."

"We'll see," Parker said.

Chapter Sixty-Eight
Day Six—April 17
Sunday Evening

_____

Alley ran over and brushed up against Teffinger's leg as soon as he walked through the front door. He picked it up, carried it into the kitchen, grabbed a can of Bud Light from the fridge and drank half of it in one long swallow. Then he put a little on his finger and gave Alley a taste. When London walked into the room, Teffinger said, "Alley likes beer."

She didn't care.

She kissed him like she meant it.

"I have three words for you," she said.

Teffinger raised an eyebrow.

"And what might they be?"

"Mile ... High ... Club."

He chuckled.

"Are you serious?"

"You have no idea."

He handed Alley to her. "In that case, I'm going to take a quick shower." Then he said over his shoulder, "Hey, would you mind driving to the airport?"

"Sure."

"I seriously need to get a few beers in my gut."

She chuckled and said, "You're such a poet sometimes."

"It doesn't come easy," he said. "I work at it."

They made sure Alley had plenty of food and water, left a radio playing on low volume, and then headed for DIA. All the while, Teffinger kept his eyes locked on the storm cells and tried to drown a bad feeling with long gulps of Bud Light. "I really apologize for not being around much the last couple of days," he said. "I feel like I invited you to a party and then left while you were in the bathroom. This is unusual, even for me. I hope you don't think this is the way I always am."

"I understand," she said. "Stop worrying about it."

"The truth is, I'm scared to death that Jena's going to end up dead and I'm going to find out after the fact that she wouldn't be if I had just been a little smarter, or a little quicker, or a little less full of coffee, or a little more full of coffee."

He drained the last of the beer.

Crushed the can in his hands.

And tossed it into the back of the 4Runner.

"She's on the news every ten minutes," London said. "Her and that guy who got killed like a vampire. Everyone in the city is obsessed with at least one of those cases."

Teffinger didn't know that.

He hadn't watched ten seconds of the news for days.

But it didn't surprise him.

"I'm not even sure why I'm going to San Francisco, to tell you the truth," he said. "This whole billboard link is a long shot to start with. And I'm spending all my time on it. All my time. I wonder if it might be smarter to just come up for air and see if there's another angle that I missed. I'm starting to wonder if I'm just making busy work to trick myself into thinking I'm actually doing something constructive."

She studied him.

"You need a good night's sleep."

They spent an hour in a dim concourse bar and then boarded the plane, which turned out to be unusually empty—no doubt because all the sane people in the world knew better than to climb into something that would in turn climb into that sky.

That insane sky.

The liftoff turned out to be even worse than Teffinger envisioned. The plane lifted off the runway and then got slammed back down immediately by a strong gust that kept it pinned to the asphalt. Then it lifted again, just before it got to the end of the runway, and bucked wildly from side to side.

Then it climbed.

Into a mean sky.

The lights of Denver got smaller and smaller and then disappeared altogether as the aircraft headed over the Rocky Mountains. Ten minutes later the twitching suddenly stopped and the plane got so still that Teffinger may as well have been at home on his couch.

No one was in their entire row, all the way across.

No one was in front of them.

Or behind them.

No one could see them from their seats.

London turned off all the overhead lights in that area of the plane. Then she put a blanket over Teffinger, unfastened his belt and slipped her hand into his pants.

"Do you want to do it in the bathroom or right here?" she asked.

Good question.

Right here would be a lot more comfortable.

Everyone in the plane seemed to be sleeping.

The flight attendant hardly ever came around.

Plus she looked like she'd understand, even if she caught them.

"Let's try here," Teffinger said.

London put a blanket over herself.

And wiggled out of her pants and thong.

Then she stood up.

Looked around.

Saw no one.

And climbed on top of Teffinger, making sure they were under the blanket, just in case.

Chapter Sixty-Nine
Day Six—April 17
Sunday Evening

———————

R ave and Parker took a cab from the LaGuardia Airport into the city just as the sun set and the lights came on.

"I'm jealous," Parker said.

"Why?"

"There are certain things that you wish you could do again for the first time," he said. "Seeing New York is one of them. Seeing it at night is even a bigger one."

Rave squeezed his hand.

"I feel so small," she said.

"That's how it always starts," he said. "Later it will make you feel big."

Rave doubted that.

She felt like an ant.

Insignificant.

She could vanish off the face of the earth right now and the city wouldn't change an iota.

"How could it possibly make me feel big?"

Parker cocked his head.

"Easy," he said. "There's so much to do and see—the shows,

the architecture, the whole sensory experience that comes with just being here. You can do more things here, which means you can have a fuller life; and when you have a fuller life, you feel bigger. You feel bigger because you are bigger, inside."

The shows.

She pictured herself on stage.

On a big stage.

With a sea of faces hanging on her every breath.

"I want to play here someday," she said.

"That'll be your choice."

"You think?"

He nodded.

"There are ten million radios in this city," he said. "Later this summer, every one of them will be playing the song you wrote this morning. Next summer, they'll be playing one you haven't even written yet."

He chuckled, as if he'd just heard a joke.

"What?" she asked, curious.

"I'm not going to start being nice to you just because you're going to be rich and famous someday," he said.

She laughed.

"You're too much."

She turned back to the lights.

And realized that right now, this minute, she wanted to live more than she ever had before; there was too much life ahead of her to die.

She held Parker's hand, leaned into his ear and whispered, "Don't let me die."

He squeezed her hand and said, "I won't."

"Promise?"

"I promise."

She exhaled.

The cab dropped them off at an incredibly luxurious building in Manhattan's upper west side. They walked across a vaulted contemporary lobby to a reception area where Parker told a nicely dressed woman, "My name is Parker. I'm here to see Twist Anderson."

The woman nodded.

Expecting him.

"Floor twenty-seven," she said.

"Thanks."

Three minutes later, they stepped out of an elevator and knocked on one of four fancy doors on the 27th Floor—2702.

A woman opened the door.

A woman about Rave's age—extremely attractive; short, stylish blond hair; blue eyes; a thin pricey dress that clung to a curvy body; a glass of white wine in her left hand; slightly intoxicated.

"You're looking good, Twist," Parker said.

She said, "You too," gave him a hug, and then looked deep into Rave's eyes.

Then, to Rave's amazement, the woman kissed her.

On the lips.

Rave must have had a look on her face because the woman laughed, grabbed her hand, and said, "Come in."

The space was huge, with lofty ceilings and a wall of windows that showcased a galaxy of city lights. Furniture was minimal and beige. Splashes of color came from strategically placed pillows, lamps and artwork. A white piano occupied a corner.

Two women sat on a couch at the far end of the room.

Drinking wine.

Smiling.

Watching.

Suddenly Parker kissed Rave and said, "Enjoy. I'll see you in the morning."

Her heart raced.

"You're leaving?"

He chuckled and said, "Don't worry. You're in good hands."

Chapter Seventy
Day Six—April 17
Sunday Night

———————————

Over expensive white wine, Rave learned a lot in a very short time. Twist was a vampire by night and an associate attorney in a mid-sized law firm by day. Unlike Parker and London, who always referred to themselves as bloodline descendents, Twist called herself a vampire. Rave wasn't sure if that was just a shortcut in the woman's dialogue or whether it meant something more.

Twist was actually her real name.

Twist Anderson.

One of the other women—the one with the thick red hair and the pale indoor skin—was Katherine Zale, nickname Kat.

Kat wasn't a vampire.

She was Twist's lover.

And a good choice, at that. The woman oozed sex in a way that Rave couldn't quite put her finger on. She was attractive but not over-the-top stunning; feminine but not overly endowed; in good physical shape but not hard-bodied; articulate but not scholarly. Maybe it was her eyes. There was something about the woman's eyes that seemed to be able to look right into your soul. However she did it, the fact remained—she oozed sensuality.

The other woman was Natalie Fox.

She was a bloodline descendent in her mid-thirties; petite; with long raven hair, engaging green eyes and lots of expensive jewelry.

Rave liked all three of them.

But if she had to live with one of them on an island forever, it would be Twist.

All three of them were longstanding acquaintances with Parker, London and Forrest.

Rest his soul.

"There are a couple of reasons Parker brought you here," Twist said. "The biggest reason was to find out if we accept you. I think I can speak for all of us by saying that we're already past that."

"No problem," Kat said.

The other woman, Natalie, nodded.

Rave didn't know what that meant, exactly, but did know that she'd rather be accepted than not; especially since she already, mysteriously, felt a connection with them.

"One of the other reasons is to find out your views on immortality," Twist said.

The word startled Rave.

"Immortality?"

Twist nodded.

"We've done a lot of research on immortality," Twist said. "The old vampires weren't immortal in the way that you hear about in the movies. They couldn't grow a new hand if it got cut off. They couldn't self-heal a wound if someone stuck a knife in their stomach. They didn't have any magical powers like that. They were just as susceptible as everyone else to mortal wounds and the effects of outside influences on the body. And, it goes without saying, they couldn't change shapes, or fly, or turn themselves into bats or anything like that."

Rave listened.

"Okay."

"But they were different from others in one important way," Twist said. "You've heard that they lived for hundreds of years. That part of the myth is actually true."

Rave studied her.

To see if she was joking.

She wasn't.

"Really?"

"There are several well documented cases," Twist said. "There was something about their internal makeup that was extremely resistant to aging. If they didn't suffer a mortal fatality, they could in fact live for a very long time. How long, we don't know, because they eventually all got killed. But a very, very long time, that's for sure."

"I'll be honest with you," Rave said. "That's hard for someone like me to believe."

"Is it?" Twist asked. "Think about it. Take a five-year-old kid. He doesn't suddenly wake up the next day fifty years old. It takes time. There's a degenerative process that takes place."

Rave nodded.

That was true.

"Everyone in the world is used to a degenerative process that roughly works the same on all of us," she said. "When we're five, we're young. When we're eighty, we're old. But the bottom line is that there's something in our makeup that causes us to get old at a certain rate. The only thing different between us and the old vampires is that they had something in their makeup that changed the rate. And like I said before, we don't know how much it changed. Maybe it extended the human cycle three-fold; or maybe it was ten-fold. We don't know. But we do know for a fact that the rate was different, dramatically different—different enough that they could literally live well over a hundred years and still look young."

That actually made sense.

And Rave said so.

"Asian women are a good modern-day example," Twist added. "It's not that hard to find a 60-year-old Asian woman who doesn't look or behave or feel any older than a 30-year-old American woman. Aging is not uniform. It's not set in stone. It's not one-size-fits-all. Mortality is not one-size-fits-all."

"True."

"Of course, the most obvious difference in life cycles is the one between the species. Humans have a much longer cycle than dogs which have a much longer cycle than insects. Compared to a fruit fly, human beings are almost immortal."

Rave cocked her head.

"So where are we going with all this?"

"We're talking about immortality," Twist said. "And let me back up for a minute and say that immortality actually isn't exactly the right word. I don't believe that even the old vampires would live forever. I believe that they had a natural life cycle, like every other living creature, that would eventually end even in the absence of a mortal wound. But since their cycle was so long, let's just refer to them, for the sake of discussion, as being immortal when compared to normal human beings."

"All right."

"So the question is this," Twist said. "How do you feel about immortality? Would you take it if someone handed it to you?"

Rave laughed.

"Sure," she said. "Give me a handful."

"I'm serious," Twist said. "How would you feel if you could live for two or three or four or five hundred years?"

Rave cocked her head.

"Let me see if I have this right," she said. "I could live for, say, three hundred years if I want to; but I could also kill myself at any time, if I chose?"

"Right."

"Meaning that I wouldn't be forced to remain alive if I didn't choose to," she said.

"Right."

"And you want to know how I'd feel about that, if it was an option?"

"Right."

"You're basically talking about the fountain of youth," Rave said. "I can't imagine a rational person who wouldn't take that in a heartbeat, if it was an actual option."

Rave drained the rest of the wine from her glass.

Twist filled it back up.

Then hers, Kat's and Natalie's too.

"Here's the reason I ask," Twist said. "Bloodline descendents of vampires have the immortality gene inside them—sleeping and dormant, but there."

Rave sipped wine.

And couldn't argue.

Conceptually, at least.

"The secret is to wake it up," Twist said.

Rave smiled.

"That would be nice," she said. "Except how do you do that?"

"We're working on it," Twist said. "In fact, we think we've already partially succeeded. Parker is taking the lead in the whole thing."

"My Parker?"

Twist nodded.

"After we learn how to fully wake it up, and become immortal if you will, the next step is to figure out how to bring others with us."

She ran her fingers through Kat's hair.

Then kissed her.

"So how are you waking it up?" Rave asked.

Twist stood up, grabbed Rave's hand, and led her to the bedroom.

The three women removed Rave's clothes.

Every stitch.

And laid her on her back on the mattress, with her arms stretched out to her sides and her palms facing the ceiling.

Rave didn't protest.

She felt safe.

She felt loved.

"The secret is in the blood," Twist said.

The other women removed their clothes. Then Twist did something to each of Rave's forearms, and to her stomach; something that didn't hurt but started a small trickle of blood at each location.

Then the three women sucked her blood.

Slowly.

Lovingly.

Rave stared at the ceiling for a while.

Then closed her eyes.

And concentrated on the sensation of the women's lips and mouths on her skin; especially Twist's mouth, which was on Rave's stomach.

She had never felt more secure.

Or more loved.

Or more right.

And realized that her life had changed, yet again.

Chapter Seventy-One
Day Seven—April 18
Monday Morning

Monday morning, Teffinger got up early and jogged down Market Street in downtown San Francisco as a cold ocean wind did its best to chill him to the bone. He planned on doing three miles, but only did two. Even now, before dawn, the city was buzzing with drivers who were no doubt trying to beat the even more oppressive traffic to come.

Because of the time constraints of last night, Teffinger hadn't called ahead to tell anyone from homicide that he was coming in this morning.

So he was prepared for a little delay when he showed up.

He checked in with the receptionist, explained who he was and that he was investigating the disappearance of a woman by the name of Jena Vellone in Denver, and got directed to the head of the homicide unit, a thin, pale man with a twitchy right eye.

A man by the name of Mark Yorke.

A man who didn't impress Teffinger much.

A man with a weak jaw.

A man who didn't drink coffee.

Or offer any to Teffinger.

Teffinger kept his friendliest and most professional face on as he explained the situation, anxious to get out of the guy's office and into a room with the file.

The file on Barbara Rocker.

Who disappeared last year.

And who had been on a billboard, the same as Jena Vellone.

"Time is of the essence," Teffinger emphasized.

The thin man stood up, smiled, escorted Teffinger to a bench in the hall and said, "Just let me make a few quick phone calls. There's coffee in the kitchen, which is right over there."

"Beautiful, thanks."

Teffinger got a cup and drank it on the bench.

Then he got a second.

Then the thin man opened his door and said, "Come on in."

Finally.

"We have a problem," Yorke said.

Teffinger wasn't sure, but it seemed like the corner of the man's mouth raised just a touch as he spoke, as if he had started to smile and then forced it down.

"What kind of problem?"

"I talked to your chief, a man by the name of F.F. Tanker, just to verify that everything is on the up and up," Yorke said. "He said that the case you say you're investigating, involving Jena Vellone, doesn't belong to Denver."

Teffinger swallowed.

Tanker would have had no choice but to say that.

He couldn't tell anyone that Teffinger was on the case only in an unofficial capacity.

"He said that the case actually belongs to Cherry Hills," Yorke added. "So I called them up. They told me that you don't have authority to be investigating the matter. In fact, according to them, you're actually a person of interest. You were the last person to see the missing woman alive. And her blood was found in your vehicle."

Teffinger cocked his head.

"I know how this looks," he said. "But trust me, it isn't anything like that. Here's the important thing. Jena Vellone is a TV reporter and her face was on several billboards in Denver. She disappeared on Tuesday and hasn't been heard from since. I've located another woman from Chicago by the name of Kennedy Pinehurst, a radio personality who was also on billboards throughout the city. She disappeared in May of last year and was later found hanging upside down in a spread-eagle position with her throat slashed. I was in Chicago yesterday, looking through the file. Then last night, I learned that you had a similar situation here in San Francisco. From what I understand, the woman's name is Barbara Rocker and she was also on billboards. These cases are all connected. I need the Rocker file right now, immediately, to figure out what that connection is."

Yorke cocked his head.

"Look," he said, "I'm not saying that you had anything to do with the disappearance of this Denver woman. In fact, you seem like a stand-up guy to me. But Cherry Hills has you down as a person of interest. How would it look to the public, or to my superiors, if I gave a confidential investigative file to a known suspect?"

Teffinger stood up.

Put his hands on the desk.

And leaned across.

"Screw the public and screw perceptions," he said. "We're talking about a woman's life."

"I understand that, but—"

"Listen!" Teffinger said. "Sometimes you just have to cut through the crap and get things done. Someone in your position ought to know that better than anyone."

Yorke stood up.

"And sometimes you just have to follow protocol," he said. "And our protocol here in San Francisco says that we don't hand our files over to suspects, even if they're detectives."

Teffinger narrowed his eyes.

"Look," he said. "You need to help me. Otherwise, the woman in Denver—Jena Vellone, who is a personal friend of mine by the way—is going to end up dead."

"How do you know she's not already dead?"

Teffinger pounded his fist on the desk.

Then he stormed out and slammed the door behind him.

The glass shattered.

Chapter Seventy-Two
Day Seven—April 18
Monday Morning

Tripp was alseep when someone shook him on the shoulder and said, "Wake up." The voice was familiar but Tripp was too groggy to place it. "It's four thirty."

The voice was VanDeventer's.

Tripp rolled to the edge of the bed and sat up.

The room was dark.

And unfamiliar.

At first he thought they were in a hotel. Then he remembered that they were in Rave Lafelle's house, waiting for her to show up, and had been waiting all night.

"Four thirty?"

"She's not coming home," VanDeventer said. The words dripped with frustration. "Let's get the hell out of here while it's still dark."

Tripp grunted.

"Yeah."

He walked to the bathroom, took a long piss, flushed, splashed water on his face, and dried it with the vampire's towel. Then he grabbed the knife, wooden stake and mallet from the nightstand, stuffed them into the pillowcase—the one from the hotel—and followed VanDeventer out the back door.

A dog barked.

From a couple of houses down.

Otherwise the world was quiet and empty.

They walked two blocks, to the car, without talking.

They encountered no one.

Chapter Seventy-Three
Day Seven—April 18
Monday Morning

———————

R ave woke up in a coffin. The lid was open and she had an unobstructed view of a ceiling twelve feet above her head. She muscled herself into a sitting position and looked around. The room was dark but there was enough light to discern that the coffin was in a bedroom, eight feet or so from a bed that showed no evidence of having been slept in.

She climbed out.

Then used the bathroom and paused briefly when her body reflected in a full length mirror.

She was nude.

The sight reminded her of last night.

Being disrobed by Twist and her friends.

And being sucked.

She checked her arms and stomach for marks but found none.

Good.

If this became a habit, she didn't want to look like a junkie.

She wrapped a towel around her waist, opened the door and was surprised to find so much light in the main room. No one was there. She checked the other bedroom—the master bedroom judging by the size—and found the bed empty and made.

She was alone.

In the kitchen, the clock on the microwave said 11:33.

A coffee pot was on and the pot was full.

Bless Twist's heart.

Rave poured a cup and then spotted a note and key on the granite countertop—WENT TO WORK ... MAKE YOURSELF AT HOME ... MY CLOTHES ARE YOURS SO DON'T BE SHY ... USE THE KEY IF YOU WANT TO LEAVE AND COME BACK IN ... I'LL BE HOME AROUND SIX. LOVE, TWIST.

Rave sipped coffee and went back to check out the coffin.

She didn't remember getting in it last night.

In fact, she didn't remember anything after the bloodsucking started.

Had the women put her in it?

Or had she climbed in herself, in lieu of the bed, of her own volition?

And if so—why?

She showered, got a fresh shirt from Twist's closet, ate, and then sat down at the piano.

She played yesterday's song four times and liked it better with each passing.

Then she paused to refill her coffee cup.

And when she did, a new melody entered her head.

Just like that.

She set the cup on the granite without even taking a sip and headed straight back to the keyboard. An hour later, she called Tim Pepper.

"I'm going to set the phone down and play a song for you," she said.

Then she did.

She picked the phone back up before the last chord finished vibrating and said, "Well? What do you think?"

"What do you think I think?" Pepper said. "What I want to know is this. Where in the hell is all this coming from all of a sudden?"

She chuckled.

"I don't know."

"Do me a favor," he said.

"What?"

"Write another one, now, this second, before whatever it is that's in you gets away."

She laughed.

"I'm serious," he said. "Sit down and write it and then call me back as soon as you finish."

She stood at the windows, drinking coffee and looking down on New York. She did that until the pot got empty. Then she sat back down at the piano and wrote a third song.

Even better than the first two.

And she played it ten times to prove it.

But there was no fourth.

Not today, anyway.

She was drained and smart enough to know it.

She didn't call Pepper even though she should.

Instead, she decided to have a look around the loft and see if she could find out what Twist-the-vampire was all about.

She knew she should probably feel guilty, snooping around, but figured that Twist owed her that much after sucking her blood last night.

Then she remembered something.

Something that happened after everyone sucked her.

She remembered having her mouth and lips and tongue on Twist's stomach. She remembered the warmth of the woman's skin and the tautness of her abdominal muscles.

And she remembered the sweet taste of blood.

She called information, got the number for Twist's law firm, and dialed. When Twist answered, Rave said, "Can you come home early?"

The woman chuckled.

"Hold on," she said.

A door closed in the background.

Then Twist said, "You want to taste me again, don't you?"

Rave hadn't realized it until now.

This second.

"Yes."

Twist said, "Welcome to the dark side. I'll be there in an hour."

Rave exhaled.

She almost hung up but then said, "Are you still there?"

Yes.

She was.

"Did I go in the coffin myself last night? Or did you put me there?"

A pause.

"You went yourself."

"I don't remember doing it," Rave said.

"Did you freak out when you woke up?" Twist asked.

"No, not really."

"You're lucky," Twist said. "I totally freaked, the first time."

"Do you still freak?"

Twist laughed.

"No, of course not. See you in an hour. I'm bringing Kat,

though."

"Fine."

"I don't do anything behind her back," Twist added, "even vampire stuff."

"Understood," Rave said. "Did we suck her last night? I don't remember—"

"No."

"Okay."

"Do you want to do that today?" Twist asked. "She doesn't mind—"

"Sure," Rave said. "But only if that's all right with you."

Twist chuckled.

"An hour, give or take."

Rave looked outside.

The sun was bright.

Extraordinarily bright.

Too bright.

"You know what," Rave said, "on second thought, I don't want to mess up your day. Why don't we just wait until tonight, when it's dark, and when we can have a few drinks and take our time?"

"You sure?"

Yes.

She was.

"Okay. Stay out of trouble until then."

Ten minutes later Parker called and asked, "Are you still alive?"

She chuckled.

"You're a tricky guy."

"I'm coming over to get you," he said. "It's time for you to get acquainted with New York."

"Give me an hour to freshen up," she said.

She hung up and then went through the papers on Twist's desk as she waited for the woman's computer to boot up.

Tell me some vampire secrets, Twist Anderson.

Chater Seventy-Four
Day Seven—April 18
Monday Morning

_____

After Teffinger shattered the glass in Mark Yorke's door, he swung back to the hotel, picked up London and said, "We're going to Plan B." Then they headed to the S.F. Public Library.

The wind stopped.

A misty fog took its place.

With the help of a wonderful librarian named Carol Smith, who bore a striking resemblance to Jena Vellone's mother, Teffinger obtained either an electronic printout or a microfiche printout of every local newspaper article that covered the Barbara Rocker disappearance.

The story was fairly simple.

Barbara Rocker was the 23-year-old daughter of Stanley Rocker.

Stanley Rocker was a filthy rich shipping tycoon.

A filthy rich shipping tycoon with an eye for history, art, the exotic, and anything off the charts, to be precise.

Each year he championed, coordinated, and funded an extraordinary event.

King Tut.

The Impressionists.

Body Works.

The publicity and promotion always befitted the stature of the event. And since Stanley Rocker paid for that publicity, he took the opportunity to put his lovely daughter front stage. It was Barbara Rocker's smiling face that announced the event in magazines, on TV and on billboards. It was daddy's way, in effect, to buy a piece of fame for his little princess.

Barbara Rocker went clubbing one Saturday in downtown San Francisco fourteen months ago, on a cold February night.

She left the club by herself.

Her Porsche 911 was later found abandoned on the north edge of the city.

She was never heard from again.

Her body was never found.

Barbara Rocker wasn't engaged or involved with anyone at the time of her disappearance.

No one demanded ransom.

The police briefly questioned a few persons of interest early on in the case, but never charged anyone. If she was murdered, the person who did it was still at large.

The victim's father, Stanley Rocker, died two months ago when his 65-foot Hatteras mysteriously went down in cold, choppy waters, twenty miles off the coast.

London said, "It looks like we're SOL."

Teffinger grunted.

"Now I understand what Yorke's problem is," he said. "This was a huge case. He wouldn't look too dandy if someone strolled in from out of town and threw some light on the picture that wasn't there before."

"You think?"

Teffinger nodded.

"He's more interested in covering his own ass than he is in solving the case," he said.

"Why don't you make an end run around him?" London asked. "Go straight to the chief, or even the mayor."

"We'll see," he said. "First we're going to talk to this guy, right here."

He put his finger on a reporter's name at the top of an article.

Peter Poindexter.

Suddenly his phone rang. Teffinger expected it to be Double-F Tanker, calling to chew him out for putting him in the middle of things. But it turned out to be Sydney.

"Did you hear what Geneva Vellone did?"

No.

He hadn't.

"Apparently on her radio show this morning, she made an offer to whoever it is that took Jena," Sydney said.

Teffinger raked his hair back with his fingers.

It immediately flopped back down over his forehead.

"Don't tell me," he said. "She wants the guy to give up Jena and take her in exchange."

"Exactly."

"Damn it," Teffinger said. "I told her not to do that."

"You knew she was going to do it?"

"No, I thought she wasn't going to do it," he said.

"But she mentioned it to you?"

Yes.

"She mentioned it, but I talked her out of it," Teffinger said.

Silence.

"How's San Francisco going?" Sydney asked.

"It's going the way my life usually goes," Teffinger said. "Do me a favor, go down to the radio station and see Geneva personally. Be sure that she doesn't do anything stupid once the weirdos start contacting her. I don't need a distraction right now."

"Nick, I really don't have time—"

"Thanks," he said. "I appreciate it."

"For the record, I'm making a mean face at you right now."

Teffinger chuckled.

"I know," he said. "I can feel it."

He almost hung up.

But Sydney said, "One more thing. We might have a break in our dead vampire case."

"Which dead vampire?"

"The male," she said. "The one by the railroad tracks."

"Forrest something," Teffinger said.

"Right, that one."

Teffinger really didn't care.

This second, he only cared about Jena Vellone.

But then he remembered the promise he made to Cameron Leigh. And he remembered that whoever killed the male vampire probably killed her too.

"What's the break?"

"Apparently, an Ohio detective by the name of Maggie Ross was in the guy's house looking around and stumbled on some male intruder who had broken in," Sydney said. "He was hiding in a closet and punched her in the face as soon as she opened the door. The thinking is that he might be the killer, or tied to him somehow."

Possibly, Teffinger thought.

On the other hand, newly dead people often end up robbed.

"Did she get a look at him?"

"Briefly."

Interesting.

"Stay on top of it," he said. "Right now I don't have time to do anything except breathe and find Jena. Keep Geneva out of trouble."

He hung up, looked at London, and said, "Wrong number."

She laughed.

Teffinger picked up the stack of printouts and said, "Let's go talk to our reporter friend."

Chapter Seventy-Five
Day Seven—April 18
Monday Afternoon

———————————

Tripp swung by Teffinger's house on Green Mountain to see if the vampire, Rave Lafelle, had moved in with her friend—Little Miss Exotic—which would explain why she hadn't returned home last night. The island girl's Camry was in the driveway; the vampire's VW wasn't. The front door was shut and so were all the windows. Given the temperature, something would be open if anyone was home.

He drove to the backside of the mountain and parked.

Then he hoofed it over the ridge, saw no nosy neighbors pointing their stupid faces towards him, and dropped silently into Teffinger's backyard.

No one shouted.

No dogs barked.

Nothing moved.

The rear sliding glass door was locked. He saw no signs of life inside the house, and moved to the bedroom window. No one was in the bedroom. The window was a vertical slider. Tripp pushed it up and was amazed to find that it actually moved.

Cool.

He put on latex gloves, removed the screen and muscled his way in.

A white cat pranced over to greet him.

Tripp picked it up and said, "What's your name?"

He carried it with him as he searched the house. "Looks like you're all alone."

Two suitcases sat on the floor in the corner of the master bedroom, one on top of the other. The vampire's? They both turned out to be empty—make that almost empty. Each one had a vinyl ID tag inside with a plastic window that said IF LOST PLEASE RETURN TO: LONDON FONTELLE, 29887 SEA BREEZE DRIVE, MIAMI, FLORIDA 80882; (283) 555-3891.

Got you.

"Her name's London," Tripp told the cat. "Do you like that? Personally, I think it's sort of cool."

London.

London Fontelle.

Are you a vampire, darling?

Or just a friend of Rave Lafelle's?

He spotted a pen and notepad next to the phone on the nightstand, wrote the information down and stuffed it in his wallet.

Then he went through the closet.

The woman had some clothes hanging, but not many. Probably only what came out of the suitcases. The rest of her stuff turned out to be in the middle dresser drawer—thongs, bras, socks and T-shirts, primarily. Tripp stuffed one of the thongs, a white one, into his left front pants pocket.

"Don't tell," Tripp said to the cat.

Then his cell phone rang.

He looked at the incoming number.

Jake VanDeventer.

Weird.

They weren't supposed to hook up until later.

"We got trouble," VanDeventer said. "How soon can you get over here and pick me up?"

Trouble?

How could there possibly be trouble?

They weren't doing anything today except staying low and waiting for tonight.

"Twenty minutes."

"Okay," VanDeventer said. "Stop at a gas station first and fill the tank."

"Why? What's going on?"

"I'll tell you when you get here."

Chapter Seventy-Six
Day Seven—April 18
Monday Afternoon

_____

Rave didn't find much of interest in the short time she had to snoop around inside Twist's loft before Parker picked her up. She did find one thing, though—namely a reference to a woman named Suzanne Wheeler from "Montreal." There was no address or phone number, but this had to be the person Parker referred to who did the genealogy work.

The person who was working on Rave's file.

Which was one of the three stolen by the slayers.

Suzanne Wheeler.

Rave memorized the name but didn't write it down.

When Parker showed up, Rave played him the two songs she wrote this morning. The expression on his face was one of awe, but he wasn't as happy as Rave expected him to be.

"What's wrong?" she asked.

"Nothing."

"No, really, I can tell," she insisted.

He paused.

Then he said, "You're going to be huge. You're going to outgrow me."

She laughed.

"Are you serious?"

He was.

So she got serious too.

"Don't even worry about it," she said.

"I already have a picture in my mind," he said. "Concerts, recording studios, managers, parties, fans—the whole superstar thing. I'll be squeezed out."

She put her arms around him.

And pulled him tight.

"That will never happen, Parker," she said. "I swear."

"You mean it?"

"With all my life," she said. "Now, show me New York."

Parker showed her New York.

Times Square.

The Statue of Liberty.

Wall Street.

"I don't want to go back to Denver," Rave said as they walked through the heart of the city; two people in a crowd of a million. "I want to stay here. I feel safe here. There's nothing left for me in Denver at this point."

"What about your gig at the Old Orleans?"

"I'm going to call Tim Pepper and see if we can get out of it," she said. "If we can't, I'll finish up, obviously. But I only have Tuesday through Saturday left, in any event. Then I'm booked for a month in Los Angeles. I'm assuming that Vegas will start within a month or two after that. Will you come with me to L.A.?"

"You want me to?"

She squeezed his hand.

"We need to stay together, Parker," she said. "I don't want to be apart from you."

He chuckled.

"What?" she asked.

"You know why you want to move to New York, don't you?" he asked. "It's Twist. She has a hold on you."

Rave considered it.

True.

But only to an extent.

"Twist is nice but she isn't you, Parker," she said.

Chapter Seventy-Seven
Day Seven—April 18
Monday Afternoon

———————————

The earliest that Peter Poindexter could meet was around one o'clock, when he'd be in the Fisherman's Wharf area. Teffinger and London got there at noon and had fresh crab for lunch. The fog lifted, patches of blue sky emerged, and the temperature climbed into the sixties. They wandered around the marina—checking out the fishing boats and watching the seagulls fight over fish guts. Ten minutes later the reporter showed up.

He turned out to be a crusty, sailor-looking man, about sixty, with a three-day shadow on his face, and gray hair slightly out of control.

Teffinger liked him right away.

They ended up sitting on a dock, dangling their feet over the edge.

"I used to fish these boats when I was a kid, during the summers, back in high school," Poindexter said. "That was more years ago than I'm going to admit. Last year, I went out for a day, just for grins. Nothing had changed. They still eat sardines out of cans, piss over the side, drink like wild banshees and shoot seagulls." He looked at London and then said to Teffinger, "I like your woman. Be good to her. Take it from someone who's been there. So, you want to know about the Barbara Rocker case, right? Is that the deal?"

"That's the deal," Teffinger said.

Then he explained the situation in more detail than he had over the phone this morning, including his run-in with Mark Yorke.

"That guy's a flaming incompetent," Poindexter said. "It's all politics, that's how he got that high to begin with. Yorke couldn't catch VD in a Singapore whorehouse." He looked at London and said, "Excuse the French."

Teffinger jumped in.

"One of your articles mentioned that a couple of persons of interest were questioned early in the case," he said.

"True."

"Do you recall who they were?"

Poindexter retreated in thought and scratched his head.

"Not offhand, but I'd have it in my notes," he said.

"So what were the circumstances?"

"One of the guys was someone she'd been drinking with at the club that evening," Poindexter said. "The other guy was someone who cruised past her house a couple of days before she disappeared."

Teffinger raised an eyebrow.

"Tell me about him."

Poindexter shrugged.

"There wasn't much to it, really," he said. "Barbara Rocker lived in a beach house that daddy bought for her. Well, beach house isn't the right term. The house itself actually sits on a bluff across the bridge, north of the city. It feeds off a public road, but has a long gated driveway with a lot of cameras. After she disappeared, the videos were pulled and the same car was seen driving by the place twice. The police ran the plates and it turned out to be a rental from Hertz out at the airport. The guy turned out to be staying in a hotel. When the cops talked to him and asked what he'd been doing on the road, he said he was driving around looking for houses for sale and getting acquainted with the area."

"And?"

"And, as I remember it," Poindexter said, "the guy didn't have an alibi for the time Rocker disappeared. However, no one from the club had ever seen him. And, it turned out, he was some rich diamond miner from Johannesburg; so he actually had enough money to buy the kinds of properties he was scouting around for. Plus, he had no motive whatsoever. So he dropped off the radar screen real quick."

Teffinger frowned.

He hoped for more.

But now saw it was nothing.

Then he raised an eyebrow and said, "Were there other houses for sale on that road at that time?"

Poindexter laughed.

"Now that is something I would have no idea of," he said. "Why?"

"You said the guy drove by twice," Teffinger said.

"Right."

"If there was a property for sale, I could see why he might drive down the road twice," Teffinger said. "But if there wasn't, I don't know why he would."

"He could have gotten lost," Poindexter said. "Those roads twist more than a hundred snakes."

Teffinger considered the theory.

Then he said, "When a guy is that rich, time is everything. Guys like him don't get lost."

Poindexter chuckled.

"You can tell that about the guy? Without ever having met him?"

"I've met plenty of guys like him," Teffinger said. "Were the two passes on the same day or different days?"

"Different, if my memory's correct."

"Can you do me a favor? Check your notes and let me know what the guy's name is."

Poindexter called his wife at home and asked her to pull the file from the basement.

Five minutes later Poindexter's phone rang.

He answered, listened, said "Thanks," and hung up.

Then he looked at Teffinger and said, "Jake VanDeventer. That's confidential, though. The police slipped me his name on the side."

Teffinger nodded.

And said, "Don't worry."

They talked for two minutes.

Then Poindexter had to run.

Teffinger gave the man a hundred dollar bill and said, "Take the wife out to dinner for pulling the file."

After Poindexter left, London asked, "Now what?"

Good question.

"Now we find a realtor," he said. "I want to know if there were any other properties for sale on Barbara Rocker's road last February. If there weren't, I'm going to get real interested in Mister Diamond Miner."

"But he has no motive, Teffinger," she said.

True.

That was the problem.

"Why would some rich guy from Johannesburg come all the way to San Francisco and kill some woman that he couldn't possibly know?" London added.

Teffinger shrugged.

He didn't know.

"Some guys don't like to pee in their own backyard," he said. "Sometimes it's nothing more complicated than that."

London punched Teffinger's arm.

"Thanks for the visual," she said.

"You're welcome for the visual," he said. "And I've got more, if you want 'em."

From Fisherman's Wharf, Teffinger and London rented a Saturn and drove north across the Golden Gate Bridge to Barbara Rocker's beach house, which had since been sold to a third party. The road weaved parallel to the coastline and fed multi-million dollar estates that sat on cliffs and overlooked the Pacific.

A mile or so down the road from Rocker's place, they came across a house for sale by realtor Jim Hansen, "Specializing in Fine Coastal Estates."

Teffinger pulled to the shoulder, killed the engine, called him, and explained the situation.

Hansen said, "February of last year?"

"Right."

"There were two properties for sale on that road," he said.

The words shocked Teffinger.

"There were?"

"Yes."

"Are you sure?"

"Yes."

"How can you be so sure?"

Hansen chuckled.

"Because I was the realtor on both of them," he said.

"Did someone named Jake VanDeventer look at either of them?"

"VanDeventer ... VanDeventer ... the name rings a bell ..."

"He's from Johannesburg," Teffinger added.

"Right," Hansen said, "the diamond miner. Yeah, I remember him now, a tough looking guy. He reminded me a little of a cowboy out of one of those old black-and-white westerns. He looked at the Fitzgerald property but didn't like it. He was looking for something a little more contemporary."

"Thanks," Teffinger said. "I really appreciate your time."

"Not a problem."

"By the way, do I know you? You sound familiar."

"I don't think so."

Teffinger hung up and slumped behind the wheel.

"Dead end," he told London. "We're back to square one."

Chapter Seventy-Eight
Day Seven—April 18
Monday Evening

The directions from Denver to Las Vegas are simple: take I-70 west until it ends, turn left, and keep going until you see the lights and hear the hollering. Tripp was at the wheel, keeping the vehicle exactly at the speed limit, leaving Grand Junction in the rearview mirror and heading into the deeper desert of western Colorado.

Jake VanDeventer sat in the passenger seat.

Reading a book called Lawyer Trap that someone left behind at a rest stop.

"Is that thing any good?" Tripp asked.

VanDeventer looked up and said, "It's got a good bad guy in it."

"What's his name?"

"Jack Degan."

Tripp chuckled.

Jack Degan.

"He sounds tough. I always wanted to be a bad guy in a book," Tripp said. "Does he look like you or me?"

VanDeventer flipped back a number of pages until he found the passage he was looking for and said, "Not hardly. Here's what the book says about him—Jack Draven know if he was an Indian, a Mexican, or just a really dark white man. Nor did he give a shit. Most people took him for an Indian on account of the high cheekbones, the thick black ponytail and the scar that ran down the right side of his face, all the way from his hairline to his chin. It had been there ever since he could remember. He had no idea how he got it, but did know that he wouldn't erase it even if he could.

"Nope, that's not you or me," Tripp said.

VanDeventer agreed.

And continued reading.

He was relaxed now, in stark contrast to when he called Tripp earlier this afternoon. Tripp had to admit, in hindsight, that VanDeventer hadn't exaggerated when he said they had trouble. A TV news report had flashed a composite sketch of VanDeventer as a person of interest in connection with the murder of Forrest Jones, who was found with a wooden stake through his heart. Obviously the female detective in Ohio got a much better look at VanDeventer than she should have.

After seeing the news report, VanDeventer's plan was simple.

Get out of Denver.

At least for a day or two.

And do it without using a bus, train or plane.

So now Tripp was driving him to Las Vegas.

Tripp would rent a room.

VanDeventer wouldn't be on the registry or use a credit card.

VanDeventer would spend the night with Tripp.

Then, in the morning, VanDeventer would buy a cash bus ticket to L.A. He'd hang out there, poised to head back to Denver in a heartbeat if Tripp needed his help.

"We're going to get to town about midnight," Tripp said. "I'm thinking that we should head over to the Spearmint Rhino and get stupid."

The Rhino?

What's that?

Tripp chuckled.

"Haven't you ever been to Vegas before, man?"

"No."

"The Rhino's one of the best strip clubs there," Tripp said. "Premium, Grade-A ass. Friendly ass. Very friendly ass."

"I thought you were getting sweet on that woman. What's her name—?"

"Brittany."

"Right, Brittany," VanDeventer said.

"That's my point," Tripp said. "I'd be with her tonight, getting some, if I wasn't out here in the middle of the desert driving in the wrong direction."

VanDeventer grunted and went back to reading.

Two heartbeats later he looked over and said, "If you really meant what you just said, I have a proposition for you."

"Shoot."

"Did you mean what you just said?"

"I did."

"Okay, then call her up right now and see if she wants to fly out tonight," VanDeventer said. "If she does, you guys can get a second room somewhere so she doesn't see me. I'll pay for everything, both rooms, her flight out, the whole thing."

"Are you serious?"

"Dead."

Tripp called Brittany.

She listened, hung up, checked with the airlines and phoned back ten minutes later.

"There's a flight I can catch," she said. "It arrives in Vegas at 11:23 p.m."

"Good," Tripp said. "When you get in, take a cab to the Mirage and call me on the way."

"This is so romantic."

Tripp hung up.

"Done deal," he said. "Thanks."

"You'll enjoy that better than the Elephant," VanDeventer said.

"The Rhino."

"What Rhino?"

"It's called the Rhino, not the Elephant."

"Whatever."

"You should get your nose out of that book," Tripp said. "You're missing some of the best scenery on the face of the planet."

VanDeventer looked out his window.

And through the windshield.

Then went back to reading.

Chapter Seventy-Nine
Day Seven—April 18
Monday Night

———————————

P arker didn't get Rave back to the loft until after dark. Twist was waiting for them, barefoot, in a simple, short white dress, looking even more incredible than last night. No one else was in the room. Twist hugged Parker and then gave Rave a long sensuous kiss on the lips.

"You taste like New York," Twist said.

"Is that good or bad?"

"I don't know," Twist said, "let me take another sample."

Then she kissed Rave again.

Longer and wetter this time.

"It's good," Twist said.

An uneasy feeling gripped Rave.

Not because she was being kissed by a woman.

But because that woman already had a lover.

"Where's Kat?" Rave asked.

"Relax," Twist said. "I'm allowed to kiss other women, so long as they're vampires. Kat couldn't make it tonight. But Natalie will be joining us."

Natalie.

Natalie Fox.

The petite, quiet vampire.

"You don't mind tasting her, do you?" Twist asked.

Rave shook her head.

No.

Not at all.

"Good," Twist said, "because she's really excited about it. Vampire blood is better for you anyway. It has more strength in it."

They drank wine.

Twist, unbelievably, had a Billie Holiday CD and put it on.

Rave felt good.

No, not good, perfect.

"I may never leave," she said.

"Then don't."

Rave looked at her.

"I want to be sure everything is out in the open," she said. "Did Parker tell you that I shot Forrest?"

Twist nodded.

"You had no choice," Twist said. "The only chance he had was for you to shoot. It wasn't your fault. You did the best you could. If Forrest was here today, he'd be the first to tell you that."

"Did Parker tell you I was drunk?" Rave asked.

The look on Twist's face said it all.

No.

Parker hadn't.

Twist had no idea.

"Both Parker and Forrest told me to be absolutely sure that I stayed totally sober all evening," Rave said. "I didn't listen to them. I drank screwdrivers. I smoked pot. Then, when I went to leave the club, Parker saw that I was in no condition to go through with the plan. He told me to abort, but I didn't. Then, because I was drunk, I ended up stopping at the wrong place. Forrest had to run a long way to get to where I was. By the time he got there, he was out of breath and no match for the slayer. So I was the one who got him into that position to begin with."

Twist looked at Parker.

"Is that true?" she asked.

Parker nodded.

Twist got off the couch, walked to the kitchen, pulled the cork out of the bottle, and refilled her glass. She almost set the bottle back down on the granite countertop, but instead walked over and topped off Parker and Rave. Then she sat back down and patted Rave's knee.

"None of us are perfect," she said. "We do what we can. The main thing is that we stick together." She clinked her glass on Rave's and added, "To the death."

Rave exhaled.

And clinked Twist's glass.

Then Parker's.

And said, "To the death."

Natalie Fox showed up ten minutes later, carrying a leather briefcase and looking like she just won the lottery. "Brought my goodies," she told Twist.

"I thought you might."

Natalie walked straight to Rave and kissed her on the mouth. "I've been thinking about this all day," she said. She drank a large glass of wine in about ten minutes and said, "Parker, will you do the honors?"

Sure.

Natalie and Parker disappeared into the guest bedroom.

And closed the door.

Rave must have had a look of curiosity on her face because Twist said, "You'll see, in a minute. We all develop our own little comfort zones on how we like to be sucked. Natalie, for example, likes to be worked into a sexual frenzy beforehand."

When Parker came out of the bedroom he asked Rave, "You

want me to leave?"

She squeezed his hand.

"No. I already told you that this afternoon."

In the bedroom, Rave found Natalie spread-eagle on the bed, naked except for a black thong. She had black leather cuffs on her wrists and ankles. The cuffs were secured to the four corners of the bed with rope.

She was stretched tight.

Immobile.

Helpless.

"No one can suck me unless you can get me to beg you to let me come first," Natalie said.

Twist climbed between the woman's legs and ran her fingers gently up and down the woman's stomach. Then she paused, looked at Rave, and said, "Pet her. She won't break."

Rave sat on the bed.

And ran an index finger in little circles on the woman's forehead.

The woman moaned and strained against her bonds.

Incredibly sexy.

Incredibly vulnerable.

"It looks like you're in our control," Twist said. Then she looked at Rave and said, "Let's tease her until she goes out of her mind."

Rave hesitated, debating, then looked at Parker and said, "Get over here and help."

"You sure?"

"Yes."

Chapter Eighty
Day Seven—April 18
Monday Night

The flight back to Denver from San Francisco was fine until they passed the continental divide. Then one lightning bolt after another ripped through the black skies, and explosions of thunder resonated with such force that the aircraft actually shook. Maniac rain tried to rip the wings off. Somehow the pilot cut through the whole mess without being swatted out of the sky and brought them down to earth alive. As they taxied to the gate, Teffinger wiped sweaty palms on his pants and said, "I am never flying again. Ever."

London chuckled.

"It was just a little storm."

"Little?" he said. "Something like that is what wiped out the dinosaurs."

On the drive home, he called Sydney.

"Tell me you got Geneva derailed," he said.

A pause.

"I went over and talked to her, like you wanted. She said all the right words and nodded when she was supposed to. But if you want my gut feeling, she was blowing me off."

Teffinger hung up and called Geneva.

She didn't answer.

"Trouble?" London asked.

"I don't know."

When they got to teffinger's house, the windshield wipers were still going full speed. Teffinger was too wound up to go to sleep, even though he should, so they opened the garage door, sat in the '67 Vette, and watched the storm.

He had a Bud Light in his left hand.

Half gone.

With a second one, still full, sitting on the floor.

Waiting its turn.

"Can you do me a favor tomorrow? Because I'm probably going to forget," he said.

"Sure."

"Google that guy Jake VanDeventer and see if you can pull a picture of him off the net," Teffinger said. "If you can, I'm going to email it to Amanda Pinehurst in Chicago and ask her if that's the guy she saw following her and Kennedy."

"I thought VanDeventer was a dead end."

"He is."

"So why are we bothering?"

"Because when you're desperate, that's what you do."

He dialed Geneva again.

No answer again.

Lightning ripped across the sky.

Immediately followed by an explosive crack of thunder.

A dog barked.

"That was close," Teffinger said. "I'll be right back."

He returned two minutes later with Alley, who curled up on his lap and purred. "I need to get out of the detective business," he said. "It's just too frustrating sometimes. I've been letting too many people down. I need a month on a beach somewhere. No bad guys; no missing people; no dead bodies. Just sand and water and sun."

"And me?"

He chuckled.

"That's understood."

"If you're serious, we can go to Jamaica," London said. "I still have relatives there, so it would be free."

Teffinger pictured it.

White sand.

Blue water.

London lying on a towel in a bikini.

"Maybe when this is all over," he said. "First I have to find Jena so I can return this animal to her." He looked down and said, "No offense, Alley."

London leaned over and put her head on Teffinger's shoulder.

Teffinger looked at his watch.

9:52 p.m.

He should head to bed.

But knew he couldn't sleep.

"I need to take a quick trip," he said. "You want to come with me?"

"Where you going?"

"To Cameron Leigh's house," he said. "She's the dead female vampire. There was something in her house that reminded me of Chicago but I can't for the life of me remember what it is. It's been nagging at me ever since I found out about the Kennedy Pinehurst case."

"Let's go."

They brought Alley with them.

Teffinger made London put on latex gloves when they got to the victim's house, same as him, so they wouldn't contaminate the scene.

They left Alley in the 4Runner and headed inside.

Everything was exactly as Teffinger remembered it.

So, where to start?

Chicago.

Chicago.

Where are you?

London spotted the wall of books and headed in that direction. "Those are all vampire books," Teffinger said.

"Wow."

"She was definitely living the life," he said.

"Can I look at them?"

He almost said no, just because his basic nature was to not mess up crime scenes, but he said, "Okay, but one at a time, and put them back exactly where you found them."

Chicago.

Teffinger gyrated towards the computer desk, which was covered with hundreds of pieces of paper; most of which contained handwriting. He started reading them when his eyes fell on a one-page calendar from last year. Each month was about the size of a business card. There were a couple of notes scribbled on the edges, with arrows drawn from the notes to a particular date.

Bingo.

One of the handwritten words was Chicago.

From that word was an arrow drawn to May 19.

"What the hell?"

He must have said the words out loud, because London walked over and asked, "What'd you find?"

Teffinger showed her.

"Chicago," he said. "This is what I remembered seeing."

"What's it mean?" she asked.

"See the arrow pointing from the word to this date?" he said, putting his finger on the date.

Yes.

She did.

Of course she did.

"Kennedy Pinehurst was from Chicago. And this is the day she disappeared."

Chapter Eighty-One
Day Eight—April 19
Tuesday Morning

———————————

Tripp was a hundred miles outside Vegas doing 85 when Brittany called with bad news. Her flight was cancelled due to a nasty storm. The next fight wasn't until the morning.

"I'll make it up to you," Tripp said.

Two hours later, shortly after midnight, he got VanDeventer situated in a suite at the Mirage. Then he took a cab to the Rhino and let the dancers dangle their legs over his shoulders and rub their crotches in his face for a couple of hours. He was down three hundred dollars and decided it was probably time to leave, before he ended up buying one of them a car.

In the morning, he dropped VanDeventer off at the bus station. Then he opened his cell phone, pulled up the address book, and wrote Lefty on a piece of paper, together with a phone number.

He handed the paper to VanDeventer and said, "Call this guy if you want some fake ID."

VanDeventer studied it.

"What can he do?"

Tripp chuckled.

"What can't he do?—driver's licenses, passports, social security cards, whatever you want."

"Can he be trusted?"

"Yeah, but he's pricey. So be prepared."

VanDeventer folded the paper and stuck it in his wallet.

"I might give him a call," he said.

"I would, if I were you," Tripp said. "Cut your hair, dye it black, get some of those big oversized nerd glasses, wear a business suit and tie—if you get all that going together with a fake name, even I wouldn't know you."

They hugged.

And parted.

Tripp wasn't in the mood to spend eleven or twelve hours on the road, so he parked the rental in the long-term lot at the airport and took a flight back to Denver. He rented a green Impala, drove downtown, parked at the edge of LoDo and hoofed it over to the abandoned warehouse.

Everything was as he left it.

Good.

Who would end up here?—that was the question.

Lauren Long?

Rave Lafelle?

London Fontelle?

Some spur-of-the-moment stranger?

Not Brittany, though.

Definitely not her.

He looked at his watch—11:48 a.m.

He called Brittany. "Are you free for lunch?"

She was.

Fifteen minutes later they met at Marlowe's on the 16th Street Mall. She wore a conservative, gray pantsuit with her hair up, very professional.

She looked nice.

"I didn't feel like driving back this morning so I took a flight instead," Tripp said. "I'm thinking that you and me can fly down this weekend, stay at the MGM for a few days, and then drive back—if you're in the mood."

Chapter Eighty-Two
Day Eight—April 19
Tuesday Morning

———————————

Unable to get out of her gig at the Old Orleans, Rave kissed Twist goodbye Tuesday morning and flew to Denver. London picked her up at DIA and told her that Teffinger took her to Cameron Leigh's house last night; and what they found.

The calendar.

Chicago.

The arrow.

"Somehow, Cameron was connected to Kennedy Pinehurst," London said. She, in turn, ended up in an abandoned warehouse, naked, suspended by her ankles in an upside-down spread-eagle position, with her throat slit from ear to ear.

"I just find it troubling that Cameron was also tied down in a spread-eagle position," London said.

"So what are you saying?" Rave asked. "That the slayers killed this woman—"

"—Kennedy Pinehurst—"

"—Right, her."

"That to me seems pretty obvious," London said. "What that means is this—if we can figure out who killed Kennedy Pinehurst, we're going to learn the identity of one or more of the slayers."

Rave chuckled.

"What?" London asked.

"How are we going to figure that out if the Chicago police haven't been able to?"

"We have two things going for us that they don't," London said. "First, we know about the connection. Second, Cameron's house is here in Denver, not in Chicago. And we have access to it."

"We do?"

"I unlocked the back door last night before me and Teffinger left," London said.

They parked two doors down from Cameron's house and headed straight for the back like they owned the place. To Rave's surprise, London pulled two pairs of latex gloves out of her pants pocket and handed a pair to Rave.

"Put these on."

Rave grinned.

"You're such an organized little criminal," she said.

"Yes I am."

They looked around.

Saw no one.

Then turned the doorknob, entered, and closed the door behind them.

"We need to be careful to not mess things up," London said. "I don't want Teffinger to know anyone's been here."

They were looking for more information on the connection between Cameron Leigh and Kennedy Pinehurst, and figured it would most likely be on one of the hundreds of pieces of paper on the desk. So that's where they devoted their attention.

They divvied up the papers.

And read every single one.

Starting with the ones on top.

Then moving into the drawers.

They found nothing of interest.

"It must be in her computer," London said. "Unfortunately, the cops took it."

"Now what?" Rave asked.

London shrugged.

Then she put a curious look on her face and said, "Maybe she stuffed it in one of her books."

They walked over to the wall of books and started leafing through them, putting each one back exactly where they found it.

"So how well did you know Cameron?" Rave asked.

"Very," London said.

"Did you ever suck her blood?"

"Many times; and vice versa."

"How about Parker?" Rave asked.

"Cameron was like Twist," London said. "There was a lot of sharing that went on." She paused and added, "Parker's fallen pretty hard for you. I suppose you know that."

Rave nodded.

"I hope you two can make a go of it," London said. "I'd like to see Parker happy. He deserves it."

"Have you ever been intimate with him?"

London shook her head.

"If you mean sex, no."

"Did you ever want to?"

"Of course," London said. "Early on. But he was always looking past me, for something more."

Rave laughed.

"More? What could be more than you?"

"You, apparently."

In one of the larger hardcover books, they discovered something interesting.

Very interesting.

Namely, several printouts from Internet searches.

Printouts of newspaper articles on the disappearance of Kennedy Pinehurst, to be precise.

Mostly from the Chicago Tribune.

"Bingo."

None of the sheets of paper had any handwriting.

"So what does this mean?" Rave asked.

"It means she was researching the Kennedy Pinehurst murder," London said.

"Why?"

London shrugged.

Then she said, "Probably for the same reason we are. She must have known that a slayer killed the woman."

"But why would a slayer kill Kennedy Pinehurst?" Rave asked.

London cocked her head.

"The same reason they'd kill Cameron, or you, or me," she said. "Kennedy must have been a vampire."

"You think?"

London nodded.

"There's no other explanation," she said.

"But you never heard about Kennedy Pinehurst before, right?"

"Right."

"So how would the slayers know about a vampire if the other vampires don't?"

London retreated in thought.

"There are only two things I can think of," she said. "Either our genealogist is leaking information; or they're doing their own genealogical research."

They got a blank piece of paper and wrote down the dates of

all the newspaper articles, so they could print them off the web later and have their own copies.

They put the originals back in the book.

And put the book back on the shelf.

And left.

Locking the back door behind them.

Outside, walking back to the car, Rave's phone rang and Tim Pepper's voice came through.

"Are you free this afternoon?"

"I can be."

"I'm going to see if I can get the guys down for a short practice session," he said. "I'd like to work up those two new songs you wrote and roll them out tonight. I want to watch the crowd go nuts."

Rave's heart raced.

Chapter Eighty-Three
Day Eight—April 19
Tuesday Morning

Teffinger got to bed too late last night and got up too early this morning. To compensate, he stopped at a 7-Eleven on the way to work and filled a thermos with coffee. Elton John's "Saturday Night's Alright" came from speakers. The kid behind the cash register stopped reading a book called Witness Chase long enough to take Teffinger's money.

"You seem familiar," the kid said.

"I stop in here all the time."

"Oh."

Teffinger was almost out the door when the kid shouted, "Hey, you want a cup?"

Teffinger ran back in, grabbed a disposable cup from the coffee area, and said, "Thanks." He had half the thermos under his belt by the time he got to the office. As usual, no one else had shown up yet, so he fired up the coffee pot before heading to his desk.

Chicago was one hour ahead of Denver.

Even with the time differential, Teffinger doubted that his counterpart, Thomas Stone, would be in yet. He called anyway. Nope, Stone wasn't in yet. "Give him another hour," the desk clerk said.

"Thanks."

Forty-five minutes later, Teffinger called again.

"I said an hour, before," the desk clerk said.

"Right, I know," Teffinger said.

"Give him another fifteen minutes."

Teffinger waited ten minutes and then called again.

"I said fifteen minutes, before."

"Right."

"Give him another five minutes."

Four minutes later, Teffinger called again.

Stone wasn't in.

"Give him another minute," the desk clerk said.

"I'm just going to wait on the line until he gets in," Teffinger said.

"Fine."

Elevator music appeared.

One minute later, Thomas Stone's voice came through.

"The desk clerk says you've been harassing him."

Teffinger grunted.

And said, "I have a second case here in Denver that I'm pretty sure is connected to your Kennedy Pinehurst case. My victim is named Cameron Leigh, twenty years old, murdered. Someone tied her down in a spread-eagle position and pounded a wooden stake into her heart—in an abandoned warehouse."

Silence on the other end.

Teffinger could almost hear Stone processing the buzz words.

Spread-eagle.

Abandoned warehouse.

"Have you ever heard of her? Cameron Leigh?" Teffinger asked.

"Can't say that it's ringing a bell," Stone said. "Tell me why you think the cases are connected."

Teffinger told him.

About the calendar.

Chicago.

The arrow.

The date.

"It sounds like you're on to something, but I don't know what," Stone said. "It's weird, though."

"What?"

"Well, you initially contacted me thinking that Kennedy Pinehurst was connected to that missing woman—"

"—Jena Vellone—"

"—Jena Vellone," Stone said. "And now you think that Kennedy's connected to this other woman—"

"—Cameron Leigh—"

"—Cameron Leigh," Stone said.

"And?"

"Well," Stone said, "if both of your assumptions are correct— namely that Jena Vellone and Cameron Leigh are each connected to Kennedy Pinehurst—then that means that Jena Vellone and Cameron Leigh are somehow connected to each other."

Teffinger raked his fingers through his hair.

"I was just about to figure that out," he said.

Stone chuckled.

They talked for another five minutes and then hung up.

When sydney showed up two minutes later, Teffinger filled her in. "I don't think it will do any good to go back through Jena's house," Teffinger said. "If the name Cameron Leigh was anywhere, it would have jumped out at us the first time. Cameron was already dead before Jena got taken."

"Agreed," Sydney said.

"Same thing with respect to Cameron Leigh's house," Teffinger said.

"Agreed."

Teffinger took a sip of coffee and found it lukewarm. He poured the rest in the snake plant and got a fresh cup.

"So what do we do now?"

Good question.

Chapter Eighty-Four
Day Eight—April 19
Tuesday Afternoon

———————————

After lunch with Brittany, Tripp walked down the 16th Street Mall under a bright blue Colorado sky, hornier than usual. The temperature was nice, about seventy. Lots of people were out strolling around.

Including lots of females.

He bought a pair of mirrored sunglasses from a street vendor for ten dollars, to better hide his face as he checked out the eye candy.

He passed the Rock Bottom Brewery, spotted a bench next to the sidewalk, and took a seat.

Someone had left a Rocky Mountain News there.

He thumbed through it.

Four or five pages in, he came across something interesting—the picture of a very nice looking woman next to an article, "Radio Personality Geneva Vellone Shocks Listeners." The article explained that Geneva Vellone is the sister of Jena Vellone, the TV 8 reporter who disappeared last week. Yesterday, during Geneva's morning talk show, she shocked listeners by making an on-air plea to the person who abducted Jena; a plea for him to take her in exchange for Jena.

Interesting.

Very interesting.

A second article on the same page was of equal interest. It had the picture of an incredibly good-looking man below the caption, "Detective Still on Case."

According to the article, Denver homicide detective Nick Teffinger had been with Jena Vellone the night she disappeared. Jena's blood had been found in Teffinger's truck, which had been confiscated by the Cherry Hills P.D. Teffinger had no authority to investigate the woman's disappearance—it wasn't a homicide, it didn't occur in Denver, and, most importantly, Teffinger was a person of interest. Last week, the Denver Chief of Police issued a public statement confirming that the investigation was being handled solely by Cherry Hills and that Teffinger was not involved. And yet, yesterday Teffinger reportedly showed up in San Francisco trying to get access to confidential police records in connection with work he said he was doing on the Jena Vellone case.

In the meantime, Teffinger was the lead investigator in connection with the murder of Forrest Jones, the man who suffered a bizarre vampire-like death with a wooden stake in his heart. That killer, ironically, remained at large.

Teffinger had a good reputation and a good arrest record.

But police protocol was clear in that officers are not authorized to participate in the investigation of a crime in which they are a suspect or a person of interest.

Was the chief ignoring protocol?

And, even worse, covering it up?

Or had Teffinger turned into a rogue cop?

Stay tuned.

End of article.

Tripp couldn't help but chuckle, especially since he had recently been in Teffinger's house. What a tangled web this had turned out to be.

He focused on the picture of Geneva Vellone.

She would be worth spending some quality time with.

Most definitely.

Chapter Eighty-Five
Day Eight—April 19
Tuesday Afternoon

———————————

After they left Cameron Leigh's house, Rave called information and obtained a phone number for one Suzanne Wheeler in Montreal, Canada; the woman who she suspected to be the genealogist working with Parker.

She dialed.

A woman answered.

"This is Rave Lafelle," Rave said. "Does that name ring a bell with you?"

A pause.

A long pause.

"How did you get my number?"

"A friend," Rave said.

"This is a breach of security," the woman said.

"Well, I just need to know a few things—"

The line went dead.

Rave looked at London and said, "She won't talk. In fact, she sounded really nervous just hearing my voice."

London nodded and said, "Good."

She didn't need to say more.

Rave understood that "Good" meant that Wheeler was following the security protocol that Parker had set up; namely, that Wheeler was only to communicate with Parker—whose voice she recognized—so that the slayers couldn't trick her into giving them information.

"Okay," London said. "So if she isn't giving information out, then the slayers must be doing their own genealogical work. That's the only reason they would kill Kennedy Pinehurst; if they thought she was a vampire."

Rave frowned.

"The poor thing," she said. "Killed the way she was, and not having a clue why."

London grunted.

"She had a clue before she died, you can bet your bottom dollar on that," she said. "I'm sure they tried to get the names of other vampires from her before they slit her throat."

Rave pictured the poor woman.

Hung upside down by her ankles.

Naked.

With cuffs on her wrists and her arms stretched down and tied to the floor. Then being pumped for information from slayers.

She looked at London and said, "I wonder why they slit her

throat instead of pounding a stake in her heart."

"Easy," London said. "They know we're mortal; they know they don't need wooden stakes to kill us. And what good would it do them to have a bunch of wooden-stake cases popping up across the country? The MO is too unique, meaning that the cases would get connected. Too many detectives would get involved; they'd share files and information; they'd be a lot smarter in a group than they would be separately."

"But now they're using stakes," Rave said.

"True."

"Why the change?"

"My guess?"

"Right."

"My guess is that they're getting bolder," London said. "They're trying to terrify us. The stakes are a way of saying that all vampires will die."

All vampires will die.

Rave had been in good spirits for the last couple of days.

Excited about her career.

Excited about Parker.

Excited about Twist.

But the words all vampires will die slammed her back to reality.

Suddenly London's phone rang and Parker's voice came through. "I just got a call from Suzanne Wheeler in Montreal," he said. "The incoming call came from Rave's phone. Did you and Rave just call her?"

"Yes."

"Why?"

"To see if she talks to anyone besides you."

"She doesn't," Parker said. "You know that's the security policy."

Yes.

She did.

"You scared her to death," Parker said.

"Sorry."

He exhaled.

"Let me call her and tell her the call was legit," he said. "The poor woman is absolutely terrified." A pause, then, "Why in the hell would you think she would talk to anyone besides me?"

"We were curious."

"Why?"

"We just wondered if she was feeding information to the slayers," London said.

"That's ridiculous," he said. "She wouldn't do that in a million years."

Chapter Eighty-Six
Day Eight—April 19
Tuesday Morning

_____

Mid-morning, Chief F. F. Tanker walked into homicide with the Rocky Mountain News in his hand and told Teffinger, "Why don't you come down to my office for a minute?"

Teffinger grabbed his half-filled coffee cup.

And followed the man.

He sensed trouble.

So much so that he didn't swing by the pot to top off. As soon as they got behind closed doors, Tanker held the paper up and said, "Did you read this yet?"

No.

He hadn't.

Tanker opened the paper to page four and pointed. Teffinger read two articles, one about him and one about Geneva Vellone. Then he looked at the chief and said, "I have a solution."

Tanker slumped into his chair and said, "Go on."

"I can't get you into trouble," Teffinger said. "I don't care about me, but I'm not going to let you go down. I'm going to the press and tell them in no uncertain terms that you had nothing to do with any of this. You never gave me authority to investigate Jena Vellone; you never covered anything up; you never knew a thing about what I was doing in San Francisco, period, end of story."

"That'll make you a rogue," Tanker said.

Teffinger shrugged.

"I'll say I took a vacation day yesterday," he said. "I was off duty, taking an extended weekend. That actually sort of makes sense because my girlfriend, London Fontelle, was with me. In fact, to make it formal, I'm giving you my notice now that I was officially on vacation yesterday. I'll fill out the paperwork as soon as I get back to my desk. Also, I'll emphasize that my trip to San Francisco wasn't funded by the department."

"Can you back that up?"

Teffinger nodded.

"Luckily, I used my own credit cards for everything. I'll never submit a reimbursement request," he said. "I'll emphasize that Jena Vellone is a longstanding friend of mine, since high school in fact, which is common knowledge anyway. Is it so wrong for one friend to worry about another? Anyway, with any luck, that will at least keep you out of it, and maybe get this thing positioned to die."

Tanker frowned.

"They're going to press for a formal investigation," he said. "I can feel it. Then the question will be whether you should be suspended pending that investigation; and maybe me too, for that matter."

Teffinger stood up.

And raked his fingers through his hair.

"We can't let that happen," he said. "If I lose my resources here, Jena Vellone is dead."

The chief nodded.

"I don't care what happens to me afterwards," Teffinger added. "I don't care if I lose my job or pension or anything else. But right now I can't afford to be jacked around. Jena's counting on me and I'll be damned if I'm going to let her down."

Tanker studied Teffinger.

"She's been gone a long time, you know."

"I know," Teffinger said. "I just can't let myself picture her dead."

"Then find her," Tanker said.

They shook hands.

And Teffinger left.

He filled out the vacation paperwork as soon as he got back to his desk, made a copy for himself and handed in the original. Sydney didn't come over, but kept him in the corner of her eye, obviously wondering if he was okay. Teffinger got a fresh cup of coffee and took a seat in front of her desk.

"The chief's going to paint his office," he said. "He wanted my opinion on colors."

She chuckled.

"What'd you tell him?"

"I suggested a light blue, to match his eyes."

"His eyes are brown," she said.

"Oops. Do you feel like taking a drive?"

She did.

And grabbed her jacket to prove it.

Chapter Eighty-Seven
Day Eight—April 19
Tuesday Afternoon

———————

B ecause she was a radio personality, Geneva Vellone had a massive web presence. In just thirty minutes at the keyboard, Tripp was able to locate dozens of photos of the woman plus more information than he would ever need. It turned out that she lived on a 5-acre horse property off Morrison Road in unincorporated Jefferson County.

Nice.

Tripp parked the Impala a half-mile south, in a scooped out shoulder that looked like it was used for parking to access a trail that snaked into open space.

He raised the hood, as if he had engine problems.

Then he walked towards the woman's house.

The temperature was nice, about seventy, but clouds rolled in from the mountains and hinted of rain tonight. He wore jeans, New Balance tennis shoes, and a dark-blue T-shirt. The woman's driveway was asphalt and long. Tripp headed up it and approached the house; to all intents and purposes, just one more poor slob who needed a jug of water to fill a leaky radiator.

He looked back over his shoulder as he came up on the house.

No one was behind him.

There wasn't a sign of life in any direction.

He didn't see any exterior surveillance cameras.

The asphalt ended at the side of the house. From there, the drive turned to gravel and continued for another hundred feet or so where it ended at a small wooden barn.

Next to the house, on the asphalt, sat a red Viper.

Good.

That meant the woman was home.

No other cars were there, meaning she was alone, unless of course she brought someone with her. Tripp heard no sounds from the house. He was close enough now that he'd hear music if it was playing.

He paused at the bottom of the front steps.

Deciding whether to knock or not.

His instincts told him not to.

So he walked around the side of the house to the back. There he found a redwood deck that came off a living room. The sliding glass door was open but the screen was shut. He tiptoed across the wood, stopped at the screen and listened.

At first he didn't hear anything.

Then he did.

Faint, but definitely the sound of a shower.

Upstairs.

He slid the screen door open.

Stepped inside.

And then silently pushed it shut.

A brown cat trotted over and stared at him.

Chapter Eighty-Eight
Day Eight—April 19
Tuesday Afternoon

Rave had been more than relieved to get out of Cameron Leigh's house without being caught. So when London said, "We need to go back," Rave's heart raced.

"Why?"

"Because we left too early."

"What do you mean?"

"There has to be more information there," London said. "We need to find it so I can feed it to Nick. The key to Jena Vellone's disappearance is somewhere in Cameron Leigh's house. The problem is that Nick thinks he found everything he needs after finding that calendar, so he's not inclined to go back. We need to go back, do a complete search, and then if we find something I'll find a way to feed it to Nick."

Rave swallowed.

Then looked at London and said, "You're nuts."

London grabbed Rave's hand and pulled her towards the car.

"Come on, we're wasting time."

Twenty minutes later, they were at Cameron Leigh's back door again, putting on latex gloves. Unfortunately, they had locked the door behind them when they left earlier. London almost broke the glass with her elbow before pausing. "Let's check the bedroom window first."

They did.

And miraculously found it unlocked.

Rave boosted London in.

Ten seconds later the back door opened and London said, "Come on."

As soon as Rave stepped inside, her phone rang and Tim Pepper's voice came through. "I have the session lined up," he said. "Can you be down at the club in an hour?"

She could come.

But she might be running a little behind.

"Wait for me if I'm late," she said.

They decided to finish searching through the rest of the books before heading to the bedroom or the basement.

Good thing, too.

Another large hardcover held a stash of eight or ten newspaper articles from the Seattle Times, printed off the web, very similar to the ones about Kennedy Pinehurst, except they pertained to someone named Destiny Moon.

"I'll be damned," London said.

"Destiny Moon," Rave said.

For some reason the name rang a bell.

"Weird name," London said. "It just goes to show; don't let your parents be hippies."

According to the articles, Destiny Moon was the lead singer in a female rock group from Seattle called La Femme.

La Femme.

"I've heard of this group," Rave said.

"You have?"

Rave nodded.

"Where?"

"I don't know," she said.

Destiny Moon, apparently, never made it home after a Saturday night gig. Her body was found two weeks later in an abandoned warehouse in a "messy condition."

They wrote down the dates of the articles.

And put the originals back in the book.

Then London said, "Let's keep looking."

Rave must have had a strange look on her face because London asked, "Are you okay?"

Rave looked London in the eyes.

"I just remembered where I heard about this group," Rave said. "My manager, Tim Pepper, mentioned them once."

"In what context?"

Rave searched her memory.

"I don't recall," she said.

"Did he manage them or something?"

Rave concentrated.

But came up empty.

"I just can't remember," she said.

"I have to feed this to Teffinger somehow," London said. "What I need to do is get him back here for some reason. Then I'll wander over here, nonchalantly start pulling books, and accidentally stumble across it."

"How are you going to get him back?"

"I don't know yet," London said. "Right now, let's see what else we can find."

Chapter Eighty-Nine
Day Eight—April 19
Tuesday Afternoon

When Teffinger swung into Geneva Vellone's driveway, he was relieved to see the red Viper parked next to the house. That meant she was home and that he hadn't wasted the trip. He topped off a disposable cup with coffee from the thermos, stepped out, and knocked on the front door.

No one answered.

He knocked again.

And sipped coffee.

No one answered.

He headed around to the back, found the sliding glass door open, and stepped inside. The sound of a shower came from upstairs.

"Anyone home?" he shouted.

She didn't hear, so he stepped outside on the deck to wait. When the water shut off, he called again and then headed up. She was toweling off when he got there. He expected her to cover up as he got closer, but she kept drying off.

He stopped at the doorway and leaned against the frame.

"Why aren't you answering my phone calls?" he asked.

"Because you're calling to chew me out."

He nodded.

That was true.

But it wasn't all of it.

"Look, I understand that you feel desperate and want to do something, but what you're doing isn't going to help," he said. "It's only going to make things worse."

"Nothing's worse," she said.

"Well, I'm here making sure you're okay instead of concentrating on her," he said. "That's worse."

"Then get out of here and do your job," she said.

Her lips trembled.

Then she cried.

Teffinger hugged her.

She buried her face in his chest.

"Have you gotten any offers yet?" he questioned.

"One."

She grabbed a pink t-shirt out of a dresser, put it on and then punched a button on the answering machine next to the bed. A man's voice came from the speaker—"I'll think about doing an exchange. To show me you're serious, and that this whole thing isn't just a publicity stunt, here's what I want you to do. Tonight at nine o'clock, go to Downing Street where it crosses above I-25. Face the freeway traffic coming from Denver. Wear a red jacket with nothing underneath—no blouse or bra. Unzip the jacket and expose yourself to the oncoming traffic. Be sure your face is visible and that you're under a light. Stay like that until 9:15. Then you can leave. If I see you there, I'll know you're serious. If I like what I see, I may or may not call to arrange something. Even if you do this, there are no guarantees."

Teffinger chuckled.

"This guy is a first-class whacko," he said. "He's going to take your picture and then either sell it to some sleazy rag or post it all over the net." He looked into her eyes to be sure she understood, but didn't see what he wanted. "Don't tell me you're actually thinking about doing this."

"What if he's legit?" she asked.

"He's not," Teffinger said. "But even if he is, that would just be all the more reason to stay away from him."

She squeezed his hand.

"I'm going to do it," she said. "Maybe you could stake the place out and spot him. Maybe you could set up cameras and get the license plate numbers of the traffic."

"The guy's a Loony Tune," Teffinger said. "Don't fall for it."

Chapter Ninety
Day Eight—April 19
Tuesday Afternoon

Tripp stood in the dark in Geneva Vellone's master closet, perfectly still, being as careful as he could to not bump into a coat hanger or make anything rattle.

His heart raced.

He breathed through an open mouth, so quietly that even he couldn't hear the passing of air in and out of his lungs.

In the master bedroom, not more than five or six steps away, Geneva Vellone and Nick Teffinger listened to a phone message from someone who wanted Geneva to expose herself to freeway traffic tonight.

Tripp was concerned with Teffinger's presence, but not scared.

If anyone opened the closet door, he'd go straight for Teffinger. The secret would be to get to him before he could get his gun. Punch him hard and heavy, right in the nose. That would disable him enough to finish him off. The woman wouldn't be a factor. She'd be too startled and scared to join in. If someone did open the closet door, it would probably be her. That meant that Tripp would have to get around her quickly to get to Teffinger.

He stood directly behind the door.

Poised.

With his fist cocked back.

Waiting.

As long as the two talked, Tripp could tell where they were. It's when they stopped that he tensed up. He didn't know if one of them was heading his way.

A minute passed.

Then another.

After what seemed like a long time, the voices trailed off and headed downstairs. Tripp stayed in the closet, but sat down to conserve his strength. Fifteen minutes later, an engine kicked over. Tripp pulled up an image of Teffinger turning his car around and heading down the driveway. Shortly after that, footsteps came up the stairs.

Geneva.

She sang a song.

Lightly.

Tripp stood up.

Ready.

And when the woman opened the closet door, he pounced.

Chapter Ninety-One
Day Eight—April 19
Tuesday Afternoon

_____

Other than the Destiny Moon papers, Rave and London didn't find anything of interest in Cameron Leigh's house. They left out the back door, locked it behind them, walked to the side of the house and paused. They scouted around for nosy neighbors, saw none, and headed towards the sidewalk.

Across the street, Rave saw a curtain move.

"I think we've been spotted," she said.

"Just keep walking."

Ten minutes later they were in London's car, driving to the Old Orleans, when London came up with an idea. "The thing we need to do is get this information to Teffinger and get it to him quick," she said. "You've never talked to him, so he doesn't know your voice. I think you should make an anonymous call and just dump it on him."

Rave contemplated it.

"He's heard me sing," she said. "He might recognize my voice."

London shook her head.

"Your singing voice is completely different," she said. "Plus, when you call him, speak different—you know, disguise it as good as you can."

"This is dangerous," Rave said.

London nodded.

True.

"This might help him find Jena Vellone," London said. "That outweighs the risk to us."

Rave chewed on it.

She had shot two men in the face.

First the skinhead.

Then Forrest Jones.

Teffinger was involved in both of those investigations.

"He really thinks that Jena Vellone is alive," London added. "He shouldn't, at least in my opinion, but he does. If we gave him something to help with that case, he wouldn't use it against us, even if he found out."

"How can you be so sure?"

"I can tell," London said. "That's just the kind of person he is." A pause, then she added, "You need to call from a payphone. If we use one of our cells, he'll be able to trace it."

They were on California Street, almost at the Old Orleans, when London spotted a public phone.

"There."

She pulled over and killed the engine.

Then she looked at Rave and said, "Are you going to do it?"

Rave paused.

Then got out of the car.

And called Teffinger.

While London stood next to her and listened.

She told Teffinger about the Kennedy Pinehurst papers stuffed in a hardcover book on the second shelf from the top; and about the Destiny Moon papers stuffed in a second vampire book near the bottom right.

"Destiny Moon?" Teffinger asked.

"Yes."

"Who is Destiny Moon?"

"I don't know."

"How do you know all of this?" he asked.

Rave hung up.

They headed straight to the Old Orleans. On the way London asked, "Do you think that your manager is involved in any of this?"

Rave cocked her head.

"You mean Tim Pepper?"

"Yes."

Rave laughed.

"No, of course not."

"Just keep the possibility in the back of your mind," London said. "He was at the club the night that Jena Vellone disappeared. Now we find out about the Destiny Moon murder, who he knew. Find out today how well he knew her and if he managed her group—what was the name of it?"

"La Femme."

"Right," London said. "If he managed them, then he knew her pretty well."

"Tim Pepper wouldn't hurt a fly," Rave said.

"Well, someone's hurting flies," London said. "You want me to hang around while you rehearse?"

Rave almost said no.

She didn't need London to baby-sit her.

But then she said, "Sure, if you want."

Chapter Ninety-Two
Day Eight—April 19
Tuesday Afternoon

A fter receiving the anonymous call, Teffinger headed
straight to Cameron Leigh's house. As soon as he came
up to the front door, he realized he didn't have a key.
He tried the knob and found it locked. Then he tried the back door,
also locked. The rear bedroom window was unlatched, however, so
he pushed it up and muscled through.

The papers were exactly where the caller said they would be.

Teffinger spent ten seconds with the Kennedy Pinehurst articles
and then set them aside.

He already knew about her.

It was the Destiny Moon articles that got his attention.

The lead singer from La Femme.

From Seattle.

Who disappeared.

And was later found in a "messy condition."

Why had Cameron Leigh been investigating her murder?

Teffinger had never heard of La Femme, but that didn't mean
that they weren't big enough in the Seattle area to get on billboards.

Had Destiny Moon's face been on a billboard?

To promote an upcoming concert?

And what did "messy condition" mean? Did that mean someone
hung her upside down and slit her throat? Or did someone pound a
wooden stake in her heart? And who was the mystery woman who

called Teffinger? What else did she know? How was she involved in all of this?

Teffinger's phone rang and he answered without even looking at the incoming number. It turned out to be Jean-Paul Quisanatte, the Paris detective working the murder of Diamanda, the model who got a wooden stake pounded into her heart.

The same as Cameron Leigh.

"We had a huge break in our case," Jean-Paul said. "I thought you'd want to know about it."

Teffinger did.

He did indeed.

"Our vice people busted a local prostitute named Rozeen," Jean-Paul said. "She said she'd give us some information if we cut her some slack. The long and short of it is that an American picked her up at about 10:30 p.m. last Tuesday, one week ago to be precise. He spent the night with her and then gave her a thousand dollars, American money, to tell the police he was with her since 7:30 p.m., if she ever got asked. She didn't think anything about it at the time."

"Okay," Teffinger said.

"The model got killed about 9:00 p.m. on Tuesday night," Jean-Paul said. "After this prostitute later read about Diamanda, she had a gut feeling that this American was the one who did it. She suspected that he gave her the money for an alibi, if he ever needed one."

"All right," Teffinger said.

"Anyway," Jean-Paul went on, "this American asked for the prostitute's cell phone number, ostensibly so he could call her the next time he came into town. Then he called her with his cell phone, to be sure she gave him the right number—that was his big mistake. She had indeed given him the right number and her cell phone rang. From that, we were able to get the American's number from her phone records. It turns out that the man is someone named Trent

Tripp. We also traced him to a flight from Paris to New York on Wednesday morning."

"Damn," Teffinger said. "I can't believe you got all of this."

"You got a pencil?" Jean-Paul asked. "I'm going to give you his address."

As soon as Teffinger hung up, he called Sydney at headquarters. "I'll be there in fifteen minutes," he said. "I want you, Baxter, and every available warm body waiting for me in the large conference room when I get there. Tell everyone to clear their schedules."

"What's going on?"

"Fifteen minutes," he said.

When he showed up, there were ten people in the room. The chair at the end of the table was empty and a full cup of hot coffee sat on a coaster. He looked at Sydney and said, "Thanks."

"No problem."

He took a sip, walked over to the white-board and uncapped a blue marker.

"We got the name of the man who stabbed the Paris model in the heart with a wooden stake," he said. "He's an American named Trent Tripp. The Paris murder is connected to our Denver case, Cameron Leigh, who was killed the exact same way. Cameron Leigh, in turn, is somehow connected to the disappearance of Jena Vellone. I don't know exactly how, yet, but there is definitely a connection. Right now, at this second, Trent Tripp is our strongest lead to finding Jena Vellone."

Someone coughed.

Teffinger looked at the person.

It was Chief Tanker.

"We're not on the Jena Vellone case," he said.

Teffinger nodded.

"Thanks for the reminder," he said. "I misspoke. Trent Tripp is connected to the murder of Cameron Leigh, which is our case. So we're going to do everything in our power to find him and catch him as soon as we can."

Teffinger handed out assignments.

Get a warrant out for his arrest.

Find out what credit cards he has, get his most recent charges, and get notified of all future charges as soon as they take place; same thing with respect to his phone calls.

Get his face on TV.

Find out what he's driving and get a BOLO out.

On and on.

"You don't think he stayed in New York?" someone asked.

Teffinger answered immediately.

"No, he's in Denver."

"How do you know?"

"Because there's too much going on for him to not be here," Teffinger said.

After the meeting broke, Teffinger met with Tanker in the chief's office, and told him about the new lead involving Destiny Moon in Seattle. "We need to run that down, right now, this minute," Teffinger said. "But I don't want to get you into another mess like I did out in San Francisco."

Tanker wrinkled his forehead.

"Let me make a few calls," he said.

Chapter Ninety-Three
Day Eight—April 19
Tuesday Afternoon

Tripp gagged and hogtied his new captive, Geneva Vellone, who wore a pink T-shirt and nothing else. He ran down the road, got the Impala and pulled to the rear of her house. He threw her in the trunk and then drove to the abandoned warehouse and parked behind the building next to the rear door. He ran up the fire escape, unchained the lock and entered. Then he grabbed a flashlight and bounded down the interior stairwell two steps at a time with the yellow beam bouncing eerily in front of him. At street level, he opened the door.

His heart raced.

He scouted around.

This was the tricky part.

He had to be absolutely sure no one saw him lifting a body out of the vehicle and carrying it into the building. If anyone saw that, even one person, they'd call the cops.

Guaranteed.

He opened the trunk and then looked in every direction.

Side to side.

Up and down.

Everywhere.

He saw no one.

He heard nothing, other than the city traffic in the distance, and a dog barking a ways off. No vehicles were entering the alley. He'd be able to hear them.

He picked the woman up.

She wasn't heavy.

A hundred and fifteen pounds at best.

He took four quick steps and had her inside the building.

The period of exposure couldn't have been more than five seconds. He set the woman on the floor, stuffed the flashlight in his rear pants pocket, stepped back outside, and closed the door. He tried the handle to make absolutely sure it had locked. Then he fired up the Impala and parked it in a $3.00-Maximum lot five blocks away. He walked back to the warehouse, down the alley and up the fire escape, two steps at a time.

Inside the building, he chained the top door shut.

There.

The building was totally secure again.

He took the stairwell down to the first floor, picked up his victim, and carried her to the top floor.

She was conscious now.

And struggled as best she could.

But the way she was tied, her twists and turns were hardly noticeable. They didn't do anything other than emphasize how helpless she was.

Which got him excited.

Very excited.

So excited, in fact, that he decided to show his little captive what a good lover he was. He put her on the floor, on her stomach, and ran his hands over her body.

"Foreplay," he told her.

Muffled words came from behind her gag.

Unintelligible.

Garbled.

"What's that?" Tripp said. "More?"

She struggled.

So nice.

He stood up and took his pants off.

Then his cell phone rang.

He followed the sound to his pants pocket and answered on the last ring. Jake VanDeventer's voice came through.

Stressed.

"What the hell's going on?" VanDeventer asked.

Tripp was confused.

"What are you talking about?"

"Your picture, man—it's all over the news."

"What?"

"They got your picture, they know your name, they even know you rented an Impala."

"What are you talking about?"

"You, man," VanDeventer said. "They have an arrest warrant out for you."

"Arrest warrant? For what?"

"For Cameron Leigh."

"The vampire?"

Yes.

Her.

"Hell, I wasn't even in town when she got killed," Tripp said. "This is stupid."

"Stupid or not, there's a major manhunt going on for your ass. Where are you?"

Tripp almost told him.

But decided it would be best if even he didn't know.

"Somewhere safe," he said.

"Here's the plan," VanDeventer said. "I'm taking the first flight to Denver to get you out of there. There's a public parking lot at 20th and Broadway. Be there at nine o'clock sharp, on the north side. As soon as we hang up, turn your cell phone off—it probably has a GPS chip in it. Don't use any credit cards. Stay out of sight. Wherever you are right now, get out of there. The cops might be closing in."

They hung up.

Tripp immediately turned his phone off.

He pulled on his pants, kicked Geneva Vellone in the ribs, and got the hell out of the warehouse, being sure it was locked behind him.

He walked briskly.

Away from downtown.

Away from where the Impala was parked.

He kept his eyes peeled for cop cars.

One approached from behind.

Tripp kneeled down, ostensibly to tie his shoe.

He kept his face pointed away.

The cop slowed down but didn't stop; then turned at the corner. A bus came up the street and started slowing down. Tripp realized that he was walking right next to a bus stop. He almost got on, but didn't because the driver would look at him while he climbed in.

He approached an intersection.

A red pickup truck pulled up and stopped.

Tripp powered his cell phone back up, cut across the street behind the pickup truck, and tossed the phone in the truck bed when he got to the driver's blind spot.

Then he continued walking.

The light changed and the truck drove off.

"Chase that," he said.

Chapter Ninety-Four
Day Eight—April 19
Tuesday Afternoon

T he afternoon rehearsal at the Old Orleans should have taken Rave's mind off Cameron Leigh, but it didn't, even though the two new songs worked out perfectly. It wasn't until Parker showed up halfway through the session that Rave relaxed.

He sat with London at the bar.

Not able to take his eyes off Rave.

Engrossed.

When the session was over, Tim Pepper came up to the stage and said, "Let me talk to you a minute." There was something weird in his eyes that Rave had never seen before. It reminded her of London's warning that Pepper might somehow be involved in all this. Pepper grabbed her by the arm, just above the elbow, and led her to the dressing room and shut the door.

Rave tensed.

This was strange.

Very strange.

Something didn't feel right.

"Let me ask you something real quick," she said. "I heard a song on the radio the other day by a group called La Femme. Is that the same one that you mentioned before?"

Pepper looked defensive.

"Probably," he said. "Why?"

"I was just wondering," Rave said. "The song was really good. Are you managing them?"

Pepper frowned.

"I did once," he said. "They're not together anymore."

"Oh."

Chapter Ninety-Five
Day Eight—April 19
Tuesday Afternoon

Teffinger was driving north on Broadway when Katie Baxter called, sounding as if she had just stepped out of a roller coaster.

"Do you have a GPS with you?" she asked.

"Hold on."

Teffinger asked Sydney.

Then told Baxter, "No, why?"

"Okay," Baxter said. "We're going to have to do this the hard way. I have Trent Tripp's cell phone company on the other line. His phone has a GPS chip and they're feeding me the coordinates. Right now he's near 16th and Washington."

Teffinger slapped his hand on the dash.

"We're on our way!"

"Don't be obvious," she said. "This is going to be tricky. When I get the coordinates, I'm punching them into the computer and—"

"—yeah, I know how it works," Teffinger said.

Five minutes later they chased down a red Tacoma, got the driver on the ground, and found the cell phone in the bed. After they checked the guy out, Teffinger helped him up, said "Sorry," and explained what had just happened.

"Someone threw the phone in your bed," Teffinger said. "I don't suppose you saw him."

No.

The man didn't.

"We're going to need a detailed account of where this truck has been," Teffinger.

The guy grunted.

"It's been all over," he said.

"Of course it has," Teffinger said. "That's the way my life works."

Teffinger was halfway done taking the man's statement when his phone rang and Chief Tanker's voice came through. "I just got a call from a friend," he said. "Geneva Vellone was supposed to be at some kind of important radio meeting at four o'clock. She didn't show up and isn't answering her phone. He wanted me to look into it, in light of the fact that she's been doing this stupid exchange talk."

"I just saw her earlier this afternoon," Teffinger said.

"You did?"

Yes.

"She was fine," Teffinger said.

"What was she doing?"

"She was at her house, taking a shower," Teffinger said. "Probably getting ready for that meeting, in hindsight."

"So why didn't she go?" Tanker asked.

Teffinger swallowed.

"She might have gotten herself into trouble." Then he told Tanker about the message on Geneva's answering machine. "Hold on, let me try to call her." He switched to the other line, dialed and got no answer. Then he switched back to Tanker and said, "I'm going to drive out and check on her."

"Do that," Tanker said. "Call me as soon as you get there."

Teffinger hung up.

The pickup driver looked at him.

Waiting to finish his statement.

Teffinger took a business card out of his wallet, wrote Katie Baxter's name and cell phone number on the back, and handed it to the man.

"Call this person and give her the rest of your statement," he said. "Please and thank you. I have an emergency."

The man looked confused.

"What?" Teffinger asked.

"I don't have a cell phone."

Teffinger reached into his pocket for a dollar but only had a five. He hesitated and then handed it to the man. "Call from a payphone."

He pointed the front end of the 4Runner towards Geneva Vellone's house and stepped on the gas.

Chapter Ninety-Six
Day Eight—April 19
Tuesday Afternoon

———————

Wearing dark sunglasses and a baseball cap, Tripp sat in the rear seat of an RTD bus, nonchalantly got off a mile from Rave Lafelle's house and then walked the rest of the way under an increasingly stormy sky.

The wind blew.

It felt good.

Wild.

He saw no vehicles in the driveway as he approached. He walked towards the house like he owned it, headed to the back, and knocked on the door.

No one answered.

Good.

He tried the doorknob, found it locked, and busted the glass with his elbow. He reached in, undid the deadbolt and entered. A white cat trotted over to meet him; the same one that had been at Nick Teffinger's house in Green Mountain.

Tripp picked it up and petted it.

"So, you're over here now, huh?"

Good.

That meant that the vampire hadn't abandoned ship and run off to some other part of the world. She'd be home, sooner or later. And when she showed up, she would die.

Whatever it took, she would die.

No matter how messy.

No matter how loud.

No matter how many protectors Tripp would have to kill first.

Tripp owed that much to VanDeventer, at a minimum, for coming back to Denver to extract him.

He made a sandwich.

And washed it down with a Diet Pepsi.

Then he scouted around for weapons. Within ten minutes he assembled a number of knives, a hammer and a crowbar. He broke a wooden leg off one of the kitchen chairs, sat down in the vampire's bedroom, and whittled it to a point as he waited.

Come on.

It's show time.

Chapter Ninety-Seven
Day Eight—April 19
Tuesday Afternoon

_____

After the rehearsal, Rave and London caught a late lunch at a mom-and-pop diner on south Broadway, then headed to Rave's place. They were just getting out of the car and walking to the front door when Rave's phone rang.

It turned out to be Parker.

More excited than Rave had ever heard him.

"Have you seen the news?" he asked.

She inserted the key into the lock.

No.

She hadn't.

"There's a massive manhunt going on right now for someone named Trent Tripp," he said.

Rave turned the key.

"Who's Trent Tripp?"

"He's wanted by the police in connection with the Cameron Leigh murder," Parker said. "My guess is he's a slayer."

Rave pushed the door open, pulled the key out and stepped inside the house. She asked London over her shoulder, "Does the name Trent Tripp ring a bell with you?"

"No."

"Me and London never heard of him," Rave said.

"Yeah, well I think you know him," Parker said. "The physical description of this guy matches the man who followed you to

Rooney Road; the one who killed Forrest."

"It does?"

"Yes, he's big, about six-four," Parker said. "Where are you right now?"

"Just got home," Rave said.

She kicked off her tennis shoes and headed to the kitchen for a glass of water. Alley ran over and London picked him up. "There's my little baby," she said.

"Listen," Parker said, "We finally have the name and face of one of the slayers. Turn on your TV and see if you can find a news report; see if this Trent Tripp is the same guy you saw on Rooney Road."

"Sure."

Rave walked over to coffee table, picked up the remote, pointed it at the TV and clicked.

"I'm doing it," she said.

"One more thing," Parker said. "If this guy is the slayer, he might feel his time's up and this is his last chance to get you. What I really think you should do is get out of that house, right now."

Rave ran the scenarios.

She had a gig tonight.

She needed a shower.

Her clothes and makeup were all here at the house.

On the other hand, Parker sounded more stressed than she had ever heard him. It wouldn't be impossible to pack everything up and check into a hotel.

"Okay," she said. "I'm going to gather a few things and be out of here in five minutes. I'm going to need a hotel, though."

"Meet me at the Adam's Mark Hotel downtown," Parker said. "I'll check in and get a room going."

"Love you," Rave said.

"Ditto."

She hung up.

London said, "I'm going to take a quick shower," and headed for the master bathroom. Ten seconds later, the woman let out a bloodcurdling scream.

Chapter Ninety-Eight
Day Eight—April 19
Tuesday Afternoon

There was no sign of Geneva Vellone at her house. There was, however, a pool of dried blood on the carpet in the master bedroom, with dried drops leading from there to the rear sliding glass door.

Which was open.

Teffinger pounded his fist on the wall.

So hard that the plaster caved in.

"Damn it!"

He attacked the furniture—overturning the couch, kicking a leg off a table, picking up a lamp and throwing it all the way into the kitchen. He heard Sydney yelling at him. He knew he should stop. He knew he was destroying a crime scene. But he couldn't stop. He ran out the back door, past the barn and into the open space. He ran until his lungs and legs gave out.

Then he walked back.

Exhausted.

Sweaty.

Sydney stared at him.

And said nothing.

He looked at her and said, "I should have done more to stop

her."

His lip trembled.

And he felt like he hadn't felt since he was ten.

Sydney put her arms around him.

And he let her.

"I should have done more," he said.

"Nick—"

"Everyone I care about is dying," he said.

They ended up sitting on the redwood deck, leaning against the house. The wind kicked up and the sun disappeared behind black clouds. They held hands and didn't talk. Then Nick stood up and pulled Sydney to her feet.

"Come on," he said. "We're wasting time."

Chapter Ninety-Nine
Day Eight—April 19
Tuesday Afternoon

———————————

Tripp surveyed his handiwork, his beautiful handiwork. The gorgeous island girl, London Fontelle, was tied spread-eagle to the bed, wearing only a white thong.

The thong was a nice touch.

She looked sexier with it on.

Tripp sat on the bed and ran his index finger in circles around the woman's bellybutton. Her tight abdominal muscles reacted perfectly, recoiling under his touch, like a fine instrument.

Incredibly erotic.

His cock stiffened.

He dragged his finger along her body, up to her right nipple, and touched it lightly. The woman pulled against her bonds but it did no good. Sounds came from her mouth but the gag kept them muted and unintelligible.

"Nice, huh?" he asked.

She wiggled in protest.

"Oh, I have a present for you, did I mention that?" he asked.

From the floor at the base of the bed he picked up the wooden chair leg that he had whittled to a sharp point. He held it in front of her face, let her get a good look, and then laid it on the bed between her outstretched legs.

"I know I don't really need that," he said. "But it makes such a cool statement."

She pulled at her bonds.

Tripp rubbed his cock.

Then he put both hands on his captive's body and felt her, all over, up and down, around and around, in and out. He continued for a long time, memorizing her muscles, gauging the sensitivity of her skin.

"I have to hand it to you," he said. "You're nice. I'm glad I didn't waste my talents on Geneva Vellone this afternoon. You know what I mean by waste my talents, don't you? I almost did, but got interrupted. That's good for you, though."

She moaned.

He took her gag off and she immediately gulped for air. "Don't scream or this goes right back on," he warned.

"Okay."

"Tell me about being a vampire," he said. "I've always been curious how it works."

She hesitated.

Weighing it.

Then she said, "Okay, but on one condition."

He laughed.

"You're giving me conditions?"

"Just a small one."

Tripp was curious.

He set a hand on her stomach and tapped his fingers.

"And what's that?"

"You tell me about being a slayer."

He tilted his head.

"Sure, why not," he said. "You first."

He ran his hands over her body as she talked. He didn't really expect her to tell him anything of substance, but she did—he could tell it was true, too, by the details.

They sucked each other's blood.

They did research.

They had a latent immortality gene.

He raised an eyebrow.

"Details," he said.

She told him that the old vampires did in fact live for a long time. They had a gene that repressed the body's natural degenerative process. This gene was present in a latent form in all bloodline descendents. A small group of descendents was working on a way to activate it.

"And how are they doing that?" he asked.

"The secret is in the blood."

Tripp cocked his head.

"Whose blood?"

"The blood of others," she said. "Blood is blood. But vampire blood is the strongest."

"So some blood is stronger than others?"

"Yes."

"And the secret is to suck the strongest blood?"

"That's our theory."

Suddenly, just like that, all the questions that had built up in his mind were answered. It all made sense, perfect wonderful sense. He couldn't wait to tell VanDeventer.

"Can you untie me?" she asked.

"Why would I do that?"

"You have me all turned on," she said. "I want to get on top."

Tripp laughed.

"Sorry baby," he said. "There's probably someone in the universe stupid enough to fall for something like that, unfortunately for you though, it isn't me."

She stared at him.

Mean.

Then she screamed.

Tripp punched her in the face until she stopped.

Then he shoved the gag in her mouth and tied it behind her head as she thrashed.

"That was a bad career move," he said.

He ripped off her thong.

And climbed between her legs.

Chapter 100
Day Eight—April 19
Tuesday Afternoon

———————

Rave pulled and twisted but couldn't get loose no matter what she did or how hard she struggled. She was on her back, tied tight to the bed, with her arms stretched over her head. Voices came from the other bedroom. One of them was London's; the other was a man's.

No doubt the slayer.

Trent Tripp.

Rave didn't want to die.

But she would.

She knew that.

Suddenly a scream pierced the air, immediately followed by the pounding of fists. Rave pulled up an image of London being beaten to death. Then the screaming stopped. Rave's heart raced so fast that she had trouble breathing. The end was coming to London.

Rave was next.

She pulled against her bonds.

Her wrists bled.

She didn't care and pulled harder.

Suddenly Parker appeared in the room. He pulled the gag out of Rave's mouth and untied her hands, working frantically, as fast as he could. "Can you untie your feet?" he asked.

"Yes."

The man's eyes were wild.

Filled with something Rave had never seen before.

Parker ran out of the room.

Two seconds later, the crashing sounds of a terrible fight came from the other room. By the time Rave got her legs untied, the commotion had reached a frantic state. She ran towards the room with a horrific fear in her spine.

She couldn't believe what she saw.

London was tied to the bed, naked, spread-eagle, watching the violence with wide, bloodshot eyes. Parker was on his back, getting beaten to death by another man who hovered over him and swung with wild fists.

She looked for something to hit him with.

Frantic.

Every second an eternity.

She saw nothing.

She turned, ran to the kitchen and flung drawers open until she found something —a steak knife. When she got back to the bedroom, Parker was twitching beneath the other man, so badly beaten that he couldn't even keep his hands in front of his face any longer.

Rave ran over.

She raised her hand and stabbed the blade as fast and hard as she could at the man's head. He must have seen her out of the corner of his eye, and turned at the last second. The blade sliced directly into his eye. It sank into his head without resistance, not hitting bone, digging deep into his brain. He made a horrible sound and twitched. His hand moved towards the knife as if to pull it out, but never got there. Instead, it fell limp.

He jerked twice.

Then stopped moving.

Blood dribbled out of his mouth.

More than an hour later, Parker recovered enough to do what needed to be done. He pulled his car into Rave's garage, loaded Tripp's body into the trunk and drove off.

His plan was to dump the body.

Then drive back to the city, call Denver homicide from a payphone, and anonymously report the location.

While parker was gone, Rave's phone rang and Tim Pepper's number showed on the display. Rave wasn't in the mood to talk to anyone, much less the man with the eerie connection to Le Femme's dead singer, but was too scared to appear as if something unusual was going on. So she answered. "The surfer guy at the bar sitting by London during the rehearsal this afternoon—I'm assuming he's the boyfriend you've been telling me about, that Parker guy."

Correct.

"Why?"

"He looked familiar," Pepper said. "I kept thinking that I'd seen him somewhere before but wasn't sure. Now I am. I've seen him before."

Rave was in no mood to care.

But she asked, "Where?"

"Do you remember the night that I discovered you, in that club down in New Orleans?"

Rave nodded.

"Well your boyfriend, Parker, was there that night."

Rave grunted.

"No he wasn't," she said.

"Yes he was," Pepper said. "He was sitting way back in the corner. He never took his eyes off you. I actually thought he was a manager, the same as me, to tell you the truth. That's why I came up to you so fast during that first break, to beat him to the punch."

Rave searched her memory.

But found no traces of Parker.

Not even a shadow of a memory.

And immediately realized something.

Pepper was lying.

Why?

She didn't know.

"If you say so," she said. "I don't remember seeing him, but that doesn't mean you're not right."

"I never forget a face," Pepper said. "Especially a man as cute as him."

Suddenly Rave thought of something—namely, a way to catch Pepper in his lie. "I'm surprised you didn't buy him a drink," she said. "I mean a man that cute, sitting back in the corner."

Pepper chuckled.

"It's ironic that you say that, because I almost sent one over."

Rave chuckled.

Then, as an apparent afterthought, she said, "What was he drinking?"

Pepper retreated in thought.

"Coors Light."

Got you, Rave thought.

Parker doesn't drink beer.

He only drinks mixed drinks.

"You have a good memory," she said.

Rave hung up, lit a joint, told London what Pepper just said and asked, "How long have you known Parker?"

London shrugged.

"Years," she said. "Five or six, I guess."

"Has he ever been to New Orleans?"

"Not that I know of."

"Would you know if he had?"

"Probably."

"Have you ever seen him drink beer?"

London laughed.

"Parker?"

Rave shook her head in disgust. "So what in the hell is Pepper up to all of a sudden?"

"I don't know," London said. "One thing I do know, though— don't be alone with him. Not after what happened to Destiny Moon."

Rave agreed.

Messy condition.

Chapter 101
Day Eight—April 19
Tuesday Afternoon

———————————

Trent Tripp's body laid in the dirt at a trailhead parking lot at the base of White Ranch Park, just south of Morrison, exactly where the anonymous caller said it would be. The body showed an inordinate amount of trauma, including a deep wound that had totally destroyed the man's right eye.

Teffinger stared at the body.

Then kicked the dirt.

Sydney stood next to him.

He looked at her and said, "He was our only lead to finding Jena."

She said nothing.

"Now we're dead in the water," he added.

The wind pushed dark clouds across the sky.

"It's going to rain," she said.

He looked up.

Yeah.

It was.

His cell phone rang and the chief's voice came though. "I just want to give you a heads up," he said. "The press has already gotten wind of Geneva Vellone's disappearance, including the fact that you were the last person to see her alive."

"Just like with Jena," Teffinger said.

"Unfortunately, yes," the chief said.

"Thanks for the warning."

He looked at Sydney.

"The press is going to have me hung out to dry by tomorrow morning," he said.

"Screw them."

Teffinger looked at Tripp's body.

Then back at Sydney.

"You know what?" he said. "I really don't even care anymore."

She scratched her head.

"Maybe Tripp wasn't our last lead," she said. "I mean, obviously, someone killed him; probably the guy who made the anonymous call. If we can find out who he is—"

Teffinger picked up a rock and threw it.

"Jena's out of time and we're out of time," he said. "I can't keep pushing reality aside any longer."

Then something happened that Teffinger didn't expect. Sydney pulled her arm back as far as it would go and slapped him across the face as hard as she could. The pain was so hot and so intense that he almost punched her.

"Get your act together!" she said.

He turned and huffed to the 4Runner.

Angry.

Frustrated.

Confused.

Apathetic.

Stressed.

Raw.

He yanked the door open, threw himself in, cranked over the engine and slammed the door as hard as he could.

Ready to drive off.

Without Sydney.

Screw her.

Screw everything.

Then he surprised himself by turning off the ignition. He sat there for a second and then filled two disposable cups with coffee from a thermos. He walked back to Tripp's body, handed a cup to Sydney and said, "Okay, let's figure out who killed this guy."

"Right."

"Did we get a recording of the man who reported the location, when he called in?"

Sydney shook her head.

"No," she said. "It didn't go to 911. It came to the main number."

Teffinger looked at the clouds.

"Of course."

Chapter 102
Day Eight—April 19
Tuesday Evening

_____

Tuesday evening, Jake VanDeventer flew through choppy skies towards Denver. He sat in first class, drinking a Bud Light and thinking about his wife, Sophia.

Rest her soul.

The soul of the only woman he would ever love.

When she disappeared, eighteen months ago, they were living in Nice, France. Jake was semi-retired, running the diamond mines through people he trusted. Sophia had turned herself into a philanthropist—rich, powerful and well known throughout southern France.

She didn't have an enemy in the world.

On a Wednesday morning, she hopped on her red scooter to buy a loaf of fresh bread, just like she did every morning. This time, however, she never returned. They found her two weeks later, in an old abandoned boathouse, hanging by her feet, naked, with her throat slit.

The police investigated.

Hard.

Under tremendous pressure from both VanDeventer and the public.

They learned a few things.

Two men had been seen in the vicinity of the boathouse during the time in question. One of the men looked like Indiana Jones, from the movies. They got no description of the other man.

That's all they learned.

The investigation slowed.

And then stopped.

That's when VanDeventer decided that he had to get things done on his own.

He learned of a similar case involving a man named Matthew Abbott, an American businessman who looked like a tattooed skinhead when he wasn't wearing a suit. Abbott's sister, Melissa, had been killed in the same manner as VanDeventer's wife, Sophia.

VanDeventer didn't tell the French police about the Abbott case.

Or the American police.

Instead, he showed up unannounced on Abbott's doorstep.

They talked.

And formed an alliance.

An alliance of justice.

An alliance of revenge.

Abbott knew a man named Trent Tripp; a large man; a capable man; a man who could be trusted; a man who might be willing to join their cause if the price was right. They met with Tripp, liked him, and made an arrangement.

Tripp took the lead in the hunt.

And found out that their two targets—Indiana Jones and the other man—were part of a group of people who believed they were bloodline descendents of vampires.

The three of them met to assess the situation.

It was their collective opinion that their two targets, and possibly other "vampires" from this group, were killing people throughout the world, most likely to drink their blood.

Over time, through the incredible digging and persistence of Trent Tripp, they uncovered more victims of the vampires.

—Kennedy Pinehurst, a radio personality from Chicago.

—Samantha Stevens, a New York socialite.

—Tristan Knox, a Los Angeles model.

—Destiny Moon, the lead singer of a female rock group called Le Femme, out of Seattle.

A pattern emerged.

The targets were always women of stature, fame, fortune or money—important women, strong women, the kinds of women who got their names and faces on billboards, TVs and radios. In each case, the woman was kept alive for a number of days, probably so that her blood could be sucked or drained over a period of time.

Vandeventer, Abbott and Tripp met to refine their goals. It wasn't their plan to randomly kill or slay anyone or everyone who might be a member of the vampire group. In fact, they only knew of two persons who were conclusively involved, namely their two target men.

Their goal was to find out the identity of these two men.

And kill them.

If they discovered other vampires along the way who were implicated in the slaying of women, then the three of them would meet and discuss what to do before proceeding. That situation, however, had not materialized to date.

Vandeventer actually thought he saw one of the two targets once—the one who looked like Indiana Jones—in San Francisco. He followed the man north of the city and saw that he slowed near an ocean estate. VanDeventer did the same, to see what the man had been looking at. He spotted surveillance cameras at the gate. Later that day he discovered that the house belonged to Barbara Rocker, the daughter of a wealthy man from San Francisco.

VanDeventer realized that she was a likely target.

And that the surveillance cameras had probably picked him up.

So he made an appointment with a realtor named Jim Hansen who had a couple of houses listed for sale on that same road. That way, if Barbara Rocker did in fact disappear, and if her surveillance cameras recorded VanDeventer's car in the vicinity, then VanDeventer would at least have an excuse for being in the area.

Twice.

Good thing, too.

Barbara Rocker did in fact turn out to be another victim.

VanDeventer got questioned by some incredibly stupid detective by the name of Mark Yorke. During that interrogation, VanDeventer asked his own questions, to see if he could find something out to help his own cause

But the detective knew nothing.

Unfortunately, VanDeventer never got a license plate number for Indiana Jones' car.

The trail died.

Then they caught a break. Trent Tripp did some work to figure out who was tapping into ancient documents that might lead to information about vampires and their bloodline descendents.

The name of a woman named Suzanne Wheeler came up.

A woman from Montreal, Canada.

Tripp flew there, broke into her place and snooped around.

Unfortunately, the woman came home unexpectedly.

Tripp scurried out the back door.

He didn't know if she spotted him or not.

When he told VanDeventer and Abbott that he was pretty sure that Wheeler was the genealogist working for the vampires, they gave him authority to break in a second time and extract anything that would tell them who their two targets were.

Tripp broke in again.

He found three files.

Diamanda.

Cameron Leigh.

And Rave Lafelle.

VanDeventer dispatched Tripp to Paris. Tripp's assignment was to see if he could get the names of the two target men from the Paris vampire, Diamanda. The theory was that each vampire knew who the other ones were. Unfortunately, Tripp got attacked by the vampire and her bodyguard and ended up with no choice but to defend himself. He was able to grab the vampire's laptop before he escaped, and brought it back to the U.S. VanDeventer cracked it, but found no information of relevance inside.

Meanwhile, Abbott went to Denver, to see what information he could get out of one or both of the other vampires.

He disappeared.

One of the vampires, Cameron Leigh, turned up dead with a wooden stake through her chest. In his heart, VanDeventer knew that Abbott didn't do it.

Abbott wasn't that kind of man.

When Abbott disappeared, VanDeventer and Tripp flew to Denver to find out what had happened, and to get whatever information they could from Rave Lafelle.

So far however, she had been a tough nut to crack.

She set up a trap for Trent Tripp when VanDeventer had to return to Johannesburg. One of the two targets, namely the Indiana Jones man, even came to Denver to help her.

But that little plan backfired on her.

She ended up shooting Indiana Jones.

Trent Tripp then dumped the man's body by the railroad tracks, and pounded a stake in his heart to send a message. At that point, they knew his name—Forrest Jones. VanDeventer wired a nice bonus to Tripp's bank as a showing of appreciation for getting one of the two targets.

That left one to go.

VanDeventer then flew to Ohio and broke into Forrest Jones' house to see if he could get information as to the identity of the second target. Unfortunately, VanDeventer got interrupted by a female detective and had to punch her in the nose. That resulted in the police believing that he was associated with Forrest Jones' murder, which in turn resulted in his composite sketch being broadcast all over the Denver news.

And a warrant for his arrest.

Now tripp was in trouble. VanDeventer would meet him at the parking lot at 20th and Broadway at nine tonight and get him out of Denver.

He leaned back in the seat and drained the last of the Bud Light from the can. His name wasn't Jake VanDeventer today; it was Ronald Ringer, thanks to the handiwork of Lefty. He wore an expensive suit, a red silk tie and leather wingtips. His hair was black now, and matched glasses that were fitted with non-corrective lenses. Even his friends wouldn't recognize him.

He closed his eyes.

And pulled up an image of Sophia.

Smiling.

Happy.

Getting on her red scooter.

Waving over her shoulder as she headed down the cobblestone driveway.

"We're half done," he whispered.

Chapter 103
Day Eight—April 19
Tuesday Evening

R ave was cleaning blood off the carpet in her bedroom when her cell phone beeped, indicating she had a voice message.

She retrieved it.

"This message is for Rave Lafelle," a woman's voice said. "This is Suzanne Wheeler from Montreal, Canada. You called me earlier. My conscience has been bothering me and I can't stay quiet any longer. Someone broke into my house a while back. I saw a man running out the back. I told Parker about it. He thought it was probably a slayer, looking for information on vampires. He said they'd probably be back and told me to leave three files where they could find them. One on Cameron Leigh, one on a French model named Diamanda, and one on you. The first two were legitimate files. They were work that I was actually doing. I didn't have a file on you, however. To my knowledge, you have no vampire ancestry. Parker told me to make up a file with your name on it. I asked him why. He said he was going to use you as bait to draw the slayers in. I did it. I shouldn't have, I admit that. I'm done with Parker and all this mess. I'm glad you're still alive and can only pray that you stay that way. Please forgive me if you can."

Rave called London into the room.

And handed the phone to her.

"Listen to this message," she said.

Chapter 104
Day Eight—April 19
Tuesday Evening

———————————

Teffinger was at headquarters, frantic, pacing, wired on caffeine, when London called. Before she could say anything, he said, "London, please don't think I'm rude, but I don't have a spare minute to my life right now."

"I'm downstairs in the lobby," she said. "Come down and see me."

"London—"

"Just do it!" she said.

"I really don't have time—"

"It's about the case."

"Jena Vellone?"

"Yes," she said. "And Geneva Vellone, too. Come alone."

Come alone?

What the hell did that mean?

Teffinger bounded down the stairwell, two steps at a time. He spotted London in the lobby and she pulled him outside where they could talk in private. Rain fell out of a twilight sky. The streetlights would kick on in fifteen minutes.

London had been crying.

"What's going on?" he asked.

She grabbed his hands.

"Do you love me?"

"Yes."

"I love you too," she said. "I'm going to tell you something but you have to promise never to use it against me or Rave Lafelle."

He studied her.

She was serious.

"Okay," he said.

"You promise?"

"I do."

"I'll tell you the whole story later," she said. "But here's what you need to know right now. Trent Tripp is the one who took Geneva Vellone. And Forrest Jones is the one who took Jena Vellone."

The words were so unexpected that Teffinger laughed. Forrest Jones was the man they found by the railroad tracks with a wooden stake in his heart.

"How could you possibly know that?"

"I'll tell you everything later," she said. "But trust me; those two things are absolutely true."

Teffinger looked for lies.

And found none.

"Forrest Jones has been dead for days," he said.

"I know."

He turned and said over his shoulder, "I'll talk to you later."

"I just found out," she shouted. "Don't hate me."

He stopped.

And looked back.

"Are you absolutely sure about this? Before I make a fool out of myself—"

"I'm absolutely positive. Trust me."

Teffinger ran up the stairs two at a time. He must have looked like an out-of-breath maniac when he ran into the room because ten pairs of eyes focused on him and didn't look away. He spotted Katie Baxter and said, "Trent Tripp is the one who took Geneva Vellone this afternoon."

She looked dumbfounded.

"How do you know that?"

"I just do," he said. "Follow the route of his cell phone this afternoon. Search every abandoned building within fifty yards of where he was."

"You're kidding, right?"

He looked around the room. "I want everyone in here to help her," he said. "No one goes off duty until we find her. I don't care if we work for two days straight." Back to Baxter, "Concentrate on his locations an hour or so after I left Geneva's place—I left at 1:30, so see where he was about 2:30. Wherever he took her, he probably took her straight there."

He pointed to Sydney and said, "I need you to come with me."

They squealed to the 6th Avenue freeway and headed west. Teffinger brought the 4Runner up to eighty and said, "Forrest Jones is the one who took Jena Vellone."

"Forrest Jones? You mean the dead guy by the railroad tracks?"

"Yes."

"What makes you say that?"

"I'll tell you later," he said.

"He's been dead for days," she added.

"I know."

"So where are we going, exactly?"

"Idaho Springs."

"What's in Idaho Springs?"

"Jena Vellone, if my gut is right."

Then he told her about the phone call he received a couple of days ago.

The display said Private Number and Teffinger didn't recognize the man's voice.

"There's a guy who got killed who's all over the news," the man said. "He's the guy who got a stake pounded in his heart, like he was a vampire or something. The one they found down by the railroad tracks—"

"Forrest Jones," Teffinger said.

"That's the guy," the man said. "Anyway, I don't know if this means anything or not, but I live up in Idaho Springs and I have a cabin advertised for rent. This guy who ended up dead called me up about it, wanting to see it. We went up there to see it but he didn't like it for some reason and never did rent it."

"Okay."

"Like I said, I don't know if it means anything or not, but I just thought I'd call because I ended up talking to someone who got killed," the man said. "Nothing like that ever happened to me before."

"I understand," Teffinger said.

Suddenly his other line rang.

"Hold on," he said, and then switched lines.

It turned out to be a wrong number.

He punched back to the first line but the man wasn't there. Then Teffinger realized why—he hit the wrong button and cut him off.

"I didn't think anything of it at the time," Teffinger said. "But now that I know that Forrest Jones is the one who took Jena, it makes sense. He must have been in Idaho Springs looking for a cabin to keep her in. He didn't end up renting the one of the guy who called me, probably because it was too close to another one. But if my gut's right, he didn't stop at that point. He called someone else and eventually rented a place. That's where Jena is right now."

Sydney shifted in her seat.

And got excited.

"If that's true, she's been abandoned for a long time."

"I know," Teffinger said. "That's why we can't mess around with search warrants."

Idaho Springs was an old mining town 35 miles west of Denver, in the thick of the Rocky Mountains. The interstate cut through it. Sydney worked the phone on the way and got the name of a realtor by the name of Theodore Brown. She called and explained the situation. He was more than willing to help.

They met him at the base of the first exit off I-70 into town.

He turned out to be an energetic, academic-looking man in his early thirties with brown glasses. As soon as they all shook hands and introduced themselves, Brown got down to business.

"There are twenty-two cabins listed for rent in the surrounding area," he said. "I've already called fifteen of them and spoke to the owners. All of them are still vacant, except for one. I wasn't able to get through to the other seven owners."

Teffinger scratched his head.

"Okay," he said. "Our man tried to rent something the first time. No doubt because he thought that just breaking into some place and squatting would be too dangerous. He needed a controlled environment. So I'm thinking that he stayed with his plan and actually rented something. So what I want to do is concentrate on the seven places where you couldn't get a hold of the owner."

"Okay."

"I don't see an alternative but to physically drive out to each one," he said. "Do you know the roads around here?"

"Like the back of my hand," Brown said.

"Let's start with the closest one."

Teffinger drove like a maniac through a thick thunderstorm but neither of his passengers complained. When they got to the first cabin, the windows were dark. They hopped out of the 4Runner and approached, leaving the headlights on the structure. The front door was locked. Teffinger looked around, found a stick the size of a baseball bat, and bashed in the front window. He muscled in and then opened the door.

The place had no public electricity.

They didn't have time to find the generator and start it.

So they searched as good as they could, using the little light that reflected into the structure from the 4Runner through the rain.

They called.

Loud and repeatedly.

No one answer.

"She's not here," Teffinger said. "Let's go!"

They fishtailed down pitch-black muddy mountain roads until they got to the next place.

Teffinger grabbed the stick from the backseat and smashed the front window without even checking the doorknob.

They entered.

The place was empty.

They repeated that scenario four more times.

No Jena.

"Damn it," Teffinger said. "We're down to one."

He stepped on the gas but drove with trepidation. If they didn't find her at this last place, he didn't know what to do.

When they arrived, the place was dark.

Teffinger smashed the window.

They entered.

And searched.

Jena Vellone wasn't there.

They searched again.

Every inch.

She definitely wasn't there.

They got back in the vehicle.

No one spoke.

Teffinger exhaled and turned the SUV around.

"Hey, wait," Sydney said.

Teffinger put his foot on the brake.

"What?"

"There's a storage shed or something back there, behind the house."

They checked it.

And found Jena Vellone inside.

Curled up in a fetal position.

Unconscious.

Chained by an ankle.

Teffinger shook her but got no response.

"Jena!"

No response.

No movement.

"See if she has a pulse," Sydney said.

Teffinger checked.

She did.

Faint.

But there.

"See if your cell gets a signal up here," he said. "We need a flight-for-life; and something to cut this chain off."

Sydney ran to the 4Runner.

"No signal," she said.

"Go down to town and call," he said. "I'm going to stay with her."

The 4Runner fired up and the back tires threw mud. Within moments the sound of the engine disappeared. Teffinger took off his clothes, down to his boxers, and covered Jena. Then he wrapped his arms and legs around her and gave her his warmth.

He had never felt such a desolate place.

And couldn't imagine what it had been like to feel only that and nothing else, day after day and night after night.

He shivered.

Thunder cracked.

And never felt better in his life.

Chapter 105
Day Eight—April 19
Tuesday Night

Three hours later, the same storm continued to fall out of the same sky. Teffinger watched it from his garage, sitting behind the wheel of the '67 Vette, drinking a cold Bud Light. London sat in the passenger seat, downing white wine faster than she should. Jena Vellone was at Lutheran Medical Center, dehydrated and malnourished, but expected to obtain a full recovery with no long-term side effects. A throng of media was camped in the hospital lobby, waiting for prognosis updates and the opportunity to actually talk to the woman.

Jena's sister, Geneva, was with her in the room.

Thanks to Katie Baxter and the team, who found her hogtied on the top floor of an abandoned warehouse.

Teffinger's cell phone was off and sitting on the kitchen table.

He watched the storm and chewed on London's story, which he fully believed.

According to London, she had no idea of Parker's involvement in anything until this evening. That's when two things happened. Tim Pepper called Rave and said that he'd seen Parker early on in a New Orleans club. Then the Montreal genealogist, Suzanne Wheeler, called Rave and said that Parker had set Rave up as bait to draw in the slayers.

Rave and London confronted Parker.

And Parker admitted, for the first time, a lot of things.

He admitted that he had in fact first seen Rave in New Orleans. He liked her, asked around about her, and found that she lived in Denver. He resolved to look her up if he ever got to Colorado.

He admitted that he and Forrest Jones had been killing women and drinking their blood—strong woman blood—in a effort to increase and activate their dormant immortality genes.

Kennedy Pinehurst.

Barbara Rocker.

Destiny Moon.

And many more.

The scenario was always the same. Parker chose the woman. He only picked women with "strong" blood, meaning women of stature, recognition, fame or money. He often used billboards to help him pick. Then, Forrest Jones did all the work, meaning the abduction, obtaining the vials of blood, and eventually killing them.

Parker and Forrest both drank the blood.

They were both chasing immortality in the worst way.

None of the other vampires, including London, had any knowledge of their activities.

Except for Cameron Leigh. Parker admitted that he found out that Cameron Leigh had grown suspicious and had started an investigation. She had obtained information on Kennedy Pinehurst and Destiny Moon. Those were the files found tucked in her vampire books.

Parker was afraid that she would go to the police.

So he decided to kill her.

That's why he told the Montreal woman, Suzanne Wheeler, to leave Cameron Leigh's file out.

Then he killed her, exactly as planned.

He pounded a stake through her heart to make it look like the slayers did it. That way London and the other vampires would never suspect him.

Parker admitted that he knew that Jake VanDeventer, Tripp and Matthew Abbott were after him and Forrest Jones. So he used Rave as bait.

To lure them in so he could kill them.

He made everyone on the vampire side of the equation—including London and Rave—believe that they were slayers, out to get all the vampires, when in fact they only wanted him and Forrest.

Parker's plan worked well, relatively speaking.

Rave ended up shooting Matthew Abbott in the face.

Rave ended up sticking a knife through Tripp's eye and into his brain.

Unfortunately for Parker, he lost Forrest Jones in the process, when Rave shot him in the face by accident on Rooney Road.

Over time, Rave became more than bait.

Parker fell in love with her.

That's why he admitted everything, in the end, so she would understand and, hopefully, stay with him.

He was wrong.

She wouldn't.

She told him that in no uncertain terms.

And Parker left.

Teffinger finished what was left in the beer can, then fetched another from the fridge, and brought London a fresh glass of wine. Jena Vellone was safe. Geneva Vellone was safe. The murders of Cameron Leigh, Kennedy Pinehurst and Destiny Moon were solved. It was now clear that Teffinger had been improperly accused as being implicated by the media in the disappearances of Jena Vellone and Geneva Vellone. Alley would move back with Jena if she wanted him; otherwise, Alley could stay here. Teffinger felt like a human being for the first time in a long time.

Lightning ripped across the sky.

Beautiful.

"The storm's getting worse," London said. A pause, then, "Have you made up your mind yet, about us?"

Teffinger nodded.

"The things you did, I can understand," he said. "I can appreciate why you helped bury the skinhead—actually, make that Matthew Abbott—in the desert. And helped get Tripp into Parker's car, to be dumped. Legally, of course, those things could be big trouble, if anyone ever found out. But I'm not telling. The only important thing to me is that you told me what you knew as soon as you knew it. That led to us saving Jena and Geneva. That trumps everything."

London exhaled.

And clinked her glass against his.

"What about Rave?" she asked.

"She did a lot of stuff," he said. "She shot Matthew Abbott, but justifiably believed he was there to kill her, so that's self-defense. She shot Forrest Jones in the face, but again, that was by accident. She was trying to save him. Then she stabbed Tripp in the eye, but only because she was justifiably trying to save Parker from a violent attack in her own home. If I was in her shoes, I would have done exactly the same thing—not to mention that I promised you that I wouldn't use what you told me against either you or her. The poor thing's been through enough. As far as I'm concerned, I hope she turns out to be the biggest singer the world's ever seen."

London leaned over and kissed him.

"I'm done with all the vampire stuff," she said.

Teffinger chuckled.

"So you're giving up on being immortal?"

"I just want to be mortal, with you," she said.

Teffinger kissed her.

"Fine by me," he said.

ABOUT THE AUTHOR

Formerly a longstanding trial attorney before taking the big leap and devoting his fulltime attention to writing, RJ Jagger (that's a penname, by the way) is the author of over twenty hard-edged mystery and suspense thrillers. In addition to his own books, Jagger also ghostwrites for a well-known, bestselling author. He is a member of the International Thriller Writers as well as Mystery Writers of America.

www.rjjagger.com